**EMMA**

EMMA'S SECRET WORLD

# EMMA'S SECRET WORLD

## Hilary James

First published in 1993 by
Nexus
332 Ladbroke Grove
London W10 5AH

Reprinted 1994, 1995

Typeset by TW Typesetting, Plymouth, Devon
Printed and bound in Great Britain by
Cox & Wyman Ltd, Reading, Berkshire

ISBN 0 35232 879 7

A young woman's trials, tribulations and eventual joyful suffering in the 'Secret World' of lesbian love and domination.

This book is a work of fiction.
In real life, make sure you practise safe sex.

# 1    A FORTUITOUS MEETING

Emma sat by herself, feeling a little forlorn, as she looked admiringly at the bronzed, lacquered bodies in the women's health club. It had been so daring to come here, but it was a mistake. How beautiful all these women were, how well groomed with their carefully painted fingers and toes, their carefully rouged and creamed cheeks, their carefully made-up lips and their immaculate hair and sleek bodies.

They must have nothing to do except laze away the hours until the evening, when their husbands, lovers or admirers would call for their presence!

What a different world hers was, she reflected sadly. She was just an Irish country bumpkin. Her rare days of inactivity were spent gardening. There was still earth under her plain short fingernails. Her body was slack, her hair untidy and her cheeks unadorned. She certainly must look out of place in this temple of beauty, even though her friends in the country considered her pretty and amusing with her plump little figure and good sense of humour.

She had come here because she was bored. What a mistake! Yet her boredom was very real.

There had, it was true, been one exciting man in her life. Henry!

She couldn't get thoughts of Henry out of her mind. The desires he had awakened in her stubbornly refused to go away.

Henry was a dashing breathtakingly attractive older man who simply regarded her as an amusing plaything. She had clandestinely met him in London several times. She still shivered deliciously when she thought of their last meeting - he had told her to meet him at the bridge over the lake in St James's Park, stark naked under her mackintosh.

It had been a supremely humiliating but strangely exciting

experience waiting for him there. Desperately anxious lest passers-by see that she had nothing on under her mackintosh, she walked meekly behind the apparent stranger like a well-trained dog; then she went down on her knees as if she had dropped something, but she was really licking the soles of his shoes as he sat on a park bench.

Then she had to follow him to his hotel, go up to his room and wait for him, naked, bending over the bed, looking at the dog whip he had left lying on it, waiting and wondering . . .

And, when he arrived, he had picked it up, slashed it down on the bed beside her trembling bottom. How she had jumped! She had felt the wind of it! She was all tensed up when he spoke: 'No time now!' he had said, with that delicious regret in his voice. 'Just wait till next time . . .' He hit the bed beside her again even more viciously, angry because of whatever had happened to interrupt them, and she shivered at the power of him. 'Next time, my dear . . .'

Yes, Henry had been really exciting. But Henry lived abroad with his wife and only came to London occasionally, so there had been no next time. Not yet anyway.

And she was married also – to John. Dull John, and even he was abroad for a couple of months – yet again.

She looked at herself in the mirror. A pretty, petite if slightly plump, blonde in her mid twenties looked back at her. She had been married for several years, but there had been no children. She had married John, she now admitted, largely because she wanted to escape from her dull life in Ireland. John's talk of romantic faraway tropical islands and long sea journeys had fascinated her and stimulated her imagination. Too late, she had found that he was a charming but rather dull scientist – an oceanographer whose job took him off to remote parts of the world for months on end, leaving her alone, very bored and not very well off in their country cottage, near the headquarters of the organisation he worked for. It was only a couple of hours from London, but she rarely went there. She had a job with a local voluntary organisation.

How she wished that John could be more assertive, more masculine, more commanding, more decisive, more anything. He seemed quite unaware of the secret yearnings of his pretty

Irish wife. Ideas of dominating her would have shocked him. He was too young and did not have the necessary strength of character. Nor indeed had most other men whom she had met. Those that did just didn't seem to recognise her innermost needs.

Naked under the towel that was wrapped around her, she was feeling more and more out of place amongst these sophisticated jet set women, these lithe models, these splendid actresses, these wives and mistresses of rich and famous men, with their beautifully kept bodies and brittle talk and empty heads.

She was relieved when she was led away into an alcove and invited to stretch out under the rays of a sun lamp. Gradually her self-confidence returned as she lay luxuriating there. Then, out of the blue, she heard a very upper-class voice.

'Goodness! What a dreadfully neglected body! You certainly need treatment! Where have you been? What have you been doing? What is your name?'

'Emma,' she managed, overcome with shame and embarrassment as she gazed up at the speaker, her new found confidence shattered again.

'Oh, don't worry,' said the woman in a more reassuring voice. 'You just need a little massage, a diet and some exercises. Then with a lesson or two in make-up you will shine like the rest of them!'

She switched off the lamp.

'Come and join the other women at the health bar,' she said, leading Emma to several women sitting on high stools, enjoying a variety of fruit drinks, served from behind the bar by a pretty young girl.

'Meet our new girl,' said the woman. 'She's Emma. Imagine what she could look like if one of you got your hands on her!'

Emma felt the eyes of these sophisticated women on her. She felt gauche and inadequate. She longed to return to her garden, her cottage, her books.

'Well, Ursula, what do you think of our country girl? What do you think we might make of her?'

'Oh, I think she's just waiting to be transformed into a fairy princess!' The voice was cultured and slow, with a hint of a foreign accent.

Emma looked up in gratitude to see that the speaker was a

tall elegant woman. She might have been forty or even fifty, but she had the skin and figure of a woman of thirty. She was dressed in a long black caftan that showed off her slim figure and gave her an artistic look. She had a long thin face with high cheekbones. Just like Garbo, thought Emma. Her hair was cut short and brushed back. Her eyes were piercing. Although in no way mannish, she had the looks and mannerisms of an ascetic youth rather than a woman of a certain age.

'Come and sit down over here, child,' she said. She had an almost hypnotic voice and was clearly used to being obeyed. She led the way to a small table set apart in a corner of the beautifully decorated bar. Entranced, Emma found herself following this woman, astonished at herself for not being angry at being called a child. Perhaps there was something psychological about the woman being so much taller than herself, making her look up at her, just as she had to look up at most men.

Emma, rather to her surprise, found herself pushing forward a chair for this strange woman, who accepted it as if of right. The girl from the bar came over immediately. Clearly her new friend was someone important.

'A glass of champagne for me and a small glass of carrot juice for my young friend.' She did not ask Emma what she would like – clearly the idea of doing so had not occurred to her, but Emma was just grateful and surprised that this sophisticated woman of the world could find a country bumpkin such as herself of any interest whatsoever.

'Now, little Emma, you are going to tell me all about yourself,' came the same quiet, hypnotic voice.

Emma found herself blushing furiously. What could she say? She simply could not admit to this glamorous figure that she was merely a housewife.

But the woman seemed to divine her thoughts and fears.

'I'm sure you do lots of interesting things,' she said with a delightful laugh. 'Anyway, a pretty little creature like you must have lots of interesting thoughts even if you have not yet had all the . . . experiences. You sound Irish, that's interesting for a start!'

When the girl from the bar had brought their drinks, the

woman drew a curtain across the alcove. Emma's self-confidence was returning fast. The privacy encouraged her to talk even more freely to this strangely commanding person, whose name, she discovered, was Ursula de Freville.

Emma found herself talking about her school days at a fashionable convent in Ireland near where her parents had lived so quietly, how she had married when she was very young to get away to England, of the meekness of John, how dull that was and a hint of the excitement of Henry . . .

'So, little girl! You'd rather be told what to do, would you? Well, Emma, would you really?'

Emma felt Ursula's piercing eyes boring into her brain, seeking out her most secret thoughts. She blushed and lowered her eyes. Ursula smiled triumphantly.

'Look at me!' she ordered. 'Look at me, Emma!' Emma raised her eyes. She bit her lips like a naughty child plucking up her courage to admit to something awful.

'There's nothing to be ashamed about. Just tell me. Would you really like decisions being taken for you? Would that make you happier?'

'Yes,' whispered Emma.

Ursula tapped her wrist encouragingly.

'There's nothing strange about that, my child!' It was the second time she had been called child. Somehow, instead of resenting it she rather liked it. Ursula had gone on speaking in her slow hypnotic voice as if she wanted Emma to remember every word. 'Most women secretly feel the same way. It's what makes them helpless slaves of the first strong-minded man who comes along – even if he's selfish and odious and behaves like a brute. But I'm not like that! No one gives me orders! Oh no! I *give* orders – especially to girls like you!'

Ursula paused, as if to allow Emma time to appreciate the significance of what she had just said.

'You'd like that, wouldn't you, Emma? Secretly, you'd like that?'

Emma found herself nodding. Yes indeed, perhaps this would not be so different from what she had always longed for in a man and only briefly found. How aloof and haughty this woman seemed, how supremely self-confident.

'The first thing I'd do with you, my girl,' said Ursula briskly, 'is put you on a strict diet.'

'But I'm not really all that much overweight,' protested Emma with a laugh, 'and anyway I haven't the will power – I've tried several times.'

'You are overweight and you'd stick to your diet all right if you were under my control, telephoning me after each meal to report what you had eaten, with the threat of a beating if you had not lost weight when you next saw me, and of a severe thrashing if you ever dared to put on any weight again.'

'A beating!' Emma did not know whether to be shocked or excited. 'A thrashing!'

'Yes. Six strokes of the cane if you don't lose two pounds. You'd find it concentrates the mind quite extraordinarily.'

'Oh!'

'And it would be twelve strokes of the cane if you ever saw this man Henry again – or allowed any other man to touch you!'

'Oh!' said Emma again. 'But . . .'

'There would be no buts about it, my girl,' said Ursula, her voice suddenly angry. 'Now, stand up!'

Shyly, Emma found herself obeying this imperious woman. She stood nervously in front of Ursula. What now?

'Unwrap your towel. Drop it on the floor.'

'But I've got nothing on!' whispered Emma, acutely embarrassed.

'Exactly! How can I see how many pounds you need to lose with that thick towel wrapped round you? Anyway the curtain's drawn, so no one's likely to see you. Now do what you're told and stop arguing! Drop the towel! At once!'

Still desperately embarrassed, Emma started to unwrap the towel. She hesitated for a moment.

'*Drop it!*'

Emma now stood naked in front of Ursula, trying to hide her body with her hands.

'Hands to your sides, you silly girl.'

Now she felt even more naked. She lowered her eyes to hide her shame. She did not know it, but it was a gesture of innocence that aroused Ursula's interest considerably. She felt Ursula's eyes roving over her.

'Turn round.'

Suddenly she felt long fingers touching her back. She stiffened. No woman had ever touched her like this.

'Keep still.'

The fingers ran down her back. They gently touched her soft buttocks. They paused there, then ran on down her thighs. No man, she thought, would be so tantalisingly demanding.

'You need only to lose a few pounds, little Emma, and to be made to do proper exercises, and you'd have as beautiful a figure as any of the women you saw earlier.'

'Oh, do you really think so?'

'Turn round again. Yes, a diet and exercises will firm up your breasts and make your waist even smaller. You could soon be a most delightful creature. Once you've learnt obedience, of course.'

It all sounded very exciting.

'Now, pick up your towel. Go to the bar and order me one of their special lobster salads. Nothing for yourself. You can have a little of mine.'

A few minutes later Emma was enviously watching Ursula eat her delicious salad. It was a long time since Emma had eaten lobster – it was so expensive. She could not help resenting the way Ursula was happily eating away. Soon there would be nothing left for her. Her mouth was watering, she licked her lips as Ursula pushed aside her plate. There was still a little lobster on it. Emma reached across the table to take the plate and received a stinging slap on the wrist.

'How dare you!' hissed Ursula, eyes blazing. 'I shall tell you when you may eat – and how much you may eat. Now light my cigarette.'

Emma felt like a naughty child. Ashamed at having angered Ursula, she quickly picked up Ursula's gold lighter and concentrated on lighting her cigarette. She noticed that Ursula did not offer her one – they were black Russian cigarettes and she used a holder.

'I enjoy the occasional cigarette with a meal,' Ursula said, 'but I don't like to see a young girl smoking. Do you smoke, Emma?'

'No . . . No, not now,' Emma replied. It wasn't quite true – she still could not resist the occasional one.

Ursula smiled. 'There is nothing like the threat of the cane to stop a young girl from smoking.'

'Yes . . . Yes, I suppose so,' stammered Emma. This talk of caning was rather exciting. Indeed everything about this magnificent woman was exciting.

'Now, you can have one little mouthful of my lobster.' She put a little piece on a fork and held it out to Emma as if she were feeding a dog. Gratefully Emma accepted it. She longed for more. She could not take her eyes off the plate, but no more was offered.

'Get dressed now,' ordered Ursula. 'I'm taking you to the gallery where some of my pictures are being exhibited. You can make yourself useful there. Clients like to have coffee whilst they are discussing prices. Hurry up!'

Emma had no time to object, even if she wanted to. That afternoon she was kept madly busy helping her new friend. She was also learning a lot about her. As Ursula dispatched her on one errand after another, she began to realise what an extraordinary woman she was. She was indeed quite well known in artistic circles in Europe, both as a wealthy patron of the arts and also a painter in her own right. She divided her time between her studio house in London and a converted Moorish palace in Morocco where she did most of her painting.

She was now in London for this exhibition and to see her friends, occasionally flying back to Morocco for a week to make sure that everything was all right at her converted villa.

She seemed to be surrounded by a coterie of artistic and rather effeminate men who treated Emma as if she were just one of Ursula's servants. Indeed Emma noticed that Ursula seemed to ignore any of the good-looking men to whom she herself was attracted.

'Stop gawking at those young men,' she ordered in a loud voice. 'You're not here to flirt with the first young man you see!'

Poor Emma could have died of shame and she saw that several of the young men were laughing at her. Ursula seemed to hate relationships with anything male. Any mention by the female staff of the gallery of normal sexual relations with a man, or even a mild flirtation, would result in a bad-tempered outburst.

'You're a fool,' she told one young woman who had been laughingly talking about throwing over her current lover and starting a new affair. 'Men are violent and disruptive creatures. Intelligent women don't need them and are much better off without them.'

It was a remark Emma would hear repeated over and over again by Ursula and her friends.

Ursula ordered Emma to bring numerous cups of coffee for herself and her women friends. She made Emma wash the cups and bring them to her to be checked for cleanliness. She made her keep a list of the paintings that had been sold and at what price, and note names and telephone numbers of possible buyers.

She even told Emma to run out and buy her some cigarettes and a large bottle of a very expensive scent that Emma had never been able to afford for herself. She gave Emma the money and then airily told her to keep the substantial change. She even allowed Emma to put a little of the scent onto the back of her neck.

Ursula made Emma feel like a favourite servant. It was all very exciting. No one had ever ordered her around quite like this.

The pictures themselves, she saw, were a mixture of exotic Moroccan scenes and of beautiful half-naked European women dressed in flimsy Moroccan dresses and kneeling in submissive or suggestive poses. They seemed popular and sold very well.

Emma blushed when she heard Ursula telling some people that Emma might well be posing for her, and laughingly enquired if anyone would like to commission a portrait of her. She was even more embarrassed when Ursula made the same remark to a wealthy Arab sheik who immediately looked her up and down, clearly wondering what she would look like half naked.

But Emma was secretly delighted to be casually introduced to Ursula's famous and wealthy women friends. She found it quite natural that she, being a much younger woman, should dance attendance on this older and infinitely more sophisticated person. It was the most exciting afternoon she had spent for years. She was only astonished that such a wonderful, intelligent and elegant woman, with all her wealth, her many interests and her fascinating friends, should bother about anyone so dull as herself.

Like Cinderella at the ball, she could hardly bear to tear herself away from it all to catch the train back to her little cottage in the country. She was delighted when Ursula gave her her card and in her long slow drawling voice whispered: 'Well, little Emma, I think we are going to see quite a lot more of each other. You'd better give me a ring and let me know whether you can come up to London in a few days time. I may want you to give me a hand here again. Now run along and don't miss your train.'

Emma was amazed at the way Ursula was already taking charge of her life. She had even specially ordered and paid for a taxi to take her to the station.

'I don't want you being picked up by some awful man on the tube,' she explained. 'And mind you don't talk to strange men on the train. I do not approve of that.'

Sitting in the taxi, Emma felt quite light-headed. After all the initial put-downs and unhappiness at the health club, the day had ended quite magnificently. Never had she felt so self-confident or happy. She felt a new glow of excitement, a woman with a new interest in life.

At the station she noticed men looking at her with unusual interest. She bought a magazine to read on the train, but her thoughts were elsewhere. She simply could not get Ursula de Freville out of her mind. She kept remembering her commanding ways, her slow cool voice and equally hypnotic eyes. She kept thinking about her haughty and disinterested manner, her obvious wealth, her artistic friends and the effortless way in which she belonged to what seemed to Emma to be the in-crowd.

She also kept thinking about Ursula's scornful attitude to men and of her sudden anger with the secretary who had been boasting of her success with them.

Emma had always thought that a woman without a man was

10

to be pitied, but there was nothing pitiful about Ursula - not since she had had a crush on the beautiful French mistress at her convent had any woman attracted her so. That had resulted only in the exchange of a few secret kisses and love notes, but this time, she instinctively knew, something far more exciting and satisfying was going to happen.

She had discovered a new and secret world - a world that had been there all around her but which she had never known even existed.

# 2     THE HEALTH FARM

Emma could hardly resist ringing Ursula as soon as she got home, but it was late and she did not want to risk a snub. All day she fought off the temptation to pick up the telephone. When she finally did ring, it was answered by a foreign sounding maid who said that Mademoiselle de Freville was out. Did madame wish to leave a message? Emma was so disappointed she simply put the phone down.

She tried again the next day and this time it was Ursula who answered. She seemed delighted that Emma had rung, and invited her for lunch the next day. She had something to discuss – it would mean Emma being very good, but she would not say more than that.

Emma was on tenterhooks as she waited at the fashionable restaurant. She had hardly slept a wink, wondering what Ursula was going to discuss with her. She had put on her smartest suit. She knew it made her look attractive and yet very young. It seemed strange dressing to look attractive to a woman.

At last Ursula arrived, looking every inch the unconventional artist, dressing in well-cut trousers and jacket, her blonde hair brushed down over her ears like that of a boy poet. She embraced Emma warmly and seemed very pleased with the trouble she had taken over her appearance.

'You must always dress well and groom yourself properly when you are meeting me,' she said. 'I think I shall send you to my hairdresser. I fancy a completely new style, something more simple and unsophisticated.'

As on their previous trip, Ursula ordered champagne for herself and a fruit juice for Emma, who didn't dare say that she longed for champagne too.

'Perhaps I will allow you to have a little sip of mine, if you are a good girl,' Ursula said when she saw the disappointment in Emma's eyes.

Once again she ordered food only for herself, a little caviar on toast followed by peaches in Armagnac.

'You can have a taste of mine,' she said, 'if you are still a good girl. I don't want you putting on any more weight. I like a girl to be really slim.'

Emma felt a little dismayed. She was a healthy girl with a good appetite. She eyed the caviar longingly whilst Ursula talked of the delights of life. Life without men, without having to pander to their brutal desires and without being financially dependent on them. She talked of her own successful career, of her life in Morocco, of Paris, Ireland and America. She talked of well-known society people.

Emma was fascinated, but she was also delighted when Ursula finally held out a tiny piece of toast with a little caviar on it. Delicious! She longed for more, but Ursula was still talking and she did not like to interrupt. At last another little piece of toast and caviar was held out as if she were a pet dog being offered a choice morsel.

She felt that her whole character was changing. Normally she was vivacious and never tongue-tied amongst her friends in the country. But here in London with this dominating woman, whether at the exclusive health club or this expensive restaurant, she became as shy as a schoolgirl amongst grown-ups.

She suddenly realised that Ursula was saying something.

'. . . that shouldn't be too difficult. You're still very young looking. You should have no difficulty in dressing as a schoolgirl.'

'But why . . . What . . .'

'You haven't been listening!' Ursula was angry. 'Pay attention when I'm speaking to you. I'm not going to take you out to an expensive restaurant and have you daydreaming all the time. I had thought of allowing you some of my peaches, but I certainly shan't now. You're a naughty and ungrateful girl and I'm very angry with you.'

'Oh, please,' cried Emma, almost sobbing, 'I'm so sorry. I'm just so happy seeing you again. Yes, yes, I'll do anything you want, of course I'll dress up as a schoolgirl.'

13

'Very well,' said Ursula, secretly pleased at how contrite Emma was. 'Are you free next weekend?'

'Yes. I think so,' said Emma. Was this what Ursula had wanted to discuss? She began to feel more and more excited.

'Then you can come with me to this health farm in the country. I have arranged to go there with several friends and I'll take you along too – as my seventeen-year-old niece, out from school for the weekend.'

'But . . . But . . . Why?'

'Because that's what I want!' replied Ursula tartly.

'It's just that it sounds so strange.'

'Of course! It is meant to! Life would be very dull if we just behaved as everyone expected! I shall pick you up at your cottage, properly dressed, which means as a schoolgirl, at three next Friday.'

'Oh!'

'And this afternoon I shall take you to a school outfitters and buy you a proper schoolgirl uniform. Let's see, a blue pleated skirt, a white blouse, white socks, flat heeled shoes, some tight jeans, a gym slip, a little party frock, a school blazer and, of course, a shorty nightdress.'

'Goodness,' said Emma. 'It's rather expensive for one week-end!'

Ursula laughed. Clearly Emma still had not realised how little such small amounts of money meant to her. 'Not at all. Schoolgirls' clothes cost so little!'

'Oh!'

'I shall take you to my hairdresser to have the curls taken out and your hair put into pigtails.'

'Oh no, I'm so proud of my curls!'

'You'll do as you're told or you won't come at all!' exploded Ursula, smacking the table hard with the tips of her fingers.

'Oh . . .'

'And you'll be taught to do your make up so that you look like a teenager. Understand?'

'Yes, yes,' cried Emma, overawed by Ursula's sudden display of temper. She remembered her similar sudden anger when they had first met and she had tried to help herself to the remains of Ursula's lobster without asking permission. She must be very careful not to cross Ursula.

'Good, then that's all settled,' smiled Ursula triumphantly.

Indeed, it was a very pretty schoolgirl who caught the train home that evening, a schoolgirl dressed in the traditional blue blazer and skirt, white blouse and short socks and sensible shoes, with her blonde hair in two little pigtails. She carried a suitcase in which were packed the grown-up clothes in which she had travelled up to London that morning and the other schoolgirl clothes she would need for the weekend.

This schoolgirl was seen off by a tall, elegant woman, her Aunt Ursula – it was a dress rehearsal to make sure Emma could act the part properly.

While they were waiting for the train to leave, Ursula suddenly said: 'Now, I want you to promise me to be a good girl until we meet, little Emma.'

'Of course, Aunt Ursula.'

'You must promise not to touch yourself. Do you understand what I mean?'

Emma blushed. This was something very private, which no one had ever spoken to her about. Left as she was for much of the time by a weak husband, she often gave herself a little relief whilst thinking of her fantasies of strong dominant men. Ursula was no fool and knew what tricks Emma was likely to get up to unless controlled, and, more to the point, that men played an important part in it all – a part which she would not permit.

'Do you promise? I shan't want to see you again unless you do!'

'Yes,' whispered Emma. She felt desperately ashamed and embarrassed.

'When I pick you up, you will have to look me in the eye and tell me that you really have been a good girl.'

Emma knew she could not lie to Ursula, but before she could say anything the guard blew his whistle and she flung herself into Ursula's arms for a farewell embrace from this wonderful woman who seemed to be controlling her very life – and all so excitingly.

As the train gathered speed, Emma felt terribly sad at being parted from Ursula. She even felt near to tears – just like a real schoolgirl. She buried her head in the girls' magazine that Ursula had thoughtfully bought for her.

Nobody would be likely to connect the normally vivacious happy-go-lucky young married woman they knew as Emma with this quiet shy young teenager.

Two days later that same shy teenager could be seen carrying her aunt's luggage up to her spacious bedroom at the health farm, before putting her own into a much smaller room along the corridor.

Minutes later Ursula called Emma in to check that she was really looking like a schoolgirl and then led the way downstairs to join her friends.

There were three other women waiting to greet her, all in their forties or fifties, beautifully dressed and exquisitely groomed. Two were very slim, with boyish figures like Ursula, but one was hugely fat.

To Emma's astonishment, each was accompanied by a young girl dressed identically to herself. As she stared at them in disbelief, she saw that the other girls were showing no surprise at the situation.

The three women greeted Ursula effusively and then to Emma's further astonishment each introduced the girl with her as her niece, just out from school for the weekend. As each girl was introduced to Ursula they gave a little curtsey – just, Emma thought, like schoolgirls in France.

'And this,' she suddenly heard Ursula saying, 'is my own niece, Emma, who has also been let out of school for the weekend.' She turned to the blushing Emma. 'Now, Emma, make a nice curtsey to each of my friends.'

Emma awkwardly copied what she had seen the other girls do. The women looked at her critically and then, ignoring her, turned to Ursula.

'My dear, where did you find such a delightful little girl?'

'Such a fresh looking child.'

'You really must lend her to me,' said the fat woman in a pronounced German accent. Emma was alarmed by the cruel smile. 'Have you yet . . .?'

16

'No, not yet,' said Ursula, with an annoyed wave of her hand. 'Not yet, Helga.'

The fat woman laughed. 'We shall watch with interest,' she said. 'I've never known you to fail.' Again that cruel smile.

'We'll meet then at dinner,' Ursula said. 'Emma you must unpack my clothes and run my bath. Run along now.'

As Emma turned to leave, Ursula stopped her.

'Give my friends a kiss, like a good little girl!'

Two of them were easy but she put off the fat woman to last and shuddered as she went to her. That kiss was horrid, specially when the woman enveloped her in a long stifling hug, but at last she escaped.

Back in Ursula's room, Emma was astonished by the lovely dresses and silk negligées she unpacked and hung in the cupboard, and the beautiful satin underwear she put away in the drawers. It seemed quite natural to do this for Ursula.

Then Ursula sent her to run her bath.

'Take care, Emma. Not too hot and not too cold. And hurry, I want you to undress me.'

As Emma scurried about, finishing the unpacking, she heard Ursula say: 'You'll make a good ladies maid, once I've trained you.' Somehow, she was pleased to hear this praise, pleased that Ursula was pleased with her.

The next thing she unpacked was a cane.

She looked at it in amazement. It was about three feet long with a curved handle. What was Ursula doing with a cane? She held it up. 'Ah, yes,' said Ursula, 'put that on the dressing table, I need you here to take off my shoes.'

Soon Ursula stood naked. She had a figure rather like a boy, with very small breasts and straight hips. There was not an ounce of unwanted fat anywhere. She made Emma lead her to the bath and then, to Emma's acute embarrassment, asked to be washed all over.

'I hope you are not going to be disobedient,' Ursula said in a menacing tone. 'The cane is there for disobedient little girls.'

It was enough. Emma applied herself to her appointed task.

'Dry me carefully and give me my negligée. I'm going to have a little rest. You can go to your room and get ready for dinner. Put on your new party dress and brush your hair straight down over your shoulders. Oh, and you can wear these.'

She went to one of the drawers and pulled out a satin slip and a pair of lace panties. Emma thought they were beautiful. She saw that they had been embroidered with Ursula's initials. The idea of wearing something that belonged to Ursula somehow seemed very exciting.

'I don't want you wearing any of your own underclothes,' said Ursula. 'Now run along to your room. I shall ring when I want you to help me dress. Make sure you are ready, and bring all your own underclothes with you. They are to be thrown away.'

In her own room Emma threw herself on the bed, her thoughts in a turmoil. What on earth was she doing, she a respectably married woman, dressed up as a schoolgirl? Acting as lady's maid to a dominating woman who seemed to have some hypnotic hold over her? It was all too silly. She would leave and go back home. But how could she? The health farm was right out in the country and she had come in Ursula's car. Ursula had told her she wouldn't need any money. It was already getting dark, the rain was beating against the window. What was she to do? She began to sob.

Suddenly the telephone rang.

'I hope you are getting ready, Emma,' came that slow hypnotic voice.

It was as if she had guessed the doubts that had been rushing through Emma's mind.

'Yes,' whispered Emma. 'Yes.'

'Good girl.'

Emma felt herself flush with the unjustified praise. She heard the click as Ursula put down the phone. Frantically she unpacked, and ran her bath. A few minutes later she was putting on the new underclothes. It was almost as though she had been marked with Ursula's initials, like a branded animal, almost as if she belonged to Ursula.

She could ring up one of her girl friends, Jane perhaps, and ask to be picked up. They could meet secretly in the grounds. She hesitated, her hand on the phone. Did she really want to run away from Ursula? Well, there was no harm in chatting to

Jane. She picked up the phone. There was a card telling her to dial '9' for an outside call. She tried it – no outside line. She dialled again, again nothing happened. Angrily she got through to reception.

'Outside calls are barred from this number,' came the voice. 'We had quite clear instructions on the matter.'

'Instructions? From whom?'

'From Miss de Freville, who is paying for the room. I have her card in front of me. "No outside calls without my express personal permission." Our engineers made the necessary adjustment. If you want to make an outside call, you must go to Miss de Freville's room.'

'Oh!' wailed Emma.

'It's a quite normal arrangement,' said the voice. 'Young girls just don't seem to appreciate the cost of calls these days, but I'll tell Miss de Freville you want to make one.'

'Oh no, please don't do that,' cried Emma. But it was too late – the telephone had gone dead.

For a moment Emma just sat there bemused. Had Ursula deliberately taken steps to prevent her from contacting the outside world or was it just a normal precaution against a huge bill being run up? But there was no time to waste.

Quickly she put on the little girl's party dress.

It was flared and flouncy and very short – unmistakably the sort of dress that a young teenager or even a much younger girl would wear. With it went white socks, flat party shoes and blue ribbon in her long hair, which she brushed straight down her back. The ribbon matched the dress – when Ursula had bought it in the girls' outfitters she had asked the assistant to show Emma how it should be tied in a little girl's way.

Emma looked in the mirror. A very pretty young girl looked back at her. The pigtails and make-up were perfect. She tied the sash bow and slid it round her waist to her back. She checked her nails for any sign of nail varnish. None. She was ready.

Almost immediately the telephone rang. It was Ursula. She sounded very cross.

'Come to my room – at once!'

Moments later Emma knocked on Ursula's door. It reminded her of her school days, of being sent for by the headmistress.

An angry voice told her to enter.

Ursula was standing in the middle of the room, still in her negligée, her hands on her hips.

'How dare you try to ring up some man behind my back, you ungrateful slut!' she stormed. She strode up to Emma and suddenly slapped her hard across the face. 'I pay for you to come here with me and as soon as my back is turned you try to ring up some man friend of yours. Well, you can go to hell. You can get out now. Leave all your new clothes behind and get out!'

Emma burst into tears.

'I didn't mean any harm,' she sobbed. 'I was only trying to ring up a girl friend.'

'A likely story! You were going to ring up some creep of a man! Admit it!'

'No, no, a girl friend, I promise.'

Softened by Emma's big eyes and her protestations, Ursula relaxed. 'Were you trying to run away?' she asked quietly. 'Were you? Were you going to ask her to come and collect you?'

'Well . . . I had thought of that . . . but then I decided I wanted to stay with you.' She flung herself into Ursula's arms, sobbing. 'I want to stay with you, let me stay with you!'

'Very well,' said Ursula. She kissed her wet eyes. 'Now dry your tears. I don't want you going downstairs looking unhappy. You're going to be a good girl, you're going to have a lovely weekend here with me and my friends. And you're going to do exactly what you are told to do.'

'Yes, yes,' cried Emma, now smiling again.

'And no more silly attempts to make telephone calls?'

'No! No!'

'Good. Now you can help me get dressed. We shall make a striking pair, the elegant famous artist and her pretty little niece.'

They did indeed make a striking pair as they entered the dining room, with its small dance floor. A pianist, a young woman, was playing in the corner. There were several groups of women, wearing evening dresses, seated at a dozen tables.

Not a man in sight!

Feeling very self-conscious in her young girl's party dress, Emma demurely followed the beautifully dressed Ursula across the room to the table at which her friends were already laughing and chattering. At the other end of the table were the three young girls she had seen earlier. Amazed, she saw that they were again all wearing blue party dresses exactly like hers and had the same ribbon tied in the same place on top of their heads and their hair straight down their backs.

It was as if all four girls had come out for the weekend from the same school – she realised that the four older women had deliberately dressed their 'nieces' identically, buying their outfits from the same shop.

'Go and join your little friends,' ordered Ursula, pointing to the end of the table where the three other girls were silently watching the older women.

As she sat down at a vacant place, Emma saw Helga, the fat German woman, look at her and then turn to Ursula.

'Your little girl is looking very pretty tonight. But has she been crying?'

'Just a small tantrum,' smiled Ursula. 'You know what teenage girls are like.'

'The only thing they respect is the cane,' said the fat woman. Emma's heart jumped. She remembered the cane sitting on Ursula's dressing table. The fat woman turned to the girl sitting next to Emma. 'And how many strokes of the cane did you get before dinner tonight, my girl? Well, Belinda, speak up!'

'Six, madam,' said the girl, looking terribly embarrassed.

'And what for, my girl? What did Miss Perkins punish you for?'

'Impertinence, madam. On your instructions she caned me for impertinence.'

'I told you!' said the fat woman, looking around triumphantly at her friends. 'The only thing these teenagers respect is the feel of the cane on their backsides. I must say Miss Perkins lays it on very well. They're really scared of her.'

Horrified by this exchange, Emma turned to look closely at poor Belinda. They exchanged little glances. Seen close up, Belinda looked more like Emma's age than a real teenager. Emma looked around. The other two girls might also have been

21

her age, and one of them, very cleverly made up as a teenager, might really have been well into her thirties. How awful, Emma thought, these women each bring a young woman here for the weekend and then treat her as if she were a schoolgirl. But in some strange way it was rather exciting having to pretend like this.

At the other end of the table, Ursula and her three friends were discussing what to order for the girls.

'I think I shall order a small helping of boiled fish for Belinda,' said the fat woman. 'I don't like her having rich food – especially when she has a busy night ahead of her.' The others laughed. Emma did not understand what she meant, but she saw that poor Belinda was blushing.

'I think a little piece of plain cheddar will be quite enough for Emma,' she heard Ursula tell the waitress. None of the girls were asked what they would like, nor were any of them given the same delicious food as the women ordered. Similarly, whilst the women all drank either champagne or a delicious fruit cocktail, the girls were left simply with water.

Stimulated perhaps, by the champagne, the women were laughing and discussing a whole range of topics from the latest gossip about the Royal Family and various cabinet members to the state of the arts in Britain and, inevitably, the utter inadequacy of the male sex. The girls were fascinated as they listened to their elders. Emma noticed that they did not join in the discussions, nor did they talk amongst themselves. She herself could not help feeling proud of the way that Ursula seemed to dominate the arguments, but even so she began to feel a little foolish at just sitting in silence. She was, after all, a well educated and intelligent young woman who, when amongst her own friends, was not backward in airing her own views.

Finally she plucked up her courage.

'How old are you, Belinda?' she whispered.

'Twenty-eight.' Belinda hesitated. 'I mean sixteen, of course.' She laid a hand on Emma's arm. 'Please, we mustn't talk.'

She was too late.

'Did I hear you say something to Emma?' demanded the fat woman. 'Did you find our conversation so boring that you preferred to talk to another little chit of a girl? Did you dare interrupt your elders and betters? Did you?'

'I'm sorry, madam,' gasped Belinda. 'It won't happen again.'

'I should think not! Little girls should be seen and not heard. I can see that the effect of your punishment before dinner has worn off.' She reached into her bag, pulled out a pen and wrote a little note. 'Take that to Miss Perkins.' She turned to her friends. 'Three on each hand should stop her interrupting us in future.'

'Oh please, madam!' She looked resentfully at Emma. 'It wasn't my fault!'

Emma had been listening to this conversation with mounting disbelief. They were sitting in a public dining room. The 'girls' were grown-up women. And yet one of them was going to be punished for merely talking, punished as if she was a naughty child.

'It was my fault,' she said. 'I asked her a question.'

'And what question was that?' came the cool slow voice of Ursula.

'I asked her how old she really was,' answered Emma innocently.

'Did you now!' said Ursula. She paused. 'Well in that case I think you'd better go with Belinda and see what happens to little girls who speak out of turn.'

She scribbled a note, folded it, and handed it to Emma.

Dumbly, Emma rose and followed Belinda out of the room. She saw the tables full of women in evening dress. She could not believe that this was really happening as she clutched the carefully folded note.

Outside the dining room, she touched Belinda's arm.

'I'm sorry. I didn't know.'

'Don't make it worse by being caught talking now,' whispered Belinda. She looked up and down the empty corridor. 'You're lucky your mistress is a beautiful and intelligent woman. I hate mine. She's so cruel.'

'Then why stay with her?'

'Because . . . Oh, I can't explain it all now. She tricked me into stealing from her, something valuable, she could get me sent to prison.' Belinda buried her face in her hands. 'I can't stand being locked up, it's claustrophobia you know, even this is better than prison . . .'

'Oh!' gasped Emma, thinking of how alarming she had found the fat woman.

'Let's just get it over and done with,' said Belinda.

Emma followed her down the long corridor, and then into an empty gymnasium. Belinda knocked on a door marked: 'Aerobics Instructress'. The door was opened by an attractive woman in her thirties, dressed in a black body stocking and leotard.

'Oh Belinda – you haven't been a naughty girl again?' She laughed. 'Well, come in both of you and shut the door. The sooner we start, the sooner it will all be over. Give me your notes.'

Silently, Belinda handed over the note from the fat woman. Emma saw that written on it was simply: 'Two times three'.

'And yours?'

Emma handed over her note. Ursula had written on it: 'To listen – as a lesson'.

'Right,' said the woman, opening the drawer on her desk and pulling out a cane. Horrified, Emma saw that it was similar to the one on Ursula's dressing table.

'Now, Belinda, stand over there with your back to the wall and stretch out your right hand, palm upwards.' She turned to Emma. 'And you, wait outside the door but leave it ajar.'

Moments later Emma heard a swishing noise from inside the room, followed by a gasp of pain. It was repeated twice. Then she heard the woman's voice. 'Now the other hand, Belinda.' Again, the swishing, the gasp of pain, repeated twice. Then out of the door came Belinda. Her face was distorted with pain. She was biting her lip to keep back her tears and the palms of her hands were tightly pressed under her arms.

'Did it hurt terribly?'

'What do you think!' Belinda replied with a sob, pressing her palms even tighter. 'And it's all your fault!'

Silently Emma followed Belinda back into the dining room. Several older women were dancing cheek to cheek with girls. Poor Belinda was still holding her palms under her arms and biting her lips. What would the dancing couples say if they knew the reason for Belinda's behaviour?

None of the four women paid any attention to them as they sat down silently, their eyes lowered demurely.

'Ah, Emma, you're back,' she heard Ursula say. 'Come and dance.'

Emma had been stunned by the sight of women dancing with girls. At first she had been shocked, but somehow it seemed quite normal in this setting. Dumbly, she let herself be taken onto the floor by Ursula. The pianist was playing a medley of slow old-fashioned sentimental tunes: '*J'attendrai*', 'These Foolish Things' and 'Day and Night'. Ursula held her as a man would. She pressed tight against her. She looked down at her and smiled, pressed her cheek against hers.

'Dear little Emma,' she murmured, 'dearest little Emma.'

Suddenly Emma felt herself go limp in Ursula's arms. She could feel excitement rising. She could feel Ursula pressing against her, she was in some sort of heaven. She closed her eyes as they danced. Occasionally she would look up at Ursula's strong face. She felt happy and cossetted, the terrifying scene in the gymnasium forgotten.

A few minutes later Ursula led her back to their table. She felt as if she were in a dream. Vaguely she heard the women talking about a race.

'We'll have it on Sunday morning. That will give them time to get fit.'

'Not less than half a mile – it's no fun if it's all over too quickly.'

'And several jumps – over fallen trees.'

'A thousand pounds entry fee – winner takes all.'

'And to make sure the lazy sluts really try hard, Miss Perkins to give the second girl ten strokes, the third fifteen and the last one twenty.'

'That should really make them try!'

Emma could not understand what they were talking about. There seemed so much about this weekend that she did not understand.

'Now Emma, it's your bedtime. Go and get into bed. Put on your new little nightdress. I'll telephone you when I want you to come and undress me.'

25

'But please – it's still early,' protested Emma. 'Can't we dance again, just once?'

'How dare you argue with me?' cried Ursula in another sudden rage. 'You silly little girl. You'll pay for this impertinence!'

At the word 'impertinence', Emma's heart sank. It was for 'impertinence' that Belinda had been thrashed by the terrifying Miss Perkins before dinner.

'I'm sorry. I didn't mean to be . . .' she wailed. To her embarrassment she saw that people at the nearby tables were looking at her.

'Very well,' said Ursula. 'Now, say good night to each of my friends and run along. And turn out the light when you go to bed. I don't want you reading.'

Ten minutes later Emma was in bed in the darkness, Ursula's last words still ringing in her ears. Somehow she rather enjoyed being treated like a child by this older and much more sophisticated woman and her equally commanding friends. Somehow she found it exciting that each of them had a young woman like herself, playing the part of a teenage schoolgirl in public. How glad she was that her mistress, if that was the right word, was the tall, slim and elegant Ursula and not that awful fat woman. She could imagine what it would be like undressing her, washing her and dancing with her. She shuddered. But Ursula? Ursula was nice . . .

The telephone was ringing. She had been dreaming of Ursula and that was her summons . . .

She found Ursula standing in the middle of the room, smoking a cigarette.

'Take off your dressing gown.'

Emma felt very naked and shy in her little transparent shortie nightdress – the one that Ursula had bought for her. She saw that Ursula was looking at her body.

'Turn round.'

She felt Ursula's hands running down her back. She quivered with excitement.

'Keep still! Head up! Look straight ahead!'

Ursula's hands ran down lower. Was it right to be touched in this way by a woman? It all seemed so natural.

26

'Oh!' she suddenly cried. Ursula took her hands away.

'Oh, no, don't take your hand away,' she heard herself pleading.

'Don't you start giving me orders, little slut,' laughed Ursula, secretly very pleased with Emma's reaction. 'Now – undress me!'

Emma had to take off each garment and fold it carefully away. Then when Ursula was gloriously naked she had to go with her to the bathroom. Ursula made her attend to her most intimate toilet. It was something she had never ever done before, but she found it gave her pleasure to be used by Ursula in this way.

Back in the bedroom, Ursula said: 'Now don't think I have forgotten your impertinence, child. I will not have you answering me back in front of my friends. I demand complete obedience and now you are to learn what happens if you are naughty. It's time you met my little cane. It's called Sambo and it likes correcting naughty little girls. Now, bring it to me – on your knees.'

'Yes,' said Emma. She felt a mixture of fright and excitement. She was going to be beaten!

'Yes, madam!' said Ursula coldly. 'You heard Belinda calling her mistress madam. From now on you will call me madam, both in public and in private.'

'Yes, madam,' said Emma happily. This rule seemed to establish the right relationship. She ran to the dressing table, picked up the cane and offered it humbly to the woman she now regarded as her mistress. How many times had she daydreamed about such a scene! Hundreds of times, ever since she had been a little girl, though never with a woman.

'Sambo, madam,' she murmured submissively, kneeling and holding up the cane.

'Now, Emma, when I beat you, which I shall do whenever it amuses me to do so as well as whenever you are naughty, you are to bend over a chair, standing on your toes, with your knees bent and your hands gripping the legs of the chair. You are to count each stroke and ask me for the next one. If you move or if you fail to count or ask for the next stroke prettily enough, then the last stroke will not count.'

'Yes, madam.' Emma was eyeing the cane nervously.

'Repeat it all back to me.'

Emma had to repeat it until she was word perfect. She had to kiss the cane and address it as Sambo. Then she bent over the chair and Ursula made her move about until she was in just the right position.

Then it started.

The whippy cane came cracking down on her tender bottom.

Ursula left a long pause between each stroke. She made Emma kiss Sambo passionately between strokes.

After three strokes Ursula touched Emma gently, and was delighted that her exploring fingers encountered the telltale signs of an increasing arousal. Excellent! Emma was learning that pleasure would only follow pain. Ursula was an experienced beater of younger women and knew the powerful effect this association could have. It was an excellent way of breaking a quite normal girl into the delights of lesbianism, though they did not become fellow lesbians in quite the same way as her three dining companions.

Like them, Ursula enjoyed the utter domination of a younger woman precisely because that younger woman was not a natural lesbian but was responding just as she would to a dominant male. The fact that the younger woman was ashamed of her response to an older woman, and being seen with her in public, made the situation more piquant.

Ursula had the whole weekend in which finally to seduce and subject Emma. She was not going to rush things. First the association of pain and pleasure must be well established. It must be mounting pain and mounting pleasure, so that the girl would end up craving the one in order to achieve the other, and recognise her mistress as the source of both. Emma was a passionate little creature with, she knew, deep-felt secret desires. She was also well educated and intelligent – this would make the seduction of her mind as exciting as that of her body.

On the fourth stroke Emma broke her position to ease the pain, so it was repeated despite her pleas and tears. And after the fifth she was so contorted and squirming that she forgot to ask Sambo for the next.

She ended up sobbing with eight weals burning into her bottom like red hot pokers.

Ursula made her kneel at her feet and promise never again to answer back under the pain of another beating. Then she took the weeping girl in her arms, comforting her, kissing her and stroking her, giving as much pleasure as she could. Emma responded passionately to the reward as Ursula stroked her.

'Young girls shouldn't have all this hair,' she murmured. 'Little girls must be nice and smooth for their mistresses.' What would have shocked Emma last week seemed quite natural now. Ursula's hand was busy, sending shivers of sheer pleasure right through her. 'I'll arrange for it to be removed tomorrow,' Ursula said. 'Then, if you're a good girl . . .'

'Oh yes, anything you say,' gasped Emma. 'I promise I'll be a good girl, madam.'

Ursula backed away and Emma gave a little cry of disappointment.

'Tomorrow!' whispered Ursula. 'Think about tomorrow!'

'Yes, oh yes!' whispered Emma.

'Now, put me into my pyjamas.' They were of black satin. Nightdresses were for frivolous girls like Emma. Ursula got into bed, then made Emma kneel at the foot of it and untuck the bedclothes.

'Suck and lick my toes, one by one, passionately and respectfully, like a cat cleaning itself,' she ordered. She lay back in the bed and felt Emma's obedient tongue, a delightful sensation.

'Now run along back to your room,' she ordered.

Twice during the night Emma's telephone rang, summoning her to Ursula's room. Once to accompany Ursula to the bathroom and once merely to kneel at the foot of the bed and suck and kiss her toes. Each time Emma found herself desperately disappointed and frustrated as she was sent back to her room. Each time she was told: 'Be a good girl, Emma. I think you know what I mean. I won't have little girls misbehaving behind my back.'

Emma tossed and turned in her bed, not daring to find the relief she so longed for. Tomorrow, she thought, tomorrow . . .'

# 3  AN EROTIC EXPERIENCE

The next morning the four women met in the grounds for an early morning game of tennis. The girls were all wearing their schoolgirl gymslips – they were not allowed to play, they simply had to act as ball girls. Two knelt, one on either side of the net just like at Wimbledon, ready to dash onto the court and pick up a ball. The other two were at either end. When each girl's mistress was serving, she had to be at that end, ready to throw her more balls. The slightest delay in picking up or feeding balls to the server resulted in a reprimand.

Ursula was a beautiful player, driving the balls with almost masculine force. Emma watched her entranced. Her standard of play was above anything that she herself had ever achieved. Her sleek body and long legs seemed to be everywhere on the court. When it was her turn to serve, Emma tried hard always to have a ball ready to throw to her – hoping to be rewarded by a smile from her wonderful mistress.

Every few games play stopped for ice-cold drinks. Each girl had to serve her mistress. Ursula hardly paid any attention to Emma. It was as if events of the previous night had never taken place. She took her drink from Emma, as she took the balls, with no sign of recognition or thanks. She was too busy talking and laughing with her friends, Emma was of no account, merely there to serve.

Emma was acutely embarrassed at the shortness of her gymslip. She kept noticing the other girls' little black knickers every time they ran or bent over to pick up a ball. Belinda, the tallest girl with the shortest gymslip, was not wearing any knickers at all, and Emma could not help noticing the red weals on her bottom. She realised that her own weals would not be fully hidden by her knickers. How awful!

Then they went to the gymnasium. Miss Perkins was waiting

to put the girls through an exhausting routine whilst their mistresses watched. When it was the turn of the mistresses, the girls were made to wait outside under the supervision of Miss Perkins' assistant. Not only were they not allowed to watch their mistresses doing their exercises – this might have given them ideas above their station – but they were also not allowed to talk to each other lest they exchange ideas on their mistresses in a disrespectful way.

When the others went off for coffee, Ursula called Emma into the gymnasium.

'Miss Perkins,' she said, 'I'd like you to have a good look at Emma and give me your advice – Emma dear, take your clothes off.'

'All – all of them?'

'All of them! We have to see how to make you fit.'

Emma had to run naked round the gym. She had to jump up and down, her breasts bouncing, her knees raised high in the air. She had to lift heavy weights, straining every muscle whilst Miss Perkins felt her thighs, her arms and her belly. She was carefully weighed and measured.

'Her breasts are slack and her stomach needs a lot of tightening,' Miss Perkins said to Ursula as Emma got dressed. 'However, with a strict diet and regular exercising, you should be able to get her down to the figure of a young girl. She needs to lose half a stone and a couple of inches around the waist. Get her down to size eight and keep her there. You'll enjoy her all the more.'

Emma blushed at hearing herself described in such a casual way, as if her own views and opinions were of no account. But to get down to size eight! She had always been at least a twelve and often fourteen.

Then it was time to move into the beauty parlour which Ursula had booked to have Emma completely depilated, just like a young girl.

To Emma's great embarrassment, Ursula insisted on watching the removal of all her body hair. It was a long and rather painful process, but Ursula seemed to be delighted as Emma was finally powdered.

'Much better!' she said. 'I like the little girl look!'

Shamefacedly, Emma looked in the mirror. She felt and looked far more naked – and just like a little girl.

'We must hurry,' said Ursula. 'We've booked the swimming pool.'

'But I haven't brought my swimming things!'

'Never mind, little girls don't need costumes.'

The women were all wearing expensive, fashionable swimming costumes, but Emma was desperately shy when, stark naked, the girls lined up on the edge of the pool. She had been so ashamed of having to show that she had lost her hair, but the others were in the same state. Each had the same little girl look that the older women obviously enjoyed seeing on their girls, though they themselves did not indulge in it.

At first each girl swam with her mistress. Ursula delighted in playing with Emma's body under the water and Emma found it madly exciting. Then Ursula told Emma to help her slip off her own costume. They were soon swimming naked together. Ursula took Emma's hands and held them to her body under the water. It was Emma's turn to give pleasure. She found it thrilling. With her natural desire to serve, it was also very satisfying.

Looking around she saw that the other three girls were all serving their mistresses in the same way in the deserted swimming pool. It was an erotic sight, even the huge fat lady was now naked and holding Belinda tight to her body. Emma could tell how Belinda hated this sort of life.

Ursula made Emma kiss her body under the water. She made her swim between her legs and gripped her head between her thighs until poor Emma thought she was going to drown.

One by one the women left the pool and lay down on a couch, ordering their girls to dry them with their tongues as they knelt alongside their mistresses' couches. Ursula steered Emma's tongue to her two nipples and then down across her stomach. Swivelling round she held Emma's head clasped between her strong muscular thighs as she talked to the fat lady, who held Belinda similarly between her huge thighs. Quite unable to move, Emma went on using her tongue as she listened to the two women discussing art and a play they had both seen recently. Never had she felt so excitingly degraded.

Then each woman went off to shower, taking her girl into

her cubicle with her. Ursula made Emma soap them both all over, and then as water slowly ran down them she pressed Emma close to her.

'Oh Emma,' she whispered, 'you're going to be a lovely little slave, perhaps the best one I have.'

But later, at lunch, there was nearly a scene when Ursula caught Emma looking round the room. She had noticed that, unusually, there were several men in the room.

'Look at her!' cried Ursula, in one of her sudden rages. 'She's making eyes at the men at the other tables like a tart! What a slut she is! Don't you dare look at any men when you are with me, Emma! You just keep your eyes down!'

Poor Emma! She had realised by now that Ursula had a strong revulsion and jealousy towards anything male. It was true that she had noticed a rather good-looking man at the next table. It was true that she had shot the occasional glance at him. She would not dare do so again.

'I have the same problem with mine,' said one of the women, the mistress of the girl whom Emma had decided was really probably in her thirties. 'We all like to have normal girls who are naturally attracted to men, but that is also a problem. The only answer is to have the girl infibulated. Two little rings and a padlock – and the girl is quite safe with men even if she can't control her passions. And yet you only have to unlock the padlock and she is immediately wide open again – if you are interested in that part of her anatomy. Not all women are, and I have a friend who had her girl infibulated with just one ring – it is brazed over so that it can't be removed, so she's closed for life, or until her mistress has the ring removed.'

Emma was appalled, listening to this. She looked nervously at Ursula. Surely she would not really . . . 'Very interesting,' she heard her say in her slow voice. 'Very interesting indeed.'

'There is another answer,' cut in the fat woman. 'It is one that Arabs and Negroes have used for centuries: female circumcision.'

'Isn't that rather drastic?' asked the first speaker. 'I'm taking my girl to Paris next week to be infibulated and I recommend that you all do the same. You can come and have a look at her when I bring her back nicely ringed and padlocked. The mere fact of being infibulated has a strong psychological effect on a girl as regards men – she will be constantly terrified lest they feel the ring and the padlock and so lose her natural desire to flirt with the first handsome man she sees. But what you are suggesting, Helga, is another ball game altogether.'

'Not really! With a grown woman it's usually limited to simply snipping off the beauty bud, and that's a tiny operation these days. But it has a powerful effect on a girl. It really stops her playing with herself – and that's something I get very angry about. Ask Belinda! But it also stops a girl getting much pleasure at all, so she's not constantly chasing after men. But, of course, she can still give a man, or a woman, just as much pleasure as before. She just doesn't get pleasure herself and that won't worry us – we all like to limit the pleasure that our girls get. So I'm seriously thinking of having Belinda done.'

Belinda's mouth fell wide open in horror.

'No! No!' She was almost screaming. Conversation at other tables stopped. 'No, please, no!'

'Don't be silly, Belinda,' replied the fat woman nonchalantly. 'There are some excellent Arab doctors in London these days who specialise in doing it. You won't even know when it is going to be done. Whilst you are asleep, you'll just be given a little prick to make sure you stay asleep whilst it is done, and then you'll wake up in the morning in the normal way – but without the tiny bud that gives you so much pleasure and which leads you into so much temptation.'

'Yes,' Emma heard Ursula say, 'I've seen several girls in Morocco who have had it done by jealous husbands. It works very well and is very effective. I've often thought about it for my girls.'

Now it was Emma's mouth which fell open in horror. Not only at the clear threat of what might happen to her, but also at the fact that Ursula apparently had other girls. Of course, it was silly to suppose that such a wonderful woman, with her independent financial means, would not have other girls. But it still came as a shock. She remembered, however, what Ursula had said in the shower about her perhaps becoming the best little slave girl she ever had. Who cared about the others, if she was the best!

34

That afternoon, Emma was summoned to Ursula's room again. She was still wearing her gymslip, but Ursula had changed into a long negligée. She hugged Emma to her and then made her stand on a chair and take off her knickers and hold up her tunic so that Ursula could look more closely at her freshly powdered little girl look.

'It's lovely,' she said. 'It's just what I want. It's a lovely fresh and plump little thing for me to play with. But you must be very careful. You heard what I said at lunch. I don't allow a girl of mine to give herself any pleasure. It must all come from me. And before there's any pleasure there must be a little pain.'

'Oh no, madam,' cried Emma. 'I've tried to be a good girl.'

'That's why I'm only going to give you ten strokes.'

'Ten!'

'Yes. You must learn that I will not have you making sheep's eyes at strange men – or indeed any man. You are mine now. No more men for my girl!'

'But my husband . . . when he comes back . . .'

'We'll see about that nearer the time,' replied Ursula firmly. She picked up the cane, swished it, and then threw it across the room. 'Now, take off that gymslip and fetch me Sambo in your teeth.'

Ten minutes later, with ten fresh weals across her bottom, Emma was kneeling, just as she had the evening before, at the foot of Ursula's bed. But this time, she knew, the sucking and licking were not to be confined to Ursula's toes. Indeed she now wore a pretty little collar, embroidered with imitation diamonds, and from that collar led a chain, under the bedclothes, up to Ursula's left hand. Emma's head was already under the bedclothes, and every few minutes Ursula would give the chain a little tug, pulling Emma's head and mouth closer and closer to what both of them realised would be its final target.

Ursula was enjoying both the feeling of power over Emma and Emma's tantalising tongue as it neared her own throbbing bud.

In her right hand she held the bedclothes, ready to lift them up at the slightest sign of recalcitrance by Emma, so that she could apply the cane which lay conveniently by her bedside.

Suddenly the telephone rang. Emma froze under the bed-clothes, but Ursula was smiling as she picked it up, and with her left hand she gave another sharp little tug to the chain, forcing Emma to bring her tongue finally to its target.

'Yes, she's just getting there,' came Ursula's cool voice. Emma, listening under the bedclothes, realised that she was talking to the fat lady she found so repulsive. 'Yes, exactly the critical moment my dear. No, she has not had any pleasure herself yet. Wait, just a moment, I think she may need a little encouragement.'

Emma felt the bedclothes being pulled back and cold air on her bare bottom, which twitched in dread of the cane. The chain leading to her pretty collar was now being held taught. She could not lower her head. Suddenly she felt a smart tap across her bottom.

'Now, listen very carefully, Emma. Imagine that you are licking the skin off a peach and don't stop.'

To emphasise the message she felt another tap, then Ursula resumed her conversation.

'Yes, my dear, of course she's very inexperienced as yet, but she's doing very nicely. Oh! Oh! Yes, very nicely indeed. Yes, I think it will be well worthwhile having her professionally trained. Yes, the same place as you sent Belinda to. Yes, I am very pleased with her so far.'

There was a click as Ursula put the phone back on its stand.

'Now, my girl,' said Ursula, 'I want to feel a little more . . .'

Half an hour later, a blindfolded Emma was lying on her back on the large bed. Her arms were tied to the two upper corners. Her hips were raised by two cushions. Ursula was alternately kneeling astride her over her head and then lying on her, hips pressed to hips, thrusting down as she cried out: 'Wriggle Emma, or I'll beat you again.'

But there was little need to beat Emma into further efforts. Exhausted as she was by the non-stop pleasure she had been giving Ursula, who had climaxed several times, she was still herself unsatisfied and was still desperately trying to seek any little movements of pleasure that Ursula allowed her. Desperately she thrust up to meet Ursula's downward thrust, but every time she felt she was moving towards satisfaction Ursula would jealously withdraw for a moment before thrusting down again. Being on top, Ursula was in complete control and able to reach the heights of yet another climax whilst keeping Emma as eager as ever . . .

'You're acquainted with Sambo, Emma. Now you're going to meet Vitellus, the little friend I acquired in Rome. Your mistress cannot be bothered to spend time and effort giving a mere slave girl pleasure. But you've tried very hard and you've made your mistress reach the heights several times. For a first time, that's very good. One day I'm going to introduce you to Duet, my other little toy, but meanwhile here's Vitellus.'

There was a buzzing noise. Still blindfolded, and with her outstretched arms still tied, Emma did not at first understand what was happening. Then the noise came very close – suddenly it was vibrating against the most intimate part of her body, the part that had been screaming for relief whilst she had been pleasing Ursula. It was driving her to the heights. Her turn had come! Ursula was using it expertly and unbelievably excitingly.

'Oh! Oh!' She cried out in sheer joy. 'Oh! Oh! Oh!'

Suddenly it was gone.

'Oh please . . . More. Don't stop now . . . Oh please!'

'Now listen, Emma. Listen carefully. You are completely in my power now. I can provide pleasure . . .' The vibrator touched her again. 'Or I can withdraw it.' The vibrator was taken away. 'Or I can replace it with pain . . .' She felt the sharp tap of the cane across the front of her thighs.

'Just remember, Emma, it was not Vitellus that was important. The pleasure came because of me, because of what I did with it. I have already told you that I shall thrash you if I even find your hands under the bedclothes. I'm telling you now that I shall also thrash you if I ever find you playing with the vibrator, or if you ever try and buy one for yourself. You are never to own one and never to use one without my express permission. Do you understand?'

'Yes, madam,' whispered Emma, suddenly frightened.

'Very well then, we can proceed.' Again the vibrator was running up and down Emma's bare body lips. Again she was soon moaning in ecstasy.

'Now listen again, Emma. Your neck and breasts are covered

in red splotches. If I were to take off your blindfold, your eyes would doubtless be glazed. You are about to reach your climax. But you will do so when I tell you and to my order.'

The vibrator was taken away.

'Do you understand?'

'Yes, madam, oh yes!'

It was replaced.

'You've been excited by a mere machine, as if you were an animal. But it will be your mistress's hand that brings you to a climax. It is her hand that you will remember with gratitude and wonder, her hand, little Emma. Mine! Just remember that! The hand of your mistress! Mine!'

The voice was hypnotic. The vibrator was taken away just at the critical moment. Instead Emma felt Ursula's hand.

'You will not dare to climax before I give you permission, little Emma, nor will you dare not to climax exactly when I tell you.' That hypnotic voice! Ursula's hand was tantalisingly slow. It made long stroking motions. Emma started to wriggle madly against it. But the long slow motions continued, teasing, titillating and keeping her dangling for what seemed like hours of exquisite pleasure.

The hand started to move more quickly.

'Now, little Emma, are you ready to yield to your mistress?'

'Yes, yes, oh don't stop, don't stop!'

'Then say it!' ordered Ursula harshly.

'I'm ready to yield to my mistress!' cried Emma.

Still Ursula kept her waiting, to impress her complete authority on the girl. She was watching her body with an expert eye. Then her hand moved again.

'Now!' she ordered.

With a sudden scream, Emma reached her climax. Never had she reached such heights, never ever!

'Oh, madam, madam!'

Ursula smiled. She had no intention of bothering to bring Emma to such heights very often. That was something reserved for herself. But the memory of those heights would keep Emma desperately keen in future to please her again and again, in the hopes of being allowed to reach them again.

Indeed, it was a strangely different Emma that sat down that evening amongst the other girls. It was an Emma clearly besotted with Ursula, an Emma who simply could not take her eyes off Ursula, an Emma who just looked silently at Ursula with wonder and adoration, an Emma who listened open mouthed to Ursula's every word as she chatted to her women friends. It was an Emma who had just lost her new virginity – not so much a physical loss as a mental one.

Later, a note was passed down the table: 'Go upstairs and wait naked under the bedclothes and apply yourself silently and eagerly to my pleasure when I come. Remember, Sambo will be waiting for the slightest sign of hesitation or slackness. And just remember that if I ever catch you playing with yourself it will be twenty strokes. And don't think that I will not know. I shall be examining you carefully to check, every time you come to London. Countersign this note to show you understand my warning and get off upstairs.'

Emma read the note three times with mounting excitement and fear. Then she signed it and sent it back before scuttling from the room.

An hour later she performed just as she had been instructed, fear of Sambo never being out of her mind for very long. Ursula had long since learnt that even the most loving girl will perform better from fear than from love.

Twice during the night Emma was sent for to perform again.

There was, of course, no question of Emma herself being allowed more pleasure. Ursula made no attempt to give the girl any, and she did not expect it. Merely giving pleasure to her mistress was sufficient reward. But, to make certain that Emma did not attempt to give herself any pleasure, her hands were fastened behind her back with a pair of handcuffs each time she was sent back to her own room by a satiated Ursula.

Emma soon learnt to open the door of her room with handcuffed hands, and to get into bed. But she could not do the one thing Ursula had forbidden her to do!

# 4    THE RACE

The next morning Ursula and her friends took their girls, as usual, for their morning exercise in the gymnasium under the orders of Miss Perkins. Then each of them was carefully weighed, naked. Emma saw that Ursula and the dreaded Miss Perkins were having a long conversation. They kept looking at her. They must be discussing her – it intrigued her and made her a little nervous. Then she was called over, still stark naked, waiting for Ursula's permission to get dressed.

'Now listen carefully, Emma. We've decided to make a start in getting your weight down.'

'But I'm not fat!'

Miss Perkins slapped her face. 'Don't you interrupt your mistress!' she shouted. Emma rubbed her cheek, not daring to open her mouth again. 'She has decided to get you down to size eight, and that's all that concerns you!'

'So you're going on a grapefruit diet for a few days, as soon as you get home,' continued Ursula calmly. 'One grapefruit three times a day instead of a meal, until I tell you otherwise. And to make sure that you stick to the diet you are to ring me after each meal – and that includes ringing me after lunch from your office. And, incidentally, with each breakfast call I shall expect a specific assurance that you've been a good girl during the night. And I shall want a report every time you go to the loo. Don't try and lie – I shall know if you do. And if I am out, you can leave a message with Rafaela, my cook-housekeeper. Understand?'

'Yes, madam,' replied Emma, blushing deeply at the thought of telling someone else about her most private bodily functions.

'You are to come to see me on Thursday. If you have not lost at least two pounds, or if you show any signs of having played with yourself, I shall beat you. If your weight is down, then you will go on this diet that Miss Perkins has prepared for you. Every time you come to London I shall weigh you and if I ever find that you have put on one ounce then it will be the cane for you, my girl. Understand?'

'Yes, madam.' She gave a little shiver. It all sounded very frightening.

'And now, Emma,' continued Ursula, 'Miss Perkins is going to show you the exercises that I want you to do every day as part of getting you sleek and fit for my better amusement. Here again, you are to report every day that you have done them properly. If you lie, then I shall see that you have remained flabby and I shall beat you. So, you see, little Emma, I am taking complete control of your body – complete control. Miss Perkins will give you a card on which you are to record details of all your bodily functions and your monthly cycle, as well as reporting them to me by phone. You are to present the card to me weekly for me to countersign. Don't forget to put down everything! Now run along and go with Miss Perkins.'

Ten minutes later a sweating and still naked Emma ran to join the other equally naked girls straining on the bicycle machines in the gym under the eyes of their mistresses. Her mind was in a turmoil. So many orders to remember, diets to be followed, exercises to be done, phone calls to be made, cards to be filled in. And at the back of her mind the knowledge that Ursula would not hesitate to use Sambo. But, after being brought to such heights of pleasure by Ursula the evening before, she was utterly besotted with the idea of serving her.

She longed, oh how she longed, for the relief that only Ursula could give. And now Ursula was also taking complete charge of her body. Could she stick to the diet? Would she dare not to! Having to ring Ursula after each meal would be a terrible deterrent!

And Ursula was insisting on her remaining completely pure. Again, could she stick to it? With John away so much of the time, and anyway not being very interested in sex, Emma had become used to satisfying herself. Now Ursula had vetoed that. Twenty strokes of the cane!

Miss Perkins had shown her cards on which she was to record her bodily functions. It even had a column headed 'Unauthorised

Masturbation' for each four-hour period, and another headed 'Authorised Relief' which Ursula herself could initial to remind herself how often she had allowed the girl to climax.

It was all terribly humiliating, but Ursula and her friends seemed to regard it as quite normal and the health farm even had the cards printed for their clients!

Emma knew that she would not be able to lie to Ursula, with her hypnotic voice and steely blue eyes. Not even over the telephone. She was really going to be under Ursula's control even when away from her.

Oh what a cruel mistress she had! Oh what a wonderful and exciting mistress! So full of surprises!

That afternoon the women were going to hold the race for their girls, with the hateful Miss Perkins organising it.

The girls were in their gymslips as Miss Perkins showed them the course. It was about a mile round the park in front of the house, so that other guests could watch. As they walked round it she reminded them that their mistresses had each bet a thousand pounds on her girl winning – they had certainly better try hard!

Four thousand pounds! That was almost as much as she earned in her office in a year. Ursula and her friends must be very rich. No wonder they could afford to spend weekends here with their woman friends and belong to expensive health clubs in London.

'And just in case any of you were thinking of slacking,' Miss Perkins was saying, 'just remember that your mistresses have asked me to give the girl who comes second ten strokes of the cane, the girl who comes third fifteen strokes and the girl who comes last twenty. The punishments will be given in the gym after dinner tonight in front of your mistresses. I warn you that I shall be laying on the strokes very hard. Much harder than your mistresses may have punished you as a game in their bedrooms. The first five strokes will be across your bottom, the next five across the back. The next five, that the last two girls will receive, will be across your tummies and the front of your thighs and the last five, for the one who comes in last, will be across the breasts.'

There was a long silence as each girl realised just what they had been let in for. Emma had listened to Miss Perkins with mounting horror. She'd won a race at school, but had never done any running since. How awful to come in last and be thrashed across the breasts!

'So each of you is going to try her utmost to win, and each of you is going to be thinking of your beating tonight if you don't win. You will be thinking of it all the time, from now until the race starts, at the beginning of the race and right at the end when you will be straining your guts to win, or at least not be last. Think of it! Look at this cane! Five strokes across the breasts. And five across the belly. Think of it. Look at the cane again.' She raised it high in the air and brought it whistling down with a crash on one of the padded gym stools. The girls all shuddered in fear. Emma even gave a little cry of sheer fright.

For a whole hour the girls were kept waiting, sitting in terrified silence in the card room whilst their mistresses finished a game of bridge. Never, thought Emma, have I been so frightened. She was scared stiff of the thought of coming last.

When Miss Perkins showed them the course, she had explained it was not just a question of the fittest girl coming in an easy first. The race was more like an obstacle course. As well as various tree trunks that they would have to jump or climb over, they also had to swim a hundred yards up a little stream, run in their bare feet, and scramble twice through a line of rubber car tyres hanging on chains from trees. The tyres were nearly six feet off the ground and it was very difficult for the girls to get through them. Miss Perkins had allowed them to have a try. Emma had found that she had to strain like mad and the other girls had great difficulty too, so clearly the race was wide open. Much would be decided in the last two hundred yards – a steep climb up a hill along a stony track.

At last the women finished their interminable game of bridge. Emma saw that they had been playing for quite large sums of money. They went out to where Miss Perkins had arranged for several chairs to be put out, together with a tray of drinks, so that they could watch in comfort as their girls strained and sweated round the course.

The girls had to take off their shoes and socks and their knickers, leaving them naked under the gymslips, their breasts rising and falling noticeably, such was their feeling of fear and anticipation as they waited for what seemed like hours as their mistresses settled into their seats near the combined start and finish.

Emma could not take her eyes off Ursula, who was casually chatting to her friends. How she longed for her touch. How she would try to win for her. Four thousand pounds! And her breasts caned if she lost!

Suddenly they were off, running like mad down the hill, their little short gym tunics flapping as they went, pursued by cries of encouragement from their mistresses. They were jumping over the big tree trunks. Emma stumbled and fell heavily. Blood on her knees, but no time to stop. She rushed after the others and jumped the next tree clear, though she saw Belinda fall, lie winded for a moment and then scramble to her feet again.

There were six tree trunks in this part of the race and each claimed two casualties. The girls were still running close to each other. Then came a patch of thick brambles and stinging nettles – the comfortably seated mistresses laughed as they heard the sudden cries of pain. They congratulated Miss Perkins at having included the bramble patch in the course. By the time the girls had got through the brambles, their legs were all bleeding and the pain from the stinging nettles was dreadful.

Now they were struggling through the tyres. Emma fell from one of them and for a moment thought she had badly hurt herself, but forced herself on to the next tyre. Belinda and the older girl were ahead of her. A picture of her breasts and belly being beaten swam in front of her eyes and somehow she drove herself on and on. She could hear the breathing of the girl just behind her. Desperately she tried to catch up the other two girls.

She was only a few yards behind them as they scrambled down the bank of the deep stream and flung themselves into the water. Emma swam like mad against the current, gradually approaching the gate that marked where they could leave the freezing cold water.

Suddenly the girl behind Emma reached forward and pushed her under, leaving her lying last. Her temper was up and by the time she reached the bank near the gate she had pushed several of the other girls under the water, had again been pushed under herself, and was now lying second. Clearly with the prospect of the terrible beatings looming closely, this was a no-holds-barred sort of race. As the girls scrambled up the prickly bank of the river, once again covered in stinging nettles, Emma saw Belinda trip the older girl and push her back into the river. Each girl was fighting desperately to be ahead of the others.

Then came a further stretch of fallen tree trunks, which once again took its toll of fallers, and then it was the uphill finish over the stretch of sharp stones. These were playing havoc with the girls' bare feet, making them look down carefully as they struggled up the steep hill, sweating freely under their now soaking gymslips. They were in sight of the finish.

Suddenly the leading girl slipped and fell. Emma found herself in the lead. The track was deeply pitted. Suddenly she stepped on a sharp stone, jumped in the air with pain, slipped in a pot hole and fell. Two girls shot past her as she desperately scrambled to her feet and struggled to the finishing line. A few yards back she had been leading, now she was third. It was too disappointing. Too unfair. Exhausted from her efforts, and trying to catch her breath back, she burst into tears as she crossed the finishing line.

Suddenly her hair was pulled up with a jerk. She saw Ursula's angry face.

'You stupid girl. You lost me four thousand pounds, you silly cow.' She smacked Emma hard across the face. 'I don't want to see you until I hear you screaming under Miss Perkins' cane.'

It was a strange scene that greeted the women later that night as they stepped into the gymnasium beautifully dressed as if for dinner and fresh from another round of bridge.

Three naked girls hung by their wrists from a beam across the gymnasium, their toes just touching the floor. Behind them was a line of chairs that faced the line of naked young female backs and buttocks. To one side stood the smiling Miss Perkins, cane in hand.

The women seated themselves. The fourth girl, the winner, dressed in her party frock, sat on the floor at her mistress's feet, a triumphant smile on her face as she looked contemptuously at the other three. She had put out of her mind the fact that had Emma not stumbled at the last moment she too would be hanging there naked awaiting the cane. She had won, and that was enough. She had won four thousand pounds for her delighted mistress. As a reward she had been allowed two chocolates, the first sweets she had been allowed in the two years she had been in her mistress's service.

The beatings started.

As the women chatted and sipped their drinks, the girls all screamed and howled as Miss Perkins went along the line, giving each girl a stroke before going back to start again.

Soon the five strokes on each girls' buttocks were completed and Miss Perkins invited the women to inspect the weals. Then it was the turn of the three losers to feel the cane across their backs. This was a new experience for Emma, who was soon howling with the other two girls as the cane was brought down across her delicate back.

Miss Perkins put the cane down for a moment and rubbed her hands. A mass beating was often part of the proceedings when these women, or their friends, came with their girls for a weekend at the health farm. She would be given a large bonus by the management, who left such matters to her, whilst charging extra on the bill for 'Special Services'. She also knew that she would be given generous tips by the women them-selves, provided she put on a good display. She now swivelled Emma and the older girl, who had come in last, to face the women, leaving Belinda, who had been second, still facing away from them with her freshly striped back and buttocks well displayed.

Soon the well insulated gymnasium was filled again with screams. Never had Emma known such pain. Never had she hated anyone as much as she now hated Ursula, who sat watching the scene with a smile on her arrogant face, smoking a cigarette in her long holder, and drinking a vintage brandy. Never had Emma felt so utterly under the thumb of another person as she now felt under Ursula's. Ursula had, quite casually, ordered her to be thrashed in this dreadful way – and was clearly enjoying the spectacle.

Emma's punishment was soon complete, but the worst part

still awaited the older girl with her full, but firm, breasts. Her cries were pitiful, but soon there were five lines across her breasts, three above the nipples and two below.

Ursula nodded appreciatively. As an experienced thrasher of young women herself, she recognised the expertise of Miss Perkins.

Miss Perkins let down the three girls and released them. Emma rubbed not only her wrists to ease the pain, but also her bottom and her tummy. She longed to reach her back, which still hurt like mad. The relief of no longer having to stand on tiptoe was enormous.

'Now crawl to your mistresses and beg their forgiveness,' ordered Miss Perkins.

Emma crawled to Ursula. She felt the hatred flowing out of her. She had, after all, cost her mistress a thousand pounds and failed to win an extra three thousand for her. She found herself begging for forgiveness, like a well whipped dog who had committed a dreadful offence.

She gave a sob of gratitude as she felt Ursula's cold hand patting her head affectionately. All was forgiven!

Still feeling like a little dog, Emma put her head on her mistress's knees. She felt so happy again, even if her back was still on fire. She looked up at her mistress with adoration, still crying from the pain of the terrible beating.

'Oh, I do love you, madam,' she whispered.

She felt again as if she had entered a new and secret world. A new and terribly exciting world that she had never dreamt existed before. A secret world to which only Ursula had the key. She would, she knew, do anything and submit to any degradation to keep the attention and interest of this fantastic, rich and sophisticated woman.

Becoming Ursula's slave was the most exciting thing that had ever happened to her.

# 5    A VISIT TO LONDON

Emma arrived home with her mind besotted with Ursula.

That night she dreamed about her. Dreamed and got too excited . . . Then, in the middle of the night, the telephone rang, making her heart thump like a wild thing.

Ursula of course!

Had she been a good girl? Had she kept her hands above the sheets? She had not! Ursula was furious, swearing never to see Emma again unless she kept herself completely pure.

The next night, when Ursula rang again, she was able to give a proper answer. To feel herself being controlled like this was unbelievably erotic, especially as it was combined with having to ring up after each meal to confirm that she had only eaten a grapefruit and to read out her list of how her natural functions had been performed – Ursula might be miles away in London, but she controlled Emma's body as if she were in the cottage.

Emma found herself thinking of nothing else day and night, and by the third day she could bear it no longer. The office was quiet at this time of the year, and she just had to take a day off, jump on a train, take a taxi to Ursula's studio and stand outside with bated breath and trembling fingers.

At last, her mouth dry, she rang the bell.

A petite foreign woman of perhaps thirty answered the door. This must be Rafaela, Ursula's cook-housekeeper.

As soon as Ursula appeared, the whole world lit up for Emma.

'Welcome, little Emma. Come, I will show you my London studio.'

She took Emma by the hand as if she were a child, and led her round the gorgeous place, really more a house than a studio. It was all beautifully decorated in white and gold, white chairs with gold cushions, white walls with the relief picked out in gold leaf; white carpets and gold lamps. Downstairs was the living room, kitchen and maid's flat. Upstairs was the huge studio where she entertained, her easel and brushes in a corner, and next to it her sumptuous bedroom and bathroom.

Emma felt such a country frump as she saw the smart London magazines, the theatre programmes, the invitations to society balls and opening nights, the signed photographs of the rich and famous.

She saw several photographs of very pretty young women, all seeming to smile shyly from their frames, and remembered how Ursula had spoken of 'her girls'. One picture was of three attractive girls dressed in transparent harem-like dresses, kneeling submissively on a tiger skin rug, and standing behind them was a burly Negress dressed like a European nanny. Two of them were the same girls whose photographs in elegant evening dresses she had just been admiring!

'Who are these?' she asked.

'Never you mind! Perhaps one day your photograph might join theirs!'

Rafaela brought in a light lunch: chilled white wine and smoked salmon.

'But first we must weigh you, little Emma,' smiled Ursula. 'Rafaela, undress our guest.'

Emma was terribly embarrassed at being undressed like a child by the Italian woman, and even more so when she stood naked in the middle of the room. She was terribly ashamed lest Rafaela might see the remains of the weals from her thrashing, and even worse her now hairless body lips. But Rafaela said nothing as she slid Emma's clothes off her. She did not even say anything when she took Emma's slip – the same slip that Ursula had given her and which was embroidered with Ursula's initials.

'Put her on the weighing machine,' said Ursula. 'Let's see how she's doing.'

Rafaela took Emma by the hand and led her to Ursula's big airy bathroom. She made Emma stand on the weighing machine and then took her back into the big room, still stark naked. She said something in Italian which Emma did not understand. Ursula, she had noticed, seemed to speak every language under the sun – she repeated to herself what Rafaela had said and consulted a little black loose-leaf book.

To Emma's surprise the book was marked 'Emma', and she saw that as well as other notes it also contained the copy of the diet and list of exercises that Miss Perkins had prepared at the health farm.

'Um, rather slow progress. Where's your record sheet, Emma?'

Still naked, Emma found her bag and handed the list to Ursula, who studied it carefully. Then she looked Emma straight in the eyes. Emma could not meet her gaze . . .

'Look at me, Emma! You've been lying!'

Emma blushed but said nothing.

'There is no way you could have only lost a pound if you had been really sticking to the grapefruit diet. You have been cheating!'

It was true. She stood awkwardly before Ursula like a naughty child.

'Rafaela, fetch the cane.'

Naked and ashamed, Emma watched the Italian woman, only a few years older than herself, go into Ursula's bedroom and return with Sambo. She began to tremble, and fell to her knees.

'Please forgive me, please, please? It was so hard to do! Please don't beat me again. Please. I promise I won't cheat on you again! Oh, please . . .'

Ursula hesitated. 'Very well,' she said at last. 'I'll let you off this time. I think you have learnt that it is no good trying to lie to me, I shall always find out the truth. I don't want to spoil what should be a happy day together.' She paused and put the cane down, and her whole attitude changed. 'Thank you, Rafaela, but before you go bring me that bottle of champagne.'

A few minutes later a very much relieved Emma was serving Ursula with a glass of champagne. She kept glancing at the cane left lying prominently on the desk – she felt like a woman who had escaped the guillotine, for the moment at least.

'Now, my dear Emma, you may have a glass too, and tell me everything you have been up to – apart from stuffing yourself with food!'

It was a lovely lunch, though she had to eat it naked. Her glass of champagne cheered her up enormously. Ursula allowed her some of the delicious smoked salmon and even let her sip the white wine. Then they enjoyed fresh coffee. And the best thing about it all was being alone with the fascinating Ursula without that awful Rafaela hanging around with her smug face, looking as if she had seen it all before.

Afterwards Emma helped Ursula to undress also, and they lay together under the sun lamp. Once again Emma admired Ursula's trim boyish figure, and thought of poor Belinda being made to serve the huge fat woman, that revolting creature who would have been flopping about like a jellyfish.

With Belinda's mistress it would have been horrible to lie side by side like this, but with Ursula it was wonderful, close together as the rays beamed down on them. The soft light made both their bodies look so nice, and in the background Ursula's stereo was playing some wonderfully erotic blues music.

Never, Emma thought, had she felt so relaxed, except perhaps when on holiday in Italy or Greece. Her mistress certainly had this international flair of making quite ordinary things seem wonderful and exciting.

She could hear Ursula's little murmurs of praise for her flat tummy and pretty shoulders. But at times there was a more brittle voice, telling her that she must get her waist even smaller and her breasts even firmer. But Emma was too happy to be upset.

Ursula moved nearer.

'Let me put some cream on you, Emma, or you will burn.'

It was not just the cream she enjoyed, for as Ursula began to spread it she could feel her pulse quickening, feel herself becoming hotter and moister.

In the corner of the room was a chaise longue. Ursula rose and spread a thick white towel on it. 'Come here, my little girl,' she said softly. 'Now, just lie flat on your front and I'll finish you off. Spread your legs wide apart so that your mistress can cream you all over.'

Emma felt almost giddy as Ursula's fingers caressed her. Could it be the champagne? Whatever it was, she adored what was happening. She had played doctors and nurses at boarding school, but this was much more exciting.

Soon she was longing for Ursula to do more. Ursula, however, was an experienced seducer of young women and was not going to hurry things along too quickly. But when Emma was feeling at her most excited Ursula again pulled her legs apart to apply yet more cream.

'Oh, Emma,' she cried in mock surprise. 'Oh, you are an excited little girl!' She bent down over Emma and kissed her fully on the lips. 'Whatever are we to do with you?'

Her tongue, like a lizard's, forced its way into Emma's mouth and right down her throat. Then she licked Emma's ears and moved on down to her nipples, which were now hard and taut.

It was so much more exciting than being with poor dull John . . .

Now Ursula put her mouth to Emma's body lips. She parted them with her fingers and let her tongue roam inside. She tickled her behind with a soft brush, until Emma felt she was exploding.

'Make me yield to you,' she screamed out.

But Ursula was not having any of that. Oh no! It amused her to bring a young woman to the point of yielding, but she would not allow her to do so until she herself had had her pleasure – and even then only occasionally.

'Please, mistress – mistress?'

The phone! The bloody phone!

Ursula was quickly off Emma, leaving her lying there in mortified frustration.

'Yes,' she heard Ursula say, 'the new one – from the country. She's here now. No, not yet. Of course I'm sure. No, I can't do that now. No . . .'

Was Ursula being challenged in some way? Asked to prove something or admit some sort of failure?

Emma saw that while she spoke she was looking into the big mirror that hung on the wall – and in that was Emma, former country bumpkin. Ursula was lying on the chaise longue, talking to some unknown person, and at the same time admiring that naked body in the mirror.

Suddenly Ursula nodded decisively, as if she had changed her mind about something.

'All right then, I will! You can listen and then apologise for doubting me! Yes, yes, if she doesn't do it you can bloody well have her, she won't be any more use to me!'

Emma had seen her clasp her breasts as she talked. She had

moved her legs apart and stroked herself between them, a sight which made Emma even more excited.

'Come here, girl,' Ursula suddenly screamed. 'Crawl, you little bitch, crawl to your mistress and please her!' She was still holding the telephone in one hand and with the other she slapped Emma across the face as she knelt hesitating between her knees.

Emma worked desperately at giving pleasure to Ursula, concentrating on her task and genuinely frightened by Ursula's sudden display of temper. She could feel the excitement rising in herself all the time. She noticed Ursula bend down and pick up something that had been hidden under a cushion. She heard a well known humming – Vitellus! She saw Ursula bend down over her and then her head was thrust down to the floor and then – in came the vibrating Vitellus!

Her hair was being pulled again. She was kneeling on all fours between Ursula's legs, controlled by Ursula's hand gripping her hair as she tried to please her whilst being driven mad by Vitellus.

Ursula looked down at the girl trying so hard to please her. She looked across at the big mirror – Vitellus was performing well. The sight of Emma grovelling at her feet aroused her further, as did the smell of Emma's own arousal.

'Not till I count twenty.' She gave Emma's hair a firm twist. 'And then instantly.'

Slowly Ursula started to count.

She still held the phone in her left hand and with her right was moving Emma's head, sending mouth and tongue up and down. The explosion hit her at fifteen. Somehow she managed to go on counting in a mounting frenzy. 'Sixteen, little slut, eighteen, nineteen, *twenty! Now! Now!*'

Emma yielded with an uncontrollable scream, and then they both curled up on the floor together.

The last thing Emma remembered was the click of the phone being put down.

Emma was now even more bestotted by Ursula and her fascinating and unpredictable ways. She thought of her all day long, of her interesting work, her sumptuous house, her widespread knowledge, her strangeness, her lesbian friends, her wealth.

It was not easy coping with Ursula's moods. On one visit she arrived late. Ursula was furious and ignored her, leaving her in the downstairs living room whilst she herself breezed in and out, hardly saying a word.

Emma was taken aback, not knowing how to handle the situation.

'Well, Emma, did I ask you to come today?' Ursula said angrily at last, looking blankly at Emma.

'Yes, madam. Don't you remember?'

But Ursula appeared to be bored. She poured herself a vodka, ignoring Emma again.

Emma was now at her wits end. She wanted to appear amusing and fun, but she realised that Ursula probably found her dull and stupid.

Suddenly Ursula said: 'Let's go to Annabel's.'

'But I haven't anything smart to wear,' wailed Emma.

'Don't worry about that,' said Ursula, starting to wake up. She called for Rafaela and told her to bring some dresses. Meanwhile she told Emma to undress, then, a moment later, she exploded again.

'My God, look at you! Just look at those drooping breasts! How can I make anything of you, you dreary little rustic? How can I go out with a peasant girl?'

She fetched the long easel brush which she often used for soft strokes across Emma's breasts, but instead used it this time to slap them.

'Get them up, girl,' she cried. 'Hold your shoulders back, you slouching animal, you. I said stick out your breasts! Up! Up! Up, damn you!'

Poor Emma was in tears. She was horrified by this sudden mood of Ursula's. It was as if she hated her all of a sudden. She felt helpless and pathetic as she stood there lashed by Ursula's thunder storm.

Then Ursula's mood changed again, like sunshine switched on.

'Now, now, there's a good girl. Hold your breasts up. Like that – yes, that's better, much better. There's a good girl. Let me wipe your tears away.'

Immediately Emma found herself responding as she never

54

had before. She knew she would do anything to please Ursula, to make herself more attractive to her. The power that Ursula had over her had suddenly entered a new dimension.

Rafaela returned with a lovely designer dress which Emma fell in love with at sight, and Ursula sent her off to have a bath before putting it on. Smiling happily, Emma set off upstairs towards Ursula's bathroom.

'Not my bathroom,' said Ursula sternly, her hard cold voice suddenly back. 'Use the maid's one.'

Crestfallen, Emma obeyed.

'Scrub her back for her, Rafaela,' called out Ursula after them. 'These rustics are filthy. I don't want her dirtying that dress.'

Half an hour later, having had a good weep on Rafaela's shoulder, feeling thoroughly demoralised and unhappy, Emma appeared again. Despite her inner distress, she looked very attractive. Under the dress she wore only a pair of Ursula's panties.

'Oh,' said Ursula, 'so my little rustic really is looking pretty this evening. Now where shall I take her?'

Emma didn't know whether to smile or cry. Was Ursula teasing her? Was she still playing games with her?

Then Ursula leaned over her, cupped her breasts, kissed her ears and murmured: 'Oh, you gorgeous little creature. Oh how I want some friends of mine to get their hands on you and really train you for me.'

Emma did not understand what she meant, but she knew that she was now longing for Ursula to strip her naked, to hold her and to play with her bare body. The last time that had happened, Emma had thought she was going to melt with excitement.

'Has my little rustic got her see-through panties on?' murmured Ursula. 'Is she going to show them to me?'

Emma was now throbbing with desire, desire for Ursula's long cool hands.

'Now my silly little rustic, let us see you put on a little show for my amusement. Take off those panties. You're going to play with yourself in front of me.'

'No, please, madam, not like this . . .'

'Shall I call Rafaela to do it – and she can see the show.'

'No, no . . .'

'Very well, go to bed instantly!' Again Emma felt a hard smack across her cheek. 'Go to the maid's spare room and stay there. I shall not be taking you out with me tonight, my girl. You're lucky I can't be bothered to beat you.'

# 6   A DINNER PARTY AND
       A NURSERY

Again Emma found herself pressing Ursula's doorbell.

'Mademoiselle is out,' said Rafaela, 'but she left this note for you.'

Disappointed, Emma opened and read it.

'It says I am to do exactly as you say, Rafaela. What does she mean?'

'She? Who is she?' asked Rafaela archly. 'Do you mean your mistress? If so, come in and say so.'

'Yes,' whispered Emma shyly as she entered the hallway. 'I mean my mistress.'

'She has a dinner party. I am to cook and you will serve it. I shall tell you what to do and show you what you are to wear.'

'What I am to wear? What am I to wear?'

'A maid's outfit, of course. You don't imagine mademoiselle would have you answering the door, offering drinks and serving dinner in your present clothes, do you?'

'Aren't I going to be allowed to join the dinner party? Aren't I a guest too?'

'Certainly not, you are a servant girl tonight and that is all you are. I believe your mistress wants to discuss your future with certain of her guests. Now, your costume is laid out in the maid's room, so you had better put it on before we practise opening doors and taking the ladies coats as well as serving. Mademoiselle does not wish to see anything of you until you show the first guest into the upstairs studio.'

So it was that three hours later it was Emma who opened the door to the first guest, a striking looking woman of about fifty. Smiling, she took her coat and led her up to the studio where a beautifully dressed Ursula stood waiting. The two friends kissed and then Emma, dressed in a black skirt and blouse with

57

a white apron and cap, offered them both a glass of sherry on a silver tray.

As she closed the door she heard the guest say: 'A new girl, Ursula? You're so clever at finding them.'

Seven other women arrived, and also a man who seemed to be one of Ursula's artistic friends. Emma was kept busy serving drinks, until Ursula told her to go down and see if dinner was ready.

This was something Emma had been dreading ever since Rafaela had told her that Ursula had left explicit instructions that she was to serve dinner wearing one less garment with each course.

By the time she served coffee she was to be down to her white cap, white gloves, black suspender belt, black stockings, high-heeled shoes – and of course her pretty diamanté studded collar!

'But why, Rafaela, why?' she had cried out in protest.

Rafaela laughed. She had seen it all before. 'These ladies like to show their new girls off to each other, like a man showing off his new girlfriend.'

'He wouldn't show off his girlfriend naked to other men!'

'Well, I suppose it isn't really like with men. These women enjoy lending and borrowing each other's girls. I am not one of them, but I can see the enjoyment of lending a reluctant girl to one's more ugly friends – think how much more she will love her own mistress when she is sent back.'

'Oh, but surely no girl would agree to that?'

'She has no say in the matter. Would you?'

Emma realised she would not. Nor could she avoid serving the dinner in the way Ursula ordered, for losing Ursula was something she just could not contemplate – even when the last guest to arrive turned out to be the hugely fat woman Helga whom she had found so repulsive even to look at at the health farm.

So it was that Emma served the delicious cold soup without her skirt, the hot salmon without skirt or blouse, and the coffee without even any panties. On each occasion Ursula took a particular delight in drawing her guests' attention to a distinctive part of Emma's anatomy, saying it was still too big or too flabby, and asking her guests for their views as to whether Emma would eventually make a suitable girl for her.

'She's certainly very pretty,' one woman said as Emma's naked breasts hung down over her as she was being served.

'Had you thought of having her breasts enlarged?' another asked. 'I mean really enlarged. I had one of my girls done. She hated it, but I found the result very amusing and stimulating. It also had the very desirable effect of making the girl much more feminine and submissive – not that you are likely to have any problems with this girl, I should think.' She laughed. 'And I see she's married. I don't expect her husband would object when he saw her breasts.'

Emma, behaving as a servant girl, listened in horror but could say nothing.

'But my dear Ursula,' said another woman, 'you really shouldn't allow the slut to go on wearing her wedding ring. It's a deliberate insult to you – a way of thumbing her nose at your authority.'

'Of course you are right!' said Ursula. She turned to Emma. 'Take off your wedding ring and engagement ring, Emma, and give them to me.'

With a sob the now nearly naked and terribly embarrassed Emma did as she was told, handing them over as humbly as she could.

'Good,' said Ursula. 'If I decide to keep you, I shall give you a new ring to wear – mine!'

This seemed a terribly symbolic moment to Emma – her relationship with Ursula was now more important than her marriage.

'Have you thought of breeding from her?' asked another woman. She was tall like Ursula and sounded French, though her English was perfect – maybe a shade too perfect.

There were a few heads shaken and a murmur of interest around the table.

'Oh, but I really enjoy supervising the breeding of my young girls as much as I do the breeding of my pedigree retrievers. It is so fascinating deciding when they should be mated, choosing the stud, supervising the arrangements. I have a little party to come and see her covered . . .'

There was another murmur round the table.

'Oh but my dears, you shall all come to the next one . . . and then there is the wait to see whether the little bitch has conceived. I get as excited about one of my girls as I do about my prize bitches, I assure you.'

'When do you tell them,' asked Helga. 'Tell them if they are, er –'

'Pregnant? Oh I don't tell them. They don't even realise I am trying to breed from them – I tell them that their morning sickness is just indigestion and often the first time they guess is when they feel the child kicking inside them.'

'Good!' said Helga. 'That is good!'

'Then of course we have tears and entreaties. But of course I make them go through with it. It becomes so exciting as the girl is made to carry her unwanted child – or better still it may be children, though never so many as my retrievers can manage. It really makes you feel like God as the girl is brought to you every day so that you can see her swelling up. You are creating something living and deciding just what you want it to be. It is fascinating using a range of different studs: Negro giants, dwarfs, huge Japanese wrestlers – and then seeing what results.'

There was another murmur of appreciation round the table.

'And her?' The woman pointed at Emma. 'My dear Ursula, this girl of yours has excellent childbearing hips. They could carry almost anything. Whenever I see a girl with a nice flat little belly like that, I immediately wonder what she would look like with a pretty round protruding one.'

'Yes,' replied Ursula. 'I have a friend in Morocco, a rich Arab woman, who shares your interest and enthusiasm in breeding from young girls. It's not something that has ever madly interested me so far – but you never know.'

Emma almost spilt the coffee as she listened. Oh no, she thought, I'm not an animal. I'm not. But secretly she realised that she would have no choice in the matter if Ursula followed her friend's suggestion.

'In any case, I think you have shown great taste in acquiring her, my dear Ursula,' came the rather precious voice of the only man present. 'With proper training you could really make something of her and give yourself considerable pleasure into the bargain.'

'Thank you, Dominic,' came the voice of Ursula again. 'That's exactly what I think too, but I wanted to show her to you all to get your views. I think she's worth spending a little time and money on. Proper professional training seems a good idea.'

Emma, now virtually stark naked, was busy serving brandy and liquers. She did not dare show by even a flash of her eyes that they were discussing her. She knew that Ursula regarded her as a mere servant. Nevertheless she felt herself go all soft at Ursula's words. So Ursula really did like her! She was prepared to spend time and money on her!

'Be careful,' Helga chipped in. 'You never know how a girl is likely to turn out before you've tried her out between your thighs. It's like buying a horse – you must ride her yourself first. Until I have done so, I wouldn't like to give an opinion, Ursula dear.'

'Well, that's easily corrected,' laughed Ursula. 'You can try her out now, whilst we finish our coffee. Enjoy your ride, my dear. Emma, take Helga up to my bedroom.'

'Oh n . . . n . . .' stammered Emma. She was utterly appalled.

'Go on, little girl,' said Ursula firmly, as if she were telling a child to show her dolls to a grown-up. 'Off you go and make Helga happy. Don't let me down, little Emma.'

Shattered and horrified, Emma opened the door for the huge woman. Then came Ursula's voice, calling after them.

'Just remember she's still pretty well untrained, Helga. You'll probably need my cane to get the best results. She knows where it is – just ask her to fetch Sambo.'

Half an hour later a smiling and radiant Helga came back into the dining room. She was followed by a subdued and blushing Emma, still dressed in just her shoes and stockings, gloves, cap, suspender belt, and collar. The guests were amused to see several fresh weals across her backside and on her cheeks: the red marks that showed she had just spent a long time clamped tightly between the thighs of a large and powerful woman.

'Well, Helga, what do you think of my little Emma?'

'Not bad, Ursula, not bad at all. My recommendation is to keep her and have her properly trained. That should perfect her technique, which is rather rudimentary at present, and also make her more submissive and pliable. That's necessary I think. I suspect she's still attracted to men, and of course that must be corrected.'

Emma was now completely under Ursula's control.

Ursula made sure in many different ways that the younger woman was always aware of this. She was not, for instance, allowed to use the seat of the loo in Ursula's bathroom. She had to accompany Ursula on shopping expeditions, naked under her dress, walking a respectful two paces behind, and carrying all the parcels. She had to throw away all her underclothes, and most of her other clothes as well, and wear only Ursula's cast-offs – all prominently embroidered with Ursula's initials. Her wastes were strictly checked and Ursula insisted on Emma filling in her record card properly and presenting it for initialling every time she came to London.

Ursula also enjoyed making her behave like a little girl, lisping her love and begging for hugs like a real child. 'You are very sweet,' Ursula would say, adding rather mysteriously, 'the sweetest of all my little girls.'

Emma enjoyed all this, thrilled by the secret world in which Ursula had immersed her. She adored her extraordinary mistress and would do anything to remain in her good books. She was terrified not only of Ursula's temper but also lest Ursula become bored with her. To prevent this, she realised, she must allow Ursula to have complete power over her. That was not only exciting, it seemed to satisfy some craving inherent within her.

She also realised now how much more seriously these highly intelligent lesbian women took their love affairs than men did theirs. They took the trouble to ensure that the minds of their pretty young girlfriends were kept fully occupied by thoughts, fears and worries about their strict mistresses.

A man might put the object of his affections on a pedestal and worship her, but Ursula and her friends, being women themselves, understood girls better. They knew that most young women secretly long to be dominated by a strong-willed man.

They also knew that a strong-willed woman could take the place of such a man, and that if the girl were kept both abject and submissive she would soon find herself adoring her controller. That was why the cane and the fear of it played such a vital role in the complex relationship between these lesbian ladies and their non-lesbian girlfriends.

Emma was fascinated by Ursula's sheer ruthlessness, strength of character, and way of life. She was hypnotised by this older woman's stare, by her voice on the telephone. Or even by a note in Ursula's handwriting . . .

She had been summoned to another weekend in London, and when she rang the door bell, Rafaela handed her a note: 'When I get back I shall expect to find you in your nursery. Rafaela will see to it.'

Rafaela threw open a door to a room that had always been locked before. Because of its very solid door and strong lock, Emma had always assumed that it was where Ursula stored her paintings. But it turned out to be a bright colourful place that had been decorated and furnished like a child's nursery.

On one wall were pictures of rabbits and bears and on another pictures of little girls in pinafores. The window had bars across it as if to prevent a child from falling out. In the corner was a large doll's house and propped against it were two delightful dolls and a range of dresses that must have cost a fortune. Several children's picture books lay on a table and on another was a child's tea set.

Hanging in a cupboard which had been left open were a row of pretty children's style dresses that were big enough to fit a grown woman – provided she was only size eight!

Up in a corner was the eye of a remote-controlled television camera that, Emma was to learn, produced a picture in Ursula's bedroom, from where it could be controlled. Later, she was also to learn that Rafaela could also see what was going on from the kitchen, so that she could keep an eye on any occupant of the nursery if Ursula was out. Either one of them could flood the nursery with bright light. There was also a baby alarm to enable Ursula to speak to a girl in the nursery.

And that was not all.

In the centre of the room was a prettily painted playpen with bars over the top that would prevent even the most active person from crawling out. Near the pen was a special child's cot, large enough to hold a grown up girl – provided she curled up – and once again with bars over the top.

The mattress of the cot, like the carpet in the playpen, was covered in a rubber sheet as a precaution against bed wetting or accidents.

The bars above the playpen and the cot had a little section that lifted upwards to allow a girl to be put into it or lifted out, with a catch on the outside that could not be opened from within.

In an alcove off the nursery was a child's bath with several plastic ducks surrounding it.

'No! No!' Emma cried.

But Rafaela's grip on her arm was tight.

'You know you love pleasing your mistress,' she whispered.

Two hours later Ursula unlocked the front door and strode into her house. She had had a successful day at the gallery and had sold several pictures for high figures. It seemed that there was a big demand for her pictures of European women, dressed skimpily and lying languidly in an eastern palace with the windows covered with beautifully decorated iron work and the walls covered with tiles. These pictures seemed, people kept saying, so realistic. The artist, they whispered, lived in Morocco – but how did she have access to such a palace and who were the beautiful girls she painted wearing so little?

Feeling on top of the world, Ursula flung open the door of the nursery, Rafaela behind her.

There was Emma, crawling in the playpen wearing plastic rompers which covered a napkin that was fastened in front with a pin. There were special gloves on her hands that prevented her from holding or undoing anything because the fingers were sewn together. A large rubber teat in her mouth, held there by a strap, stopped her from talking – because of the gloves she could neither remove the teat from her mouth nor the rompers from her bottom.

'She looks charming.' Ursula clapped her hands in delight. 'You have done very well, Rafaela. Let us have a closer look at my little girl.'

She slid back the catch and opened the top of the playpen, then leant down and lifted Emma out, just as if she were a baby. Thrilled, she sat the silent and almost naked girl on her knees.

Emma looked up at her, trying to talk from behind the comforter but only able to make gurgling noises like a baby.

'When was she last changed?' asked Ursula.

'Two hours ago, mademoiselle.' Rafaela went to a cupboard and pulled out a child's pot. 'Should I start training her?'

'Yes, you start that whilst I'm changing to go out for the evening. And then you could put her to bed in her cot. I'll look in to see her before I go out. Oh, but has she had a feed yet?'

'No, mademoiselle. It's ready but I thought you would wish to start her.'

Rafaela handed Ursula a baby's feeding bottle with another big teat, then unfastened the strap that held the comforter in Emma's mouth. Before Emma could say a word, Ursula had thrust the teat of the bottle of warm specially sweetened baby milk into her mouth – and Emma found herself sitting on Ursula's lap and sucking eagerly at the bottle.

'What a lovely little girl you are,' said Ursula encouragingly. 'The nicest of them all. You're going to love this little nursery. When you're a bigger girl I shall let you play with your dolls, but for now you'll be in the playpen during the day, all weekend, except when Rafaela puts you into your cot for your afternoon rest and in the evening. I want my little girl to have plenty of sleep – and who knows? – her mistress might come to see her during the night. And you're going to really look forward to your bottles. Perhaps another time, when you are bigger, we might let you have a little baby food out of a tin.'

She glanced at her watch, then stood up and handed Emma and the bottle to Rafaela.

'Goodness, I must fly. I'm going to the theatre, little baby. I'll look in later before I leave and when I get back to make sure baby is all right.' She patted Emma's cheek and turned to Rafaela. 'She's a really lovely little girl. I've got several friends coming to lunch tomorrow. They'll be fascinated to see her being given her feed. You'd better change her just before they arrive – I don't want any unpleasantness.'

With a wave to the 'baby' she hurried from the room.

A few minutes later, the bottle being empty, Rafaela replaced the big teat in Emma's mouth and fastened it again behind her neck. Then she unfastened Emma's nappy and put it in the laundry basket before seating Emma on the pottie. Emma was now desperately trying to say something, but all that came out were gurgles as nature took its course.

'That's a good girl,' said Rafaela, 'your mistress will be very pleased.'

Then she put a clean nappy on a couch and lay Emma on her back on it. She powdered her well and then fastened the dry nappy. Then she put Emma into the cot with its rubber sheet and the beads on the side for Emma to play with. Emma curled up in the cot.

'Now go to sleep, little one, until your mistress comes to kiss you goodnight.' She lit a night light and switched off the light. She set a baby alarm by the cot. It would enable every little whimper Emma might make to be heard in Ursula's bedroom or the kitchen. Then she shut and locked the door, leaving the key in the lock so that Ursula could visit the nursery whenever she wished.

An hour later a beautiful tall woman quietly entered the nursery. She tiptoed to the cot, put her hand through the bars and stroked Emma's long hair, listening approvingly to the little gurgling noises.

'Good night, little Emma. You have pleased your mistress very much and if you are a good girl she will come and visit you later during the night. You'd like that, wouldn't you, my beautiful little Emma?'

The reply was another delicious little gurgle.

Ursula smiled in delight and turned to go.

'Night-night, little Emma.'

The experiment had been a great success, thought Ursula, as the taxi took her to the theatre. She had really enjoyed seeing Emma in the playpen wearing her rompers. The joy of the nursery was that its inmate could also be made to play the part of a little girl of five or six, and she could have a strict governess instead of a proud mama.

It would, she thought, be amusing to give Emma lessons in reading and writing, in colouring and drawing, and to keep her in the nursery, unable to get out, only allowed to play with dolls or look at picture books. To punish her when she was naughty. To put her into her cot for her afternoon rest and to watch her on the internal television to make sure she remained a good girl and did not get up to any naughty tricks – tricks that carried the automatic penalty of twenty strokes of the cane.

She might even suggest to some of her friends that they bring their girls over for a children's tea party. Balloons, pretty party dresses, a competition for the prettiest little girl and doll . . . The possibilities seemed endless and would all serve her desire to dominate the younger woman.

There might even be a baby girl's party, with half-a-dozen little creatures, naked except for their rompers, all crawling round the playpen, making little gurgling noises behind their teats, and each trying to please its mistress by making her feel that she had complete power over her girl – even the power to reduce her to the status of a baby girl.

She would still use Emma as her maid when it suited her, of course. But the nursery offered a whole range of alternative ways of dominating the young woman – and excuses for beating her.

Yes, she felt, the nursery was a great success.

# 7    BOURNEMOUTH

Ursula genuinely felt that men were evil and treacherous.

When Emma arrived from the country and went to the studio, Ursula would interrogate her angrily, cane in hand, as to whether she had been seeing any men, whether any had been invited to her house, and Emma even had to account for her relationship with the milkman, the postman, the gardener, the newspaper boy, and even with her next door neighbour, a retired army colonel.

Ursula was suspicious of all these men, and regarded Emma as a trollop who would happily have sex with all or any of them. She even made Emma swear that she had not spoken to any men on the train and began to send a minicab with a woman driver to pick Emma up at the station because she was frightened that Emma might otherwise go shopping or visiting friends on her way to the studio, and start talking to a man.

So when Emma's husband, John, returned, it naturally put a great strain on both of them.

Ursula started to pay a regular allowance into Emma's bank every month and told Emma to tell John that she now had a part-time job in London as Ursula's assistant and to show him the bank statements. This explained Emma's frequent absences, and John was delighted that his wife had a new and absorbing interest that was also obviously well paid. What he did not know was that Ursula kept Emma's cheque book and credit cards under lock and key, paid her bills, decided what she might buy for herself, and allowed her only a little pocket money, with a separate account for her housekeeping allowance from John.

Emma asked Ursula to stop beating her, but Ursula refused, so that Emma had great difficulty in hiding the inevitable weals from the cane called Sambo.

'What's that mark, darling?' the naïve and innocent John would ask.

'Oh, it's where I tripped up coming down the stairs.' Emma would say, or something equally inadequate.

She just had to do something about it.

'Ursula,' she said timidly one day, 'John is getting very suspicious. Please, you really must stop beating me so hard.'

'Nonsense, little Emma,' said Ursula sternly. 'That is quite enough of that, so kindly do not ask me a third time. You can tell that pig of a husband what you like, but don't try and use him as an excuse for avoiding a beating or two. It's good for girls to be regularly beaten. Besides, I enjoy beating you, so if you want to go on seeing me then you must accept it.'

Emma was terrified of losing Ursula and the new world to which Ursula had introduced her. So she accepted the beatings. Indeed, she found them and the long drawn out anticipation of them very exciting and was becoming addicted to them.

But Ursula was also very disturbed by the thought of John making love to Emma.

She made Emma promise to sleep apart from John, making the excuse that she was not well. She insisted on Emma telephoning her each morning as soon as John had left for his office to say whether or not she had slept in John's bed.

Emma found all this attention very exciting – she felt like a young girl being pursued by a handsome prince, except that in this case it was a handsome princess. But it was not at all pleasant when Ursula rang one night to check that Emma was on her own, only to hear a breathless John in the background complaining at being disturbed, for although Emma wished John would dominate her in the bedroom she nevertheless enjoyed making love to her gentle husband occasionally.

Emma was immediately summoned to London and a truly terrible scene followed. There were accusations that Emma was a liar and unfaithful to her mistress. There were tears and screams and a thrashing. Ursula took Emma to see her own woman doctor and told her that Emma, who hardly dared to open her mouth, was not strong enough to submit to sexual relations with her husband.

They came out with a note confirming this and saying that Emma must sleep in a separate room.

Not content with all this, Ursula decided to strengthen her control over Emma even further by taking her to Bournemouth for a few days. She was having an exhibition there. There had been a lot of publicity in the local press and the mayor was to open it. The local gallery had booked a suite for her in the best hotel, and she, in turn, booked a small room at the back for Emma.

Only when Ursula had rather mysteriously gone off for a few days to her villa in Morocco had the reins on Emma been eased. Now they were to be shortened again.

Ursula drove down to Emma's cottage in her smart car. Emma found it highly embarrassing having to introduce Ursula to her husband, especially as Ursula had previously given strict instructions that she was to be naked under her tweed suit when she arrived.

But John was not aware of that and all went well. Ursula showed great interest in his work as an oceanographer and thanked him for 'lending' her Emma for a few days to help out with her exhibition. He, in turn, the innocent that he was, thanked Ursula for taking such an interest in his little country mouse of a wife and for having given her new interests.

Emma listened with growing embarrassment as the two of them discussed her education in the artistic world as if she were a child. But worse was to follow. Hardly were they out of sight of the cottage when Ursula stopped the car and got out.

'Now, if I'm paying for you in Bournemouth, little Emma, I shall expect good service – starting with driving the car.' She produced a chauffeur's cap. 'This will clearly establish your status. Put it on and drive me to the Royal Hotel in Bournemouth.'

She then settled down nonchalantly in the back seat to read the latest reviews of her exhibitions whilst Emma, not daring to open her mouth, drove carefully off.

When they arrived, Emma had to unload all Ursula's luggage and park the car before taking her own little suitcase to her own small back room. Hardly had she entered when the phone rang. It was Ursula imperiously demanding when she was going to come and unpack for her.

'At once, madam!' She sped up to Ursula's spacious suite, happy to be needed. It was indeed a lovely room with several armchairs and a sofa, a balcony, and a gorgeous view over the sea to the Isle of Wight in one direction and Poole Bay in the other. There were numerous bunches of flowers from well wishers and from the local gallery, which Ursula told Emma to put into vases after she had fetched her a drink from the well-stocked bar.

As usual, Ursula had brought a lot of luggage. One piece seemed to Emma to be rather strange.

'What's this?' she asked. 'What should I do with it, madam?'

'That, little Emma,' replied Ursula, 'is a sleeping bag, and what you are to do with it is sleep in it – on the floor by the side of my bed. Then, should I snap my fingers, you will be ready to kneel up, put your pretty little head under the bedclothes and apply your tongue and the tips of your fingers to giving me pleasure. Then, when I am ready to go to sleep again I need only snap my fingers to put you back on what we might call "stand by".'

'I see, madam.'

'And you will find that Rafaela has packed Sambo too. You may place him on the bedside table, and, whilst you are pleasuring me, just remember he is there in case I consider you lacking in diligence.'

'Yes, madam.'

'Now you may run my bath. I shall require you to wash me, dry me, oil me and give me a massage.'

Emma enjoyed serving Ursula in this way, but not the extra little attentions of an intimate nature that, she knew, she would also be called on to perform.

'Then,' Ursula continued, 'you will serve me dinner here in this room, and I shall use Duet on you. You love Duet, don't you, little slut?'

Emma blushed. She had been introduced to the dual delights of Duet in Ursula's studio. Its name arose from the fact that it was intended to be played with by two women.

Emma hated it.

Ursula, already penetrated by one half of Duet, would lie on her back and make Emma straddle her hips and allow the other half of Duet to penetrate her as well. She would then have to lean down low and play with Ursula's small, almost boyish, breasts, whilst maintaining a regular to and fro motion with her hips. This would have the effect of driving Ursula almost crazy with excitement, whilst severely limiting Emma's own pleasure. Which, of course, was just what Ursula intended, for the knowledge that Emma was suffering pain rather than pleasure made her own pleasure all the greater.

The evening passed just as Ursula had planned it.

A naked Emma bathed, cleaned, prepared and massaged Ursula. A naked Emma waited on Ursula at dinner and, when it was over, was allowed to kneel on all fours and, without using her hands, gobble up off one plate the various scraps of smoked salmon, soup, fillet, ice cream and Camembert cheese that Ursula had left, all mixed together in a horrid looking mess.

Sambo had to be brought into action before the bowl was licked spotless by Emma's tongue, even though, on Ursula's strict instructions, she had had no lunch before Ursula had arrived to pick her up.

The relaxing bath and massage, the delicious meal and the view over the lit-up sea all combined to make Ursula enjoy Duet even more than usual. She kept Emma hard at it for what seemed hours as she reached one peak of ecstasy after another, her cane in hand to keep Emma moving at just the right speed. Several times she pretended that she was going to allow Emma to yield, but then every time changed her mind, leaving Emma almost out of her mind with the intense frustration.

Finally, feeling herself near to climaxing yet again, she ordered Emma to do likewise, but strictly to her order. The sight and noise of Emma yielding to her just when instructed to do so made her own climax even more mind-blowing.

An hour later the exhausted Emma, lying uncomfortably in her sleeping bag on the hard floor, heard the snap of Ursula's fingers. She knew what she had to do and she did it. Then later, whilst Ursula once again lay dreaming in her soft bed, Emma, even more exhausted now, was trying and trying to get to sleep on the hard floor – still on 'stand by', as Ursula had called it.

In fact, Emma was frequently summoned during the night by the snap of Ursula's fingers to arouse her and to relieve her almost insatiable passions. Twice she had to accompany Ursula to the bathroom. Every time she managed to fall asleep, it seemed to her, she was awakened by another snap of Ursula's fingers – reinforced by Sambo if she were not quick enough in responding.

It was indeed a tired and still sexually frustrated Emma who served her mistress with breakfast in bed in the morning, once again bathing and drying her, and dressing her for her big occasion – the ceremonial opening of the exhibition of her paintings. Thoroughly satisfied by both her physical and mental domination of Emma during the long night, Ursula looked radiant when the big hired car came to take her to the gallery.

Ursula had made Emma empty her purse and now left her with just a few coins. Enough, perhaps, to buy a simple sandwich and a cup of coffee, but certainly not enough to take a taxi to the gallery. After walking there, with no special invitation to allow her into the private reception, she had to stand amongst the public whilst Ursula munched delicious dainties.

Standing unnoticed amongst the spectators, Emma heard the mayor praise Ursula's skills. She applauded when Ursula fluently replied. Oh how proud she felt to be the friend of such an extraordinary woman! She saw that Ursula had noticed her, and although there was no sign of recognition she felt prouder than ever.

Then something happened.

She caught the eye of a very good-looking man in the official party. He came down and spoke to her. He was kind and solicitous, and she warmed to him immediately. She saw Ursula glaring at her, but before she could protest the handsome young man had swept her out of the room and everything prudent out of her mind.

He offered to show her the town. He took her to the pier and then the amusement park. They laughed together as he drove their bumper car into all the other cars full of young men with their girls, and clutched each other like any ordinary couple on the switchback.

Emma was learning again what fun it could be to be with an

attentive and charming man. She thought of nothing else, especially when his hand, perhaps accidentally, perhaps not, brushed her breasts, and later her thighs.

He suggested that they meet for a drink that evening and go dancing. Emma was thrilled. 'Yes, yes,' she said. So why not, she thought? Ursula had to go to an official dinner in her honour, something to which Emma was not invited.

But it was a furious Ursula that was waiting for her on her return to the hotel.

'Where have you been, you slut? Who gave you permission to go slinking off? I saw you making sheep's eyes at that young man you went out with! You know very well I will not have you talking to men and yet you disobeyed me blatantly! Right in front of me! How dare you! How dare you try to defy me? Who do you think you are? You're just nothing without me, you . . .'

'Please, please,' interrupted Emma, sobbing hard, suddenly realising the enormity of what she had done. 'Please, oh please, I didn't mean to go against you, I just . . .'

'You just thought you could get away with it!'

'No, no . . .'

Ursula's eyes narrowed. 'And I suppose you thought you could take advantage of my going out to dinner tonight by arranging to meet your young man this evening. Well, have you, Emma?'

'Yes, madam,' whispered a white and trembling Emma.

'Very well.' Ursula suddenly laughed. 'Keep your date with your odious young man, but I shall take certain precautions – and I insist that you are back in your room by ten, waiting for me to summon you to lie by my bed. I may well be later, of course, but that need not concern you.'

So it was that when two hours later Emma met her young man in a pub, she was feeling distinctly uncomfortable. She was, it was true, looking ravishingly pretty in her most fetching dress and with high heels and stockings.

But Ursula, as she threatened, had taken her precautions. Under the dress Emma was locked into her rompers!

The poor young man could not understand why the precocious young woman of the afternoon had turned into the intensely shy and distant person he now found himself with. She seemed to cringe away from his every touch as if she were frightened he might discover something, and she seemed distracted and preoccupied all the time. All in all he was quite relieved when she said she had to be back at her hotel by ten.

Emma was inwardly seething with rage as the disappointed young man took her back to the hotel and she made her way, alone, back to her small cheerless room. Ursula, that jealous bitch, had completely spoilt what should have been a fun evening with a touch of romance. Who knows, they might have ended up in the back of his car! And now she just had to sit and wait for Ursula to return from her evening's pleasures and summon her to her degrading duties.

She wanted desperately to spend a penny – and she couldn't with this damn thing locked around her. She took off her dress and looked down at herself. That cunning little locking pin of Ursula's! How awful it would be to wet her rompers! How shame making! She remembered Ursula's joke about the rompers being in their pristine state. She just could not wait any longer. She felt like a naughty little child as she wet herself – which, she realised, was just what Ursula had intended.

Suddenly she revolted. She wouldn't stand any more of this. She found the scissors and cut away the wet plastic covered towelling. It fell away from her.

She felt wonderfully free as she dried herself.

Then the awful realisation of what she had done hit her. Ursula had been angry before, now she would be livid, absolutely and terrifyingly livid.

Never mind. She would stand up for herself. Let the phone ring. She deserved her sleep and she would damn well have it. She took the receiver off the hook and was soon dreaming of an angelic young man, while touching herself in a way that Ursula had forbidden.

So it was that just after seven in the morning a silently furious Ursula flung open the door, pulled the sleeping Emma out of bed, and frogmarched her along the deserted corridors and up to her own suite.

Not until the door shut behind them did she say a word. Even then her rage was strangely contained.

'I suppose you think you have been very clever, Miss! Well, you are not as clever as you think, not as clever as me. You are going to learn that she who pays the bills calls the tune, my girl.'

She paused, glaring at Emma, who just stood there mesmerised at the realisation of what she had done and by Ursula's piercing eyes.

'I shall say no more. You know exactly what you have done and you know exactly what the punishment is. You are to have ten strokes now and another ten when I get back from the gallery – and then you can go and catch your train. Now, bend over that chair.'

Ursula proceeded to cane Emma in a slow and methodical way. Several times she took a little run, so as to bring the cane down harder on Emma's behind. She ignored all Emma's cries of pain, her fervent protestations of adoration, her desperate promises never to do it again, and finally her screams for mercy.

When the ten strokes had been delivered, Ursula ordered the sobbing girl to stand in the corner in disgrace whilst she herself bathed, dressed and did her hair. The fact that these were all tasks which, normally, Emma would have helped with, drove home the disgrace with which she was now regarded by her mistress.

For the next hour she was ignored, except for being banished to the bathroom whilst Ursula's breakfast arrived.

With Emma standing in the corner with her naked back towards her and her nose touching the wall, Ursula sat back and enjoyed her breakfast and made several telephone calls to friends in London. Emma, in disgrace, was completely ignored.

Then, without a word, Ursula pulled Emma over towards the curtains. They had big soft silken cords to keep them back and Ursula used these to tie Emma to a chair. She was quite helpless with ankles, belly and chest all tightly bound to the chair. And her wrists were bound back to her upper arms so that by swaying her body slightly she could just pick up the phone and answer it, but not dial.

Ursula rang room service to say that she did not wish to be disturbed and put the telephone alongside Emma. Then she picked up the 'Do Not Disturb' notice to hang it on the outside of the door and without saying another word went out. Emma heard her hanging the notice on the other side of the door, and then the door itself being locked.

Emma realised to her horror that she was now locked in the room and that no one would come to release her until Ursula herself returned. And when she did, Emma thought with mounting fear, she would give her the remaining ten strokes. Never had she seen Ursula so cool, so calculating, so inwardly furious and yet so outwardly calm. So dangerous. Yes, dangerous summed it all up.

She tried to ease her bonds, but only succeeded in making them tighter. She just had to sit there, quite still, and wait for Ursula's return. She thought of calling out, but she knew that the walls and doors of this old-fashioned hotel were exceptionally thick. If no one had heard her cries when she was being thrashed, they would not hear her now.

So there she sat, alone with her thoughts. What a fool she had been, what a complete and utter fool. How stupid she had been to start playing around with a young man when she was with Ursula. She knew very well that men were anathema to Ursula.

Even more, how stupid to indulge herself by cutting away her rompers and giving herself pleasure. She knew very well that Ursula regarded the prevention of that the very touchstone of her control over a girl, and that all pleasure had to come from Ursula's own hands and not the girl's.

Yes, how stupid she had been to think she could get away with touching herself – even if it had been for the first time since she had come under Ursula's spell.

She should have known that Ursula would regard any such act as a blatant unfaithfulness and a deliberate attempt to throw off her hold over her. Surely she had known that Ursula prided herself on being able to detect when a girl had been naughty and would catch her out?

If ten of the strokes had been for going out with a young man without permission, for cutting off that thing round her loins and for leaving the telephone off the hook, then she was lucky to be getting only another ten for pleasing herself without permission. Ursula had seen through her all right, she had known for sure.

Suddenly the telephone rang.

Awkwardly she picked up the receiver with her tied hands.

'Well, little Emma, was it all worthwhile?'

'No, madam,' sobbed Emma.

'Do you know what the remaining ten strokes will be for?'

'Yes, madam, I think so.'

'Yes, and you are lucky to be getting only ten for that, are you not?'

'Yes, madam, very lucky,' whispered Emma.

'And are you now feeling ashamed of yourself for doing it?'

'Yes, madam, very,' said Emma in a voice like a little contrite schoolgirl. She really meant it.

'It will be ten strokes that you will not forget in a hurry – ten strokes that you will remember when you are next tempted to be unfaithful to your mistress.'

The phone went dead. Carefully Emma struggled to replace the receiver. She did not want another scene.

It was another hour before she heard Ursula's key in the lock. Without a word she untied Emma and pointed to the chair.

'I want you to call out each stroke aloud,' she said. 'Now, before we start, kiss the cane and say that you deserve every stroke of your thrashing, you disgusting little girl.'

Even Ursula was surprised with the genuine fervour with which this grown woman acknowledged the righteousness of her punishment and the wickedness of her behaviour. But that did not stop her from applying the strokes with double her normal zest, making sure that each stroke left a weal that fitted in neatly below the previous one. The final effect was a perfect ladder – Ursula was, of course, an expert in the art of thrashing a young woman.

It would be amusing, she reflected between the cries that marked the application of the sixth and seventh strokes, to know what excuse Emma would give to that rather wet husband of hers to explain why she could not sit down for a day or two.

# 8　　HENRY AND RETRIBUTION

In all the excitement of learning to serve Ursula, Emma had almost forgotten Henry, her former occasional and dominating lover. She had once laughingly told Ursula about him, but Ursula had not been amused.

'He's obviously just another male brute,' she had said. 'You must promise me you will never see him again.'

And, happily absorbed by her new and exciting relationship, Emma had given her promise.

Then suddenly Henry sent her a note – he was coming to London on business for a couple of days. She was to meet him at his hotel as she had before. He would expect to find her hidden under the bedclothes at six o'clock sharp. The following day he would be busy in the City but that evening he would be taking her to a particularly amusing cocktail party for which she must look her best – she would have the day free to amuse herself and have her hair done.

Furious at the way Henry took her for granted, Emma decided that she was too busy to meet him. This was indeed half true since Ursula had already summoned her to London on Henry's second day, the day of the cocktail party.

But when Henry rang to confirm the arrangements and she heard his attractive commanding voice, Emma's resolve melted and past pleasures surfaced in her mind. Perhaps she could fit it all in, stay with Henry and see Ursula during that second day without even missing the cocktail party. A daring thing to do? It was indeed, but what a thrill it would be if she could meet both her male and female lovers the same day!

Life had never been like this before.

Ursula must never know, never, never, never! Never!

That was what she was still thinking a few days later as she lay curled up under the bedclothes in Henry's hotel room. She was wearing the prettiest nightdress as, madly excited, she awaited his heavy step – for he was a big man in every sense of the word.

He would, she knew, expect her to remain hiding under the bedclothes, getting more and more excited whilst he undressed, had a bath and then got into bed to read a book as the exquisite little creature under the bedclothes did her utmost to please him.

Only later would he reach down and pull her out by her hair and allow her to fling her arms round his neck whilst she told him all her news.

What to say about Ursula?

Nothing! Neither must know about the other!

Deliciously aroused and trembling with anticipation, she lay in the dark until she heard the door open. What a man Henry was, what a thrilling man, she would soon be sensing just what a real man he was . . .

Next morning, feeling very small and helpless, Emma lay contentedly in Henry's strong arms, reaching up every few minutes to lick his chin as a kitten might. They had enjoyed an evening of lovemaking, followed by dinner and a night of yet more love.

Wonderful! So wonderful! It almost made one forget Ursula!

Then, later, as she got out of her bath, Henry laughingly produced a strange looking object which, he explained, was a cricketing box – normally worn by men for protection against fast bowlers. It could be used as a chastity belt, he thought. The elastic straps which went round her hips, and down between her legs, held the padded elastic shield tight over her body lips. Of course, the belts could easily be slipped down or a naughty finger inserted under it, but it would have a psychological effect on a girl waiting to meet her dominating lover.

'I want you to wear this all day,' said Henry before he left for the City. 'It will keep you thinking about me all day and make you long to be back in my bed again after tonight's cocktail party. It's got a little grill so you can spend a penny without taking it off, so don't. Understand?'

'Yes, Sir,' replied Emma shyly as she put it on under Henry's watchful gaze.

But after he had gone she was left in a quandary. She had

been told to wear it – but she was due to report to Ursula shortly, and if Ursula saw it . . . Well, she shuddered to think what would happen if Ursula saw it.

She was only having lunch with Ursula. What the hell! She felt a sense of adventure since Henry had forced himself back into her life.

A little later she could have been seen tripping along Bond Street as if she had not a care in the world. She looked in all the shops and in one boutique saw a lovely dress. She was about to go in and ask to try it on when she remembered the belt across her hips. What had originally seemed to be just a good joke now seemed a more serious matter as the time of her date with Ursula drew closer.

Perhaps she could exchange the damn thing for a pair of panties at Ursula's house before Ursula got to her . . .

Rafaela opened the door and told her that Ursula was waiting for her upstairs.

'Look, Rafaela, can you lend me . . .'

But then came a voice from upstairs, deceptively pleasant in tone. 'Is that you, Emma, darling?'

Emma held her breath in sudden panic and turned to run, but Rafaela had already closed the door and locked it.

'Is that you, Emma? Why don't you answer me?' This time the tone was much harsher. There was a pause and then a very angry shout: 'Emma! Come upstairs at once, do you hear? At once!'

All pretence of pleasantness had been completely dropped. Ursula was obviously furious about something. But what had she done wrong?

Emma hurried upstairs like a naughty schoolgirl summoned by her headmistress. In her dressing room Ursula stood waiting for her. She was dressed in exquisite silk satin pyjamas. Obviously she had only just got up. She had that early morning look that seemed to be natural in women who are interested only in other women. She regarded Emma icily, but when she spoke her tone was quite pleasant again.

It was this constant contradiction in mood that never failed to unnerve Emma. One moment she would be longing to please Ursula, and the next she was almost hating her.

'So, little Emma,' said Ursula in her most schoolmistressy voice. 'Would you care to have breakfast with me and tell me all that you have been doing?'

Emma hesitated. She sensed that Ursula was up to something and she had a guilty conscience. But there was no way Ursula could know about Henry.

'Well, if you've lost your tongue, my naughty little Emma, tell me whether you had a good journey up to London this morning?'

'Yes, thank you,' said Emma.

'Then how is it that your daily told me on the telephone early this morning that you had gone to London yesterday afternoon?'

'Oh!'

'To stay with a friend!'

'Oh!'

'Well? I'm waiting for your explanation – and it had better be a good one!'

Emma saw Ursula glance towards her dressing table. There, lying waiting on it, was a cane. It was not Sambo but a heavier one. Emma's mind was racing. How ever could she get out of this predicament? It was thrilling all right, but just a bit too much so, just a bit nasty . . .

More than a bit nasty!

At that moment Rafaela came into the room with breakfast. Emma saw that the tray was laid for two, with lovely warm croissants and a pot of steaming hot coffee. Emma licked her lips in anticipation as Rafaela left the room, hoping that a cosy breakfast would make Ursula forget her awkward questions.

She smiled nervously and helped herself to a croissant.

'*Put that down!*' shouted Ursula, slapping at her wrist. 'You're having nothing, you little tart! Go and stand in the corner! At once! Keep your face to the wall and don't you dare say a word until I tell you!'

Emma listened to Ursula drinking her coffee and shivered with dread. Then she could hear her spreading butter and jam on her croissants. Next another cup of coffee. What was going to happen? She cringed inside at the memory of the sight of the heavy cane, obviously put out ready for her arrival. Sambo was bad enough, but this one . . .

She went on trembling as she stood like a naughty child in the corner of Ursula's bedroom.

Suddenly she heard Ursula put down her cup with a decisive bang. She longed to look around, but did not dare to do so. She heard Ursula ring for Rafaela, who came into the room within seconds. She always seemed to appear, Emma thought, as if she had been standing just outside the door, listening or waiting to be summoned.

Emma felt utterly stupid standing in the corner with the housekeeper in the room. How dare Ursula humiliate her in this way? Hatred and anger began to replace fear. Then, as if deliberately intending to humiliate her further, she heard Ursula speaking to Rafaela in a very familiar tone.

'Well, Rafaela, that was a delicious breakfast. Thank you. Of course you will realise that that disgusting girl, Emma, is not having any?'

'Yes, mademoiselle.' She could imagine Rafaela's smile of contempt. She hated her and her smug voice and her superior air – and she was only a servant!

'Well,' purred Ursula in a soft and menacing tone, 'perhaps it would be more appropriate for her to be naked when I ask her some simple questions about what she was doing and where she has been. She probably smells like a tart. I can't bear to go near her. So, Rafaela, would you be so kind as to start taking her clothes off?'

Emma was appalled. Never before had Ursula used Rafaela to undress or humiliate her.

But, of course, Rafaela always did as she was told. She went over to the cringing figure of Emma, who was wearing a smart navy suit with a well-cut skirt, a bolero top and a shirt. Rafaela carefully removed the bolero, then Emma gave a little sob as the shirt went next. It was all so degrading!

Luckily she was wearing a slip under her suit. She began to break out in a sweat at the thought of what would happen if Rafaela removed it. She simply could not stand the indignity of Rafaela discovering Henry's so-called chastity belt.

'Please!' she cried out to Ursula, without daring to turn round. 'Please, don't let her take off anything else. Stop, Rafaela! Stop! Don't touch me! Keep away!'

This was greeted with a little laugh from Rafaela and a furious retort from Ursula.

'How dare you speak to Rafaela like that. I told you to keep quiet until you were given permission to speak. I'm going to have you beaten for insolence, you loathsome little bitch!'

Emma was startled by Ursula's fury. Before she knew what had happened her slip was gone.

'So!' said Ursula, in genuine surprise. 'What have we here? What funny little thing is this you have on? Let us have a better look at it. Rafaela, turn her towards me.'

Ursula was appalled by what she saw. There was a long pause and then she told Rafaela to bring Emma closer.

'So what is this?' she demanded. 'Some sort of chastity belt, is it? Who's been putting this on one of my girls? Who? Who?'

Poor Emma was too frightened to open her mouth. She just stood there petrified and embarrassed beyond belief.

Ursula's voice had now become quiet, but even more menacing.

'I'm going to have to beat the truth out of the stupid creature!'

There was a deathly silence in the room.

'Rafaela,' said Ursula slowly, 'bring me the cane and clear away the breakfast things. Thank you. No, don't go. Now, Emma, spread yourself across the table.'

It was a low coffee table with an unbreakable glass top. Dumbly, not knowing what else she could do, Emma knelt down over the table. The ice-cold feeling of the glass on her naked breasts made her shudder and then jump up quickly.

'Get down!' cried Ursula. 'The little bitch! Rafaela, tie her to the legs of the table. You'll find some elastic in my drawer. Meanwhile, Emma, you just remain kneeling over the table and don't you dare move one inch!'

Rafaela hurried back with the elastic cord. Emma was still not properly prone over the table. She knew that if she was not, then she would be pushed down. She lowered herself down until her breasts were flattened by the cold glass table top. She felt Rafaela seize one wrist and tie it tightly to a table leg. Then the other wrist was tied. She felt helpless. But the so-called chastity belt stopped her tummy from being quite flat on the table.

Suddenly there was a streak of fire across her bottom.

'Flatten yourself!' ordered Ursula coldly, tapping Emma's bottom with her cane. 'You're just a lump of meat to be tenderised. Do you understand?'

Poor Emma tried desperately to obey Ursula, but the raised front of the cricketing box prevented her from flattening her belly.

'Very well,' said Ursula with deliberate coarseness, 'then raise your arse up in the air.'

This was slightly more comfortable for Emma, but she blushed at the thought of how she was now having to display herself – especially to a servant.

As Ursula watched the wriggling Emma being finally tied down, bottom raised, she could not help liking what she saw, despite her genuine fury. Here was the beautiful and proud Emma having to show herself off like a bitch on heat or a mare in season. She was going to have some fun punishing this disloyal creature! She prodded Emma's bottom with the end of the cane, then turned to Rafaela as she finished tying Emma's legs.

'You know, Rafaela,' she said, 'I can't help thinking that there is something in this idea of a chastity belt. Perhaps we can make a proper one – one which could not be removed. We'll go out shortly, after I've dealt with this matter, and see if we can find some suitable materials. But before you go you can give the girl a stroke of the cane for speaking to you so insolently.'

She tossed the cane to Rafaela, whose eyes lit up at the thought of being allowed to give the stuck-up Emma a good hard stroke. A moment later Emma gave a cry – not merely a cry of pain, though Rafaela had used her muscular peasant arm to good effect, but also of shame, shame at being beaten by Ursula's foreign servant.

'Thank you, Rafaela, that will be all,' said Ursula. A moment later Emma heard the door of Ursula's bedroom being closed. She was now alone with an angry Ursula – alone and tied down. Despite her fear, excitement was rising in her.

'Now Emma,' Ursula said in a quiet but ominous tone, 'we are going to have a little punishment and then a little confession.' She parted Emma's flaring buttocks. 'And we might even have a little torture as well as a caning – it will depend on how quickly and fully you confess about whatever you have been up to behind my back.'

Emma knew that she simply could not confess to the truth about Henry and the chastity belt. But she also knew that Ursula would flog the truth out of her in the end.

'Right,' said Ursula. 'I have all day in which to beat you until you talk. The longer you take to confess everything, and I do mean everything, the more I shall enjoy myself. We'll start with two strokes – nice and slow with a long gap between each stroke during which you can think about the ones to come. I expect you will be begging to confess before they are over, but you'll still get them all, and another two five minutes later just in case you are thinking of telling me a pack of lies. After that everything will depend on what you decide to tell me.'

After two strokes of the heavy cane, Emma was pleading for mercy and swearing she would tell Ursula everything. The appalling five minute wait for the next two was terrible. Emma was crying and begging very prettily, thought Ursula, as she walked round the room swishing the cane and rearranging the flowers.

Emma could hardly believe that she was really going to be given the other two strokes when she was already prepared to tell all, but two more strokes she received. By this time she was screaming that she would confess everything if only Ursula would release her from the table.

'Don't try to bargain with me, you hussy,' said Ursula. 'For that you get another two strokes – across the back. Now, arch your back for the cane.'

A few seconds later two awful yells could be heard, even down in the kitchen where Rafaela gave a smile of contentment. That girl Emma was really learning that her mistress would not tolerate anything but complete loyalty and obedience from her girls.

Ursula looked down on the now well-marked body of the sobbing Emma. She was clearly broken. She unfastened the girl's arms only.

'Kneel up!'

Awkwardly Emma knelt on the table, her thighs still tied down. She rubbed her bottom, feeling the weals and trying to ease the awful pain. She longed to be able to reach her back and ease the pain there too.

'Head up! Hands on your head! Get that back straight, you slovenly bitch!'

Ursula walked round her, tapping with the cane.

'Now thrust your breasts out – that's better!' She touched each breast with the cane, making Emma shiver in fear. 'Now, the slightest hesitation in answering a question and this is where the cane will strike next!'

Naked, cold and terrified, Emma knelt on the table. All her resolutions about being brave and not saying anything about Henry were gone. Now she was just longing to get back in Ursula's good books and avoid a further beating by confessing everything.

Ursula stood behind her, the cane tapping the sides of her breasts.

'Speak!'

At once Emma poured out everything about Henry.

Ursula went white. She was stunned as the full implications dawned upon her.

That innocent convent educated look hid desires far deeper than she had realised, and made her the more desirable.

But . . .

But Emma had a masochistic relationship with a man! A relationship that paralleled and rivalled her own!

This was serious, this threatened her hold over Emma!

Something had to be done about it.

Something most definitely had to be done about it . . .

# 9 URSULA'S REVENGE

Ursula was stunned that Emma could so easily betray her. She was also stunned that Emma should be so malleable and have allowed herself to be talked into going to bed with a mere male brute. Emma was certainly not going to any party with that brute, tonight or any night. She was astonished that Emma could have every contemplated any such thing.

The truth about Emma's real relationship with Henry had dawned on Ursula. It was a masochistic relationship that rivalled her own. Clearly it was not a simple one – or else how could Emma have even dreamt of deceiving her, or of being unfaithful to her? She was determined to find out what was really in Emma's mind, and the best way would be to degrade the girl and then gradually reward her. That innocent convent girl look about Emma, Ursula was now discovering, hid desires far deeper than she had realised. Ursula was determined to stamp them out.

She rang for Rafaela, who as usual came instantly.

'Come down to the kitchen,' Ursula said to Rafaela. 'I want you to give this little slut some work to do – work that will make her realise that she is just my skivvy, a skivvy who exists only to obey her mistress. A skivvy who has no private life of her own and who has to be completely faithful to her mistress.'

Moments later all three women were in the kitchen, with Emma still naked. As usual, the kitchen was immaculate, for Ursula insisted on a high level of hygiene.

'Well Rafaela, you do have this looking nice. But I am afraid that we shall have to dirty it a bit, if the slut is going to learn to scrub and clean as well as you do.'

Emma was livid at being referred to as if she was a servant like Rafaela. She stamped her feet.

'How dare you talk like that about me in front of Rafaela!'

Ursula just laughed. 'I'm really going to give you something to complain about.' She turned to Rafaela. 'Make the kitchen floor as filthy as you can.'

Rafaela was delighted. Eagerly she emptied the contents of the rubbish bins all over the floor and added gravy, yoghurt, some awful scraps of meat and rotting fish and vegetables. The floor now really looked a revolting mess.

'Right, Rafaela, you can have the afternoon off once you feel that Emma has got the floor back to the same pristine condition that it was in before,' Ursula smiled. Then she turned to Emma. 'Now get scrubbing! And all the time you are scrubbing you are to say over and over again: "I am scrubbing that brute out of my life." Now scrub Emma! Scrub! Harder! Say your little prayer out loud. I want to hear you say it. Now! That's better. Make sure she scrubs hard, Rafaela, and make sure she also repeats her little ditty.'

Ursula left the kitchen, leaving Emma scrubbing the floor under the watchful eye of Rafaela as she cried out aloud, over and over again, 'I'm scrubbing that brute out of my life.'

It took two hours of hard work before Emma thought that the kitchen was back to its former immaculate state. But Rafaela told her that it was still not clean enough. She must scrub the whole floor yet again. 'I want to see the floor really shining,' she said in her Italian accent.

Emma decided that she was under no obligation to take orders from Rafaela, no matter what Ursula had said. She decided to stand her ground. She put down the scrubbing brush and stood up. She would not do any more scrubbing!

'Since I cannot tell madame that the kitchen is properly clean,' said Rafaela, 'I shall have to tell her that you have refused to work properly.'

Emma felt that Rafaela was being petty and vindictive. She would ignore her – that would put her in her place again. With a toss of her head, she went out of the kitchen and upstairs to report to Ursula that her punishment had been completed. But meanwhile Rafaela was putting a pile of dust into one of the kitchen corners.

'I've finished, madam,' said Emma with a little curtsey.

'Good,' replied Ursula, putting down her book. She was now dressed to go out, Emma noticed. 'And is Rafaela satisfied?'

'Oh, she is never pleased,' replied Emma angrily.

'Don't be a stupid little girl, Emma. If the kitchen floor was really clean, then Rafaela would be pleased. I'd better come down and see for myself.'

Ursula came downstairs. Emma proudly showed her what seemed to be a spotlessly clean floor. Ursula turned to Rafaela, 'Are you satisfied, Rafaela?'

'No madame,' came the reply. 'She works in such a slovenly way. Look at all the filth she has left in this corner, for instance.'

Emma was furious. 'That wasn't there a few moments ago,' she burst out.

'So!' said Ursula. Her voice was icy. 'Not content with lying to me about where you have been, you also lie to me when I give you a punishment to carry out. You are to scrub the whole floor again until Rafaela is satisfied. You are to obey Rafaela. You are under orders. Do you understand?'

Emma burst into tears. She felt that she did not understand anything any more. They were playing games with her – one minute pretending to be pleased with her efforts and the next dashing her hopes. The tears ran down her cheeks.

But despite the tears and despite her protests, Emma, like a naughty schoolgirl, had to do what she was told and scrubbed the whole floor yet again. She was tired and weary, when at last Rafaela said: 'That will do now. I will tell madame.'

Ursula came down and again inspected Emma's work. There was no praise, just a grunt, then Ursula ordered Emma to go upstairs to the bathroom. Emma rushed upstairs with relief. But hardly had she got there when the door was shut. She heard it being locked fron the outside and the key taken out. She heard Ursula's footsteps going away.

So it was that Emma, still stark naked except for Henry's chastity belt and with only a loo, a bidet and a bath for company found herself locked into the little room which only had one small window. How long was she going to be kept there? Where had Ursula gone? She remembered Ursula's remark about going out to see if she and Rafaela could find some suitable materials to make a real chastity belt. Then she remembered that Ursula had given Rafaela the afternoon off. So many thoughts were racing through her mind. How on earth was she going to rejoin

Henry in time for the big cocktail party? Could she get out through the window? Would she get caught? And anyway she was naked! And how was she going to keep her appointment at Harrods hair salon?

She had no watch. About an hour seemed to have gone by without any sign of Ursula or Rafaela.

She began to think seriously about getting out through the little bathroom window. It faced a small courtyard whose walls were covered with a climbing plant. She was naked and might be seen from the house next door! But if she were to wrap a towel tightly round her, she could probably climb down to the ground. She knew that during the day Rafaela often did not bother to lock the door from the kitchen into the back yard. If she could get down to the ground and into the kitchen, then she could come back upstairs and find her clothes again. But had Ursula switched on the burglar alarm before she had apparently gone out? She had no idea how to check, nor how to switch it off. The thought of being found by the police naked under a towel was too awful to bear thinking about. But she had to try and escape!

Somehow, just wearing a towel, she managed to scrape out through the small bathroom window. Somehow, she managed to get down to the ground. The kitchen door was open! Hesitantly, for fear of setting off the alarm, she made her way upstairs. The house was empty. There in a corner of Ursula's bedroom were her clothes.

She quickly dressed, scared lest Ursula might return at any moment. She rushed out, found a taxi and got to Harrods a little late for her appointment. They did a quick job and she rushed on to Henry's hotel.

She found him having a bath, and sat down to gather her thoughts.

Emma felt terribly guilty about escaping from Ursula and about disobeying her. Ursula was still her beloved mistress and she could not help feeling that Ursula had every justification in being furious at her behaviour and that she had deserved her punishment. The bathroom door was closed. She dialled Ursula's telephone number.

Ursula was fuming with rage.

'I never want to see you again,' she screamed down the telephone.

Emma saw the bathroom door open.

'Keep your voice down,' she begged, fearful lest Henry would hear Ursula's angry screams. She could hear him moving around the bathroom.

'Why should I keep my voice down?' screamed Ursula, even more angry than before.

'Because he'll hear,' whispered Emma.

'He! He! That brute!' yelled Ursula. 'You mean that you are with him again? You harlot?'

'Please don't scream,' cried Emma. 'I promise I'll explain everything tomorrow. I might even get away to you tonight. Please don't be angry.' Then in an even lower voice, she whispered: 'I'll do everything you want tomorrow. I promise. I'll be your little girl again. Just wait a little . . . He's coming out of the bathroom. I must hang up.'

She put the phone down quickly.

'Everything all right?' asked Henry. 'You look flustered. Who were you ringing?'

'Oh, I'm fine, sir,' lied Emma. She knew he liked her to call him 'sir' and to behave as if she were his slave girl. 'I just wanted to make sure that everything was all right at home. I didn't want to disturb your bath by asking for your permission.'

Henry smiled. She really was a deliciously submissive young woman.

The cocktail party was very amusing. As Emma chatted away to a bevy of admiring men, she could not help wondering what these sophisticated people would think if they knew that she was only there because she had escaped from an upstairs bathroom window? What would Henry say?

Emma was too worried to respond to Henry properly that night. Henry was furious and threatened to beat her. Oh no, not you too, thought Emma. Still she could only think about Ursula and what would happen when she went back to her house the next day after Henry had left. She knew she just had to go back and face the music. If she did not, then Ursula really would not see her again – and that was something she just could not accept.

Henry left the next morning, still furious and refusing to speak to her. Emma was almost relieved. She could now truthfully tell Ursula that she had broken with Henry. Indeed she decided that, although it was still only half past eight in the morning, she would go straight round to Ursula's.

'I've come to apologise,' said Emma quickly, as Rafaela showed her into Ursula's spacious and beautiful bedroom. 'It's all finished now. I won't be seeing him again.'

'Well, we'll record that little statement on my video camera later on,' said Ursula. 'Meanwhile it's fifteen strokes of the cane for you my girl. I don't allow my girls to two-time me and get away with just a little apology. You've got to learn your lesson. Fetch the cane!'

A few minutes later, Emma was bent over the back of a valuable Sheraton armchair, her hands gripping its arms. She really felt that she deserved her punishment.

'Why are you being punished, Emma?' asked Ursula icily.

'Because I was unfaithful to my mistress,' replied Emma with a little sob of shame.

'Are you ready to ask to be punished?'

'Yes, madam, yes. I deserve to be punished for deceiving my mistress. I beg to be punished and forgiven.' There was no mistaking, Ursula realised with satisfaction, the fervour in Emma's voice.

'Do you realise that only the cane can wash away your disgusting behaviour with a mere man?' came Ursula's hypnotic voice.

'Yes, madam.' Emma's voice was very contrite.

'Then before each stroke, I want to hear you say, 'I will remain faithful and obedient to Miss de Freville and I will not see that brute again'. Now lift up the back of your dress for your caning. Bend over more. Head down lower. Up on your toes! That's better.'

Ursula swished the cane through the air several times.

Emma was terrified, but nevertheless she could feel herself becoming aroused.

'Now call out the first stroke and make your promises. There will be an interval of one minute between each stroke and you must count the sixty seconds exactly to yourself and then call out the number of the next stroke and your promise once again. Now off we go with the first stroke, Emma.'

The first five strokes, which took five minutes to administer, were given with Emma's panties still on.

'Now for the next five strokes,' Ursula said, 'I want to hear you saying, loud and clear, "I hate Henry. I hate his revolting penis. I will never let him near me again". You must say it convincingly or else the previous stroke won't count and let's have your panties down now. Yes, right down. And bend over again so that I can have a good look at you.'

Emma felt Ursula's hand between her legs. She felt deeply ashamed, for despite the agonising pain of her slowly drawn out beating, she knew that it had aroused her. She could not help it – it was her built-in masochistic nature.

Ursula, however, was delighted to find that being beaten by her mistress had such a powerful effect on Emma's sensual feelings. She simply could not take her eyes of Emma's glistening body lips as she applied each stroke and as she listened to Emma counting the sixty seconds in a little whisper and then saying her new little piece about Henry. She made Emma raise her head as she said it and several times made her say it looking into Ursula's eyes. She was satisfied with the apparently genuine fervour with which Emma said it.

After the tenth, very painful, stroke, Emma could hardly go on gripping the arms of the chair. The thought of another five strokes to come was almost too much. But at least, she thought, Ursula was using her usual light whippy cane and not that awful heavy one that she had used the previous day.

'Now for the next five strokes,' said Ursula, 'you are to say, "I hate all men with their revolting penises and their mean selfish minds. It's Ursula that I love. It's Ursula that I love." '

At last the fifteen strokes were over. Never had Emma experienced such a long-drawn-out beating. Never had she experienced pain over such a long time. It was a beating that she would certainly not forget in a hurry – not merely for the pain, but also because what she had had to say before each stroke. The words were etched into her memory – just as Ursula had intended them to be.

But Ursula had not finished with her brain-washing rituals.

'Get undressed and stand in the middle of the room,' she ordered.

She set up a video camera and tape recorder. She adjusted the lighting. She made Emma have several rehearsals until she was word perfect. She made her practise lisping until her voice was indeed that of a little girl. Then she made a perfect recording of the naked Emma, lisping the same little chants that she had to say whilst she was being beaten.

The video tape was locked away. It would amuse Ursula's women friends when they next called for a chat and would provide after dinner entertainment – especially if it was being served by a blushing Emma.

The tape however was destined to be used more often. First of all, Emma had to listen to it now, over and over again. Then Ursula gave her a walkman, with instructions to put it on whenever she was in a bus, train or tube. It would, Ursula said, stop her from making eyes at every man she could see. Although to a casual observer she was just another young woman listening to her favourite pop music, she would in fact be hearing her own voice, lisping over and over again her love for Ursula, her promise to remain faithful to her and her hatred for all men and their revolting penises and for Henry in particular.

Overcome with the feeling of Ursula's complete authority over her, Emma found herself crawling to her feet. She licked them happily. She had been naughty and had been punished for it. Now she could return to being Ursula's little girl again. It was so exciting. She had genuinely forgotten all about Henry. She loved her mistress. She looked up at the imposing figure standing over her in her well cut satin pyjamas.

'Oh, madam,' she cried, tears of happiness in her eyes, 'I've been such a fool. I do love you. I really do.'

Delighted with this spontaneous display of affection and submissiveness, Ursula stroked Emma's hair. 'Tomorrow we'll drive out to your house and you're going to give me everything that Henry has ever given you or written to you – everything. You're not going to have anything to remind you of him. He's right out of your life now. Sit down and write a letter to him saying that you do not ever want to see him again.'

Poor Emma could not help having a lump in her throat as

she wrote the fateful letter. Ursula stood over her and dictated it. Then when Emma had signed it, she rang for Rafaela, handed it to her with instructions to post it immediately and to come back and tell her when she had done so. Emma gasped as she heard Ursula's hard words, but she knew in her heart that it was all for the best. She was Ursula's girl now.

Then she had to sit quietly in the corner of the room, listening to the recording, whilst Ursula bathed and dressed. Rafaela came back and reported that the letter was in the post. It seemed to Emma that a little bit of her life was being ended.

'I want you to put Emma into her baby rompers,' Ursula told Rafaela. 'Put her into the playpen in the nursery for the rest of the day. I've got quite a lot to do. You can give her a bottle every four hours, but make sure she's got her baby gloves on and don't let her say a word all day. She's got plenty to think about!'

All day Emma crawled about her playpen. The big comforter was firmly strapped into her mouth, allowing her only to make little babyish gurgling noises. She was naked except for her baby rompers and two little ribbons in her hair. She looked a very pretty little girl. The fingerless gloves were fastened onto her hands making it impossible for her to grip anything, unfasten the comforter or undo her baby rompers. The bars over the playpen kept her in it.

Rafaela had put a teddy bear into the playpen for her to play with. She could also play with a row of beads fastened to the bars, but otherwise there was nothing for her to do except think what a fool she had been over Henry and how wonderfully masterful Ursula was. The combination of her gloves and the thick material of the rompers made it impossible to while away the time by touching herself – just as Ursula had intended, she thought ruefully.

At lunch time and again later on in the afternoon and evening, Rafaela came in, unfastened her comforter and made her take the teat of her bottle of warm baby milk between her lips through the bars of the playpen. After her lunch time bottle, Rafaela allowed Emma to sit on the little pot that was kept in the nursery cupboard, but it was the last time that she was allowed to do so. When her next bottles were brought, Emma, unable to speak, pointed desperately to the cupboard. But Rafaela appeared not to understand her and left her alone in the room, her bladder bursting – until nature took its course, making her feel utterly ashamed.

Not until after dinner did Ursula reappear and this time with a couple of her women friends. Emma did not know whether to feel humiliated or proud at being shown off by Ursula to her friends. She was acutely conscious of the state of her rompers.

'Why, it's the girl in the video!' exclaimed one of the women.

'Doesn't she look sweet,' said the other woman reaching through the bars to caress Emma. Suddenly the woman jumped back. 'Oh, Ursula, the little girl's wet herself!'

Ursula's eyes glistened. Rafaela had carried out her instructions well. She feigned anger.

'How disgusting,' she cried, calling urgently for Rafaela. 'We've already started training her to use the pot. Obviously she needs more of the cane to make her learn properly!'

Rafaela came quickly. 'She's wet,' said Ursula with mock disgust. 'Put her on the pot and then change and powder her. Then go and fetch my cane.'

Ursula turned to her two friends. 'There's only one way to pot-train a bigger girl – fear of the cane.'

Poor Emma did not know which was more degrading: to have to perform into the pot in front of these strangers; to have to lie on the nursery table whilst Rafaela washed and changed and powdered her under their interested eyes; to have to listen to the women discussing her realistically babyish body lips with their complete absence of body hair; to have to kneel with her head in the horrible wet used rompers, whilst Ursula gave her her three strokes of the cane, each punctuated with cries of 'Naughty! Naughty!' from Ursula and her friends; or finally being put to bed, apparently for the night, in the little child's cot, whilst Ursula pointed out to her friends the watching television camera, the baby alarm, the night light and of course the rubber under sheet.

'So you can really see her on the television screen by your bed at any time during the night?' asked one of the women. 'That's wonderful! Ursula you are a genius when it comes to handling reluctant young women.'

They all left the room, leaving Emma curled up on the rubber sheet of the cot, the comforter still strapped to her mouth. She felt very sad. She had so hoped that Ursula would take her to her bed that night.

She was therefore thrilled when, an hour later, the nursery door was unlocked and in came Ursula. She was wearing a long satin negligée with nothing on underneath. In her hands she held a cane. She was looking radiant.

Silently she unfastened the top of the cot and lifted Emma out. She pointed to the floor. Emma knelt down on all fours like a little dog. Still on all fours Emma followed Ursula up the stairs to her bedroom. She knelt by the side of the bed, as Ursula got into it.

There was a pause. Then Ursula clicked her fingers. Not a word was spoken. Obediently Emma crawled into the bed and down between Ursula's thighs. Ursula still had the cane in her hands, and not until Emma was properly in position did she remove the big comforter from Emma's mouth. Then, giving Emma's naked bottom a sharp tap with the cane, she lay back to enjoy what she felt was her just reward after all the excitements of Emma's disgraceful behaviour. She felt like a deceived husband whose cringing wife, after due punishment, was being allowed to show real love for her husband.

No attempt was made to unfasten Emma's rompers and indeed they remained on all night – a night in which Emma was to give her mistress repeated exquisite pleasure whilst receiving none herself.

The next day it was again a tearful Emma who under Ursula's gaze went through her cupboards and her desks removing every article of clothing that Henry had given her and every letter he had written to her.

They had driven down to Emma's cottage in Ursula's fast car. Ursula had told Emma to make sure that her husband was at his office and that the cottage was empty. Ursula had not said a word during the drive. Her mouth was set in a grim look as she thought about the important task that lay ahead of her: the removal of everything that might remind Emma of Henry and of her former free life. For Emma, it had been a traumatic journey as she silently thought of the implications of what lay ahead.

'You can keep your country clothes,' said Ursula harshly, looking at the pretty little frilly things that Henry had given Emma, 'but from now on in London, apart from anything I may buy for you, you will wear only my old throw-outs, my underwear, my old nightdresses and my discarded dresses and suits.'

Emma nodded. The fact that Ursula's underwear and night-dresses were all embroidered with Ursula's initials would make it doubly exciting. It would make her feel even more that she belong to Ursula – just as Ursula knew it would.

Ursula glanced through the pile of letters and instructions from Henry that Emma had handed her and put them aside.

Later that day, back at Ursula's house, Emma stood by Ursula's side as she put the letters into her shredder. She could not help but feel a little pang in her heart. It all seemed so final.

There felt an even greater pang in her heart a little later when Ursula threw all the lovely clothes that Henry had bought her onto the fire in the drawing room. As she watched them disintegrate, she felt as though her affair with Henry had also disintegrated. She smiled. How much more exciting, she thought, was her affair with Ursula. Not only was it more exciting, but it was also so much more time consuming. It occupied every moment of her life, whereas the affair with Henry had just been something which had been picked up every now and then.

'Now you really belong to me, and to me alone,' murmured Ursula, giving Emma a hug. 'Go upstairs and wait for me in my bed and if you are a good girl, I might let you have a little fun as well.'

Emma looked at her adoringly. Then, excited beyond all bounds she turned and ran from the room.

# 10    THE DANCING CLASS

It was four days after the date when Ursula had been expected back from her Moroccan trip, and two weeks after the disastrous meeting with Henry.

Emma had persuaded Ursula to let her take her to the airport and to Emma's great delight and relief there had been a further reconciliation and they had, apparently, parted on wonderful terms. Ursula had been at her nicest, whispering little murmurs to Emma that: 'You are my favourite child, little Emma. You are my sweet, good, little girl.'

Emma still cherished the memory of having lunch with Ursula in the V.I.P. departure lounge and lisping like a little girl – just to please Ursula. Ursula had been delighted. Emma had worn her pretty little girl smock-dress with a pink ribbon in her hair. She had to pluck up all her courage to wear such a childish outfit in such a public place as an airport. Ursula had always told her that she could carry it off and no one seemed to stare unduly at her. Only she, Ursula, her mistress, would know that she was dressed like that because she was her little slave girl. She was now Emma, a little girl with quite hairless body lips, all soft and powdered like those of a baby girl.

To please Ursula all the more, she had even put on her rompers and tied them just like Rafaela did. Ursula had been keen to inspect this, so they had gone to the V.I.P. loo together and there Ursula had made her inspection.

'Yes, you are trying to be a good little girl again, aren't you?' she said. 'Now don't cry when your mistress goes. Just go back to the studio and tell Rafaela that I want you to spend the rest of the day in the playpen. She's even got a new harness for you – just like a child's. I shall think of you, during my flight, sitting in your playpen, playing with your beads and your little furry animals – under the watchful eye of Rafaela and the television camera.'

Back in the lounge, Emma had been overcome with sadness when it came to say goodbye. There had been tears in her eyes.

'There, there,' Ursula had laughed in front of the rather surprised ground hostess. 'Don't cry, I shall soon be back. Remember all the rules whilst I am away and don't forget to ring me twice a day on the special number I gave you to say that you are obeying them. I want you to keep nice and pure for me – and no talking to strange men!'

With that she had gone, leaving Emma feeling inadequate on her own and longing for her return. Sadly she had driven Ursula's car back to the studio, rung the bell and waited for Rafaela to open the door. She still did not have a key of her own.

Now here she was, four days after Ursula was due to return, ringing the studio, but only getting the answering machine – yet again.

She finally rang the health club. Oh yes, they said, Mademoiselle de Freville had been there two days ago for her regular Thursday massage and work-out. She had been with a very pretty young girl. They had seemed such a charming and happy pair.

Furious with rage and jealousy, Emma had put the telephone down with a bang. She was so angry that she could hardly speak and then in the middle of this crisis, her husband, John, had tried to persuade her to spend the night in his room, but the only person she craved was Ursula.

How could Ursula be such a bitch, she asked herself over and over again? She couldn't have forgotten all those humiliating telephone calls she had made – just as Ursula had instructed. It had been so difficult with John in the house all the time.

How silly she had been to imagine that women like Ursula have any real feeling or care for anyone else, never mind love anyone else. 'Love,' she had once said mockingly, 'is just a fairy story.' Emma had thought that she was joking. She certainly loved Ursula all right. She had been brought up on Nancy Mitford's *Love In A Cold Climate* and on Jane Austin and she really believed in love. But Ursula had quite a different

101

make-up. Her thing was dominating girls – and having lots of them. She hated men, except of course her pansy artistic types who were like herself. Emma had noticed how Ursula and her friends had their own jokes and their own language from which she was cut off.

Two more terrible days passed. Still she could not get through to Ursula. She wondered if she had another secret telephone number which she had not told Emma about. She left messages at the health club, but Ursula never rang, although they said they had given her the messages. They told her that she had been there with several different girls . . .

Finally Emma could not stand it any longer. She would call in at the studio to see for herself what Ursula was up to. She told John she had to go up to London. He told her to give Ursula his regards. 'What a delightfully intelligent woman she was,' he remarked. Emma bit her tongue to prevent herself from saying the truth.

When she arrived, somewhat breathless, she rang the studio door bell, her heart pounding. Surely Ursula would be delighted to see her, now that she was actually there.

Rafaela opened the door in her usual polite manner that she used with strangers.

'Ah, Miss – what is your name? Who do you want to see?' she asked, her face a mask.

'I'm Emma,' she cried. 'You remember me!'

Rafaela did not flicker an eyebrow. She was clearly well versed in how to deal with Ursula's cast-offs, or, as in this case, with girls with whom she was displeased.

'Would you come in?'

She left Emma in the downstairs study. In the distance, Emma could hear soft music and laughter, the clink of glasses, girls giggling and Ursula's cool, distinctive voice. At least she's here, Emma thought.

She was left for over half an hour on her own, feeling more and more thwarted as she listened to all the merriment from which she seemed to be excluded. What was going on?

She decided to go upstairs to the long studio room, where Ursula usually did her entertaining, to see for herself. She crept along the landing and up the stairs, nervously watching out for

Rafaela. When she got to the door of the studio, she did not dare go in. It seemed silly with all the noise to knock. She looked through the key hole.

The sight that met her eyes left her feeling astounded. This couldn't be true! She felt herself breaking out in gooseflesh all over. She had to muffle her cries of horror and hate. But she could not tear her eyes away from the key hole, for there, right before her eyes, was Ursula, looking superb and statuesque. There were four extremely pretty girls in ballet dresses, but with no panties on under their tutus. They were bending over, swaying and dancing and displaying their little hairless bodies to the music, looking enchanting with lovely painted faces and brushed back hair. Their eyes were fixed on a long cane that Ursula held in one hand whilst she controlled and encouraged them with the other.

It was difficult for Emma to tell their ages. She knew only too well herself how a twenty-six-year old could be made up to pass herself off as a thirteen-year old, which is what they appeared to be. A teenage dancing class!

Their beautiful little frilly dancing costumes spread out sideways above their tiny little powdered bottoms and their beautifully painted body lips. On two of the little bottoms – a mere size eight Emma guessed enviously – a pretty coloured flower motif had been painted or tattooed.

Emma was spellbound. She listened hard at the door. She could hear Ursula's voice at its most hypnotic and seductive.

'Ah, my little cygnets, my little swans.' Emma realised that the music was the 'Dance of the Cygnets' from *Swan Lake*. 'How beautifully you've been performing. What good little girls you have all been! And which of my little swans is going to attend on me this evening?'

The four little swans sank into a deep curtsey. 'Me! Me!' they all cried in tiny little high-pitched childish voices.

Emma could stand it no longer. She rushed into the room, screaming at Ursula. But Ursula was at her most cool and calm. She looked down with disdain.

'Well,' she demanded, 'what are you doing here, you ugly little country bumpkin? What makes you think anyone wants to see you?'

103

Hearing these cold, brutal remarks, Emma stopped dead in her tracks. She was completely silenced, appalled. How could this horrible woman deceive her with all these girls and then treat her with such venomous cruelty? She simply could not believe what she was seeing and hearing. She, who had given up everything to become Ursula's slave, given up all her men friends, given up her lover, virtually given up her job and almost given up her marriage, was now being treated like a complete stranger. Ursula had been so friendly, tender and loving to Emma when she left for Morocco. Now Ursula's whole attitude to her had changed. Had Emma's role also changed? Had she been demoted to some new and inferior status below that of these girls?

Then as if Ursula was reading Emma's thoughts and wished to confirm them, she went on in her cold authoritarian voice.

'You've arrived just in time to attend on my little swans – when you have smartened yourself up and put on the new maid's uniform I've specially bought for you and which you will find hanging in the maid's room, your room, next to Rafaela's in the servants' quarters. I think it will suit you very well. It's a real servant's uniform.'

The thought that Ursula had actually bothered to buy something for her and that, despite her hostile reception, was apparently still expecting her, delighted Emma. She was suddenly thrilled. Ursula was at least talking to her again. So what if she had to demean herself? So what if she had to dress as a servant and live in a servant's room?

'Then I shall want you to bathe my little swans, do their hair and get them ready for my dinner party this evening – at which you will be helping Rafaela to serve my guests. Now go and get changed in your room and then come back here and run the bath for my swans and for myself.'

Emma ran happily down the stairs again. Who cares, she was thinking, if I am temporarily out of favour? She'd soon show those wretched little swans what she was made of! She'd soon show them how much better she was than they at giving Ursula the intense pleasure that she craved. She would soon again be the centre of Ursula's life.

But meanwhile, she asked herself agonisingly, why did her

beloved mistress have to be so cruel? It was like being in the harem of some rich Pasha, she thought. A girl only remained the favourite whilst it was she who gave the greatest pleasure. At any second she risked being demoted by new, fresh faces and then having to fight her way back to favour. She remembered the Ursula she had known when she was favourite. The Ursula who had adored her, the Ursula who, when they played nanny and little girl, had told her that she was the one and only little girl who could give her such ecstatic pleasure. She remembered how Ursula had delighted in making her bend over, spread her buttocks and offer her excited juices to Ursula to taste. She tasted better, sweeter and fresher than any other girl, Ursula had declared.

But supposing she was not as good as Ursula's other girls? She remembered how at that first dinner party she had waited on, they had discussed the need to have her properly trained. 'Professionally trained,' had been Ursula's mysterious expression. Supposing, just supposing, that Ursula found those beautiful lithe ballet girls more exciting in bed than her? Suppose that she had enjoyed the excitement of seducing and initially dominating Emma, but now found her inexperienced and gauche by comparison with those pretty, supple and submissive girls? Suppose that she had had them 'professionaly trained', to a level of expertise that gave her much greater pleasure than anything she now experienced with Emma, now that the novelty had worn off? To win back Ursula, should she volunteer to be 'professionally trained'?

Thinking back to the simile with the harems of rich Pashas, she remembered that she had read that the Negro eunuchs in charge of Turkish harems had been responsible for teaching new girls all the initimate tricks of giving a man real plasure. She remembered being shocked to read about white slave girls being similarly trained by the slave dealers' servants, before being sold. Would she too have to be trained in all the exquisite techniques in giving a woman real pleasure if she were to stand a chance of regaining her position as Ursula's 'favourite little girl'?

But there was no time for all this now. She must hasten to get changed into her new servant costume. Her heart fell when she saw it. It was not at all like the frilly, sheer, French maid's costume that she had to wear at the last dinner party. It was a rather ugly eighteenth-century servant's smock and bonnet. Putting it on made her feel like she was now nothing more, in Ursula's eyes, than a servant girl, a labourer, a skivvy. She was a slavey rather than a slave. This, of course, was a feeling that was greatly heightened by having to get the four ballet girls looking radiant for the dinner party. They were gorgeously painted and powdered, whilst her cheeks remained just scrubbed. They were dressed in lovely evening dresses, whilst she remained in her degrading smock and bonnet.

The feeling was further heightened during the dinner, when she had to serve the beautifully dressed and gaily chattering women and girls – this time there were no men present. She had to keep a respectful silence. The women guests complemented Ursula on the beauty and submissiveness of her four little swans, no one mentioned Emma or even seemed to notice her in her ugly costume.

After the meal, the women drew lots to take one of the girls to bed in Ursula's bedroom. No one thought of including her in the lottery. She simply had to make the bed again as each woman, including Ursula herself, satisfied herself with the girl of her choice. No one even considered choosing her, and certainly not Ursula, who made Emma come into the room, turn out the light and stand holding a lighted candle to make her lovemaking with one of the girls more romantic. To have to stand holding up a candle by the side of the bed and silently watch whilst Ursula took her pleasure with another girl was a humiliation that was almost more than Emma could stand. Only the sight of Ursula's dreaded cane, Sambo, lying ready on the bedside table, kept her quiet. But at least I am here again in Ursula's house, she kept telling herself.

When all the guests had left, Emma had to put the four swans to bed in Ursula's large bed. Then she had to help Ursula to undress and to climb into the middle of the bed so that she had two girls on either side of her. The four girls crowded round Ursula, each busily trying to catch her attention.

Ursula sent Emma off to bed in the little cot in her dressing room that was simply an alcove off the bedroom itself. Emma scarcely knew which was more degrading, to be present in Ursula's bedroom as she enjoyed herself with another girl under her nose, or to lie awake, alone, frustrated and torn by jealousy, as she listened to the girlish squeals coming from the bedroom and imagined what was going on.

Emma remembered that Ursula was a patron of a ballet school and so presumably not only was her word law there, but the girls also knew that; if they really pleased her, then she would help them in their careers. This thought made Emma feel even more resentful and dispairing. How, she asked herself, could she ever begin to compete with such lovely creatures, each so strongly motivated to please Ursula?

Next morning, again dressed as a skivvy, she had to bring Ursula and her little swans breakfast in bed. The girls treated her with contempt as they snuggled up to Ursula, each whispering a reminder of how she in particular had given Ursula intense delight during the night. It was a scene that made Emma, once again, feel madly jealous. The last straw for her was when Ursula looked at her archly and said: 'Well Emma, aren't you sorry now to have deceived me with your dreadful man? You could have been one of my little swans. Just think of what fun you have been missing – all night.'

Soon the girls went off to their rehearsals at the ballet school – with strict instructions to hurry back that afternoon to provide Ursula with more amusement and pleasure.

Emma was sent off home again with merely a vague promise from Ursula that she would be in touch again soon – and a warning that meanwhile she was not, of course, to have sex with her husband or see Henry again.

# 11 EMMA TRIES TO ESCAPE FROM THE GILDED CAGE

When Ursula went off to her mysterious villa in Morocco for a couple of weeks, Emma had time to sit down and wonder about their relationship.

Here am I, she thought, a happy, vivacious, and respectable young married woman, playing the role of the servant girl, or helpless slave, of a rich and dominating older woman.

Admittedly, Ursula had introduced her to a new and sophisticated world, of whose very existence she had previously been largely unaware. Admittedly too she had found that having to be submissive to Ursula satisfied her secret masochistic longings. Admittedly that was often; also madly exciting, even when painful. Admittedly, moreover, she had found Ursula to be a highly intelligent and fascinating woman, even if she was also a cruel and demanding mistress.

Was it time to call a halt before she was sucked even deeper into the maw of the secret world of Ursula and her friends?

She felt like a trapped animal, like a bird in a gilded cage. Could she ever really escape from the cage?

She angrily put down the child's book that Ursula had given her to read whilst she was away. Initially Ursula had taken a delight in educating Emma into the secrets of the artistic world and in broadening her mind. But since her escapade with Henry, Ursula had seemed determined to reduce her intellect to that of an innocent little girl, forbidding her to read grown-up books and insisting that she read only children's ones.

There seemed to be a sort of insurmountable barrier, almost like a class difference, between, on the one hand, Ursula and her women friends, the mistresses, and on the other, their girls, their playthings, whom they treated with contempt as inferiors – as if they were mere slaves.

Henry, she thought with a smile, treated her as a slave girl in the bedroom. That was rather exciting! But outside the bedroom he treated her like a princess. Ursula just treated her like dirt all the time.

It wasn't fair!

Idly turning over all these thoughts in her mind, Emma looked at the invitations over the fireplace.

She recognised one as being for a cocktail party being given by some friends the next day. She had longed to go to it – there was always amusing people there. But as John was away for a few days, Ursula had refused her permission, as usual, to go on her own. Ever since her meeting with Henry, Ursula had refused to allow her to go to parties by herself.

'You're such a little tart, Emma,' Ursula had said. 'If I or your husband aren't with you, then you can't be trusted not to go off with the first good-looking man you see.'

Ursula had no objection to her going to parties in the country with her husband, but even here insisted that Emma should ring her, or her housekeeper, before leaving and again when they got back – making up some story to explain to her husband what she was doing. The general rule was that Ursula had to know where Emma was at all times.

Emma pursed her lips in irritation. It was rather exciting being under such strict control by Ursula, but she had so much wanted to go to the party. She would go in her prettiest dress and have her hair done specially.

As the time for the party loomed closer, the idea of going to it without Ursula's permission, and indeed behind her back, became increasingly exciting. It reminded her of the forbidden dormitory feats at her convent school!

There was the usual amusing crowd at the party.

Emma was thoroughly enjoying herself flirting with a number of men, many of whom she knew quite well. They all seemed surprised at how much more slender and sophisticated she had become, and how well informed she was about the art world. 'What have you been up to, Emma?' everyone kept asking. 'You seem a new person!'

Emma could not help laughing to herself at how shocked

they would be to learn the truth: that it was all because she had become the sexual slave of a ruthless older woman who was an expert at disciplining young women like herself – and at making them please her.

None of these men could have any concept of the degree of control that she had willingly submitted to, nor of how daring she had been to come to the party at all.

No, she thought, none of these men could begin to understand her need to be dominated by a strong-willed man – or woman. Henry understood this, of course, but he was abroad and anyway Ursula had forbidden her to see him again.

These thoughts were flashing through her mind, when suddenly she noticed a well groomed young woman looking at her quizzically across the room, a dark haired, petite woman of her own age, dressed in the height of fashion. The two women smiled at each other across the room. Emma made her way over towards her.

'Aren't you Emma?' the young woman asked in a casual tone. 'I think I've met your husband. Anyway, I'm Sonia.'

They talked and found that they had much in common: friends, love of country things and of gardens. Sonia was chic, soft-spoken, well-off and recently divorced.

'Why don't you come and have a drink tomorrow evening?' she asked, looking Emma in the eye. 'We could continue our talk alone.'

'Why not?' laughed Emma returning her look. 'I'd love to!'

Blushing, Sonia lowered her eyes.

In bed that night Emma felt very excited as she thought about her meeting with Sonia the following evening.

She was tired of being a puppet on a string – of being Ursula's little plaything. This was going to be a new and startling venture. For the first she was actually going to be master of her own life. She herself was going to be taking the initiative. Thanks to her new found self-confidence she was actually going to be the seducer and not the seduced!

She was going to be a free woman! Or was she deceiving herself that she could really get away from Ursula's domination or from her own masochistic longings to be dominated?

Anyway, she decided, she was jolly well not going to go on making those humiliating daily telephone reports to Rafaela. She was a big girl now with a girl of her own! Rafaela could go and jump in the lake.

As Emma pressed the doorbell, the feeling of thrilling anticipation that had been building up inside her was overwhelming. Then suddenly there was Sonia, standing in the doorway. She looked stunning in thigh-length boots, leggings and a short top.

'Oh, my dear, do come in,' she smiled.

'What a lovely house,' said Emma as Sonia led the way through two different rooms to a beautifully furnished long room in which a fire was burning. Sonia just sat down on the floor by the fire as if their meeting was nothing out of the ordinary. Emma gazed at her admiringly. She was loathe to make the first move, but she felt that both of them knew what was going to happen.

After some initial small talk, Emma said: 'And what about your husband? Has he gone for ever, or do you think you might perhaps have him back?'

'Have him back!' cried Sonia. 'You must be joking!'

Emma felt that this was perhaps the signal for her to get closer to Sonia. But it is difficult to make such an approach if you are in country clothes! So, knowing that Sonia was fashion-mad, she said: 'Have you had any new clothes, any new ball dresses, I can look at?'

Delighted, Sonia whisked Emma upstairs to her bedroom. Off the bedroom, instead of a dressing room, was a virtually walk-in wardrobe.

'Oh do try on that marvellous see-through top and lovely skirt,' cried Emma.

'Let me just help with the buttons at the back. Oh! Your hair has got caught. I'll just loosen it for you . . .'

The sight of Sonia's protruding nipples and beautiful figure made Emma impetuous. In fastening the buttons, she moved her hand slightly forward to touch Sonia's left breast.

At first Sonia was slow to respond, but when Emma persevered and touched her other breast, she could feel Sonia leaning back against her. They stood clasped like lovers for a full minute. Emma saw that Sonia's eyes were glistening. Instinctively she felt that Sonia could be hers.

Emma was indeed stunned at how easy it had all been. She began to feel what she thought a boy must also feel on his first serious date with a girl: a thrilling throbbing sensation. Indeed, she now realised that to have a beautiful and compliant woman in your arms was almost suffocatingly exciting. No wonder men chased girls! No wonder Ursula and her friends chased girls!

'Let's dance,' she whispered.

'Dance!'

'Yes! Let's pretend we are at a party!'

'Oh, Emma! You really are too silly,' said Sonia, getting cold.

Emma wondered what on earth she should do to retrieve the situation. She stroked Sonia caressingly. But Sonia was too taken up with admiring herself in the mirror to notice any of Emma's attempts at seduction.

'Wait here!' Emma cried desperately. 'What you need is a drink.'

She rushed downstairs, brought up a bottle of gin and some tonic, and poured two large gins. Outside it was now raining. The rain beating against the windows seemed to make Sonia amorous again. She tried on some exotic panties and a sexy-looking basque. She stood admiring herself, looking breathlessly beautiful. The gin was beginning to have its effect. Emma could see that Sonia was ready for something more. Why else would she have put on the basque and panties – hardly to excite herself!'

'Where did that gorgeous basque come from?' Emma asked.

'Oh, Jean-Paul sent it from Paris.'

Emma knew nothing about Jean-Paul, but the gin was taking its effect on her too and, with Sonia looking so ravishing, she was damned if she was going to have Jean-Paul, or anyone else, stop her from enjoying her.

'Lie down, my little Sonia,' she murmured, deliberately mimicking what she thought Ursula might have said in a similar situation. 'Lie down, my little girl.'

Sonia lay stretched out on the bed.

Emma came beside her. Gently at first, she began to touch her. Soon they were rubbing against each other and holding each other. Sonia's breasts got bigger and bigger. She pleaded with Emma to bite her nipples. Emma felt wonderfully masterful. It was the most fantastic sensation that she had ever experienced. Instinctively she knew, just as, she thought, a man would know and Ursula would know, that this was the critical moment. It was now all or nothing!

She had by now removed all her clothes. She peeled the basque and panties off Sonia. Their naked flesh touched with every movement. Emma was awash with arousal. She felt the most extraordinary urge to penetrate Sonia like a man. She wished she had one of Ursula's dildos that she could strap on round her loins. She put her hand down onto Sonia's beauty bud. But to her astonishment Sonia suddenly went cold, pushing Emma's hand away.

'What's the matter, my little Sonia? Don't be frightened. I'm not a brutal beast of man! I'll be very gentle with you. I'm not going to hurt you. You're going to love it, just you see! I know you need me.'

Sonia was indeed responding, but with the top half of her body only: her mouth, her nipples and her eyes. But alas for Emma, her bottom half just didn't seem to function.

Emma was desperate. She realised that this was a case of utter frigidness. A man, she felt, would know what to do, but she herself had simply no idea; she had no experience whatsoever in dealing with this kind of situation. She had never even read much about it in books.

She felt madly frustrated. She wanted Sonia more than anything she had ever wanted, and yet she had to content herself with a sort of robot who only functioned on the top. No matter how much Emma caressed, tickled, stroked or rubbed Sonia's beauty bud, there was just no reaction.

She felt mortified. She longed to know what made Sonia respond. Was it Jean-Paul? Did she need to be beaten? Was that it?

Sonia refused to speak. She got up off the bed and dressed. She turned to Emma.

'You can see yourself out, Emma, when you are ready.'

It was a very sad Emma who closed the front door without even saying goodbye to Sonia. It had been a very sad non-event.

By the time that Emma got home she was in the depths of despair and disappointment. She felt simply awful. She longed to get advice from someone, to ask what she should have done. But whom could she ask? Ursula would simply laugh at her if she told her about her failure. If she told Henry then he would probably tell her it served her right, and anyway Ursula had made her break with him.

She spent a moody few days trying to forget about Sonia and to concentrate on other things. Then suddenly the phone rang.

It was the vampire, as Emma had secretly christened Ursula, back a few days early from Morocco. Surprisingly, instead of speaking harshly to Emma, as she often did on the telephone, Ursula was friendly and charming.

'Oh, Emma, I did so miss you.'

Emma's self-confidence was at such a low ebb that she was immediately seduced by these words. But she tried to be cold and distant, as she had resolved to be before her own failure to seduce Sonia.

'All right, Ursula, what do want?' She was astonished at her own bravery at speaking in such a way to Ursula. There was a long pause, as if Ursula was considering the implication of being spoken to in such a way by someone she regarded as her servant girl. Emma was expecting an explosion down the telephone but instead Ursula was at her most cloying.

'Nothing at all! I don't want anything, my darling, except you. It's you we want. You're fun. We like you. We want to see you again . . .'

All this was music to Emma's ears. Her determination not to see Ursula again, not to fall under her thrall again, was evaporating fast.

'. . . and all my friends are asking where my lovely little friend Emma is!'

After the humiliation of being brushed off by Sonia, Emma now had no difficulty in persuading herself that she should see Ursula again after all.

'So when are you coming up to London to see me?' asked Ursula. Emma tried to rescue what was left of her self-esteem by saying that she was so busy, that it was difficult to get away, that . . .

But Ursula wasn't going to be put off like that. Sensing that the battle was now won, her tone changed abruptly.

'Emma! You'd better come up tomorrow afternoon.'

Emma abjectly conceded defeat.

'Yes,' she said.

'Yes what?'

Emma swallowed hard. All her former resolve had now gone.

'Yes, madam,' she said in a humble little voice.

'Good little girl!' came Ursula's voice. 'Good! We shall be alone.'

Going up in the train the next day, Emma was furious with herself at having been so weak in giving in so abjectly to Ursula. Why did she always go back to her every time she snapped her fingers?

Emma didn't particularly like her, even if she did find her fascinating. Ursula enjoyed making her do such degrading things. She treated her like dirt. So why was she going back to her? Was it just because her attempt to prove her independence by seducing Sonia had failed so ignominiously?

She felt a great rage swelling up inside her. On the one hand she wanted to stand up to Ursula, but on the other hand there was the terrible failure with Sonia still hanging over her.

Suddenly she saw the answer. She would tell Ursula about Sonia without saying anything about the dreadful failure at the end. She would even taunt Ursula about Sonia. She would let her think that she was now like Ursula's women friends: that she had a girl of her own.

That would make Ursula treat her with respect, as an equal. That would change their whole relationship for the better. She would now treat her just as an intimate woman friend with whom she could have a highly enjoyable relationship in bed, and not as merely a servant or slave.

Yes, indeed, Emma thought, she would turn the Sonia episode to her own advantage and re-establish her relationship with Ursula, but on a completely new footing – one that was not, for once, dominated by her fear of Ursula's cane.

As Emma rang the door bell she felt a little shiver of apprehension. Was Ursula the spider and she the fly, innocently being lured into the trap of the spider's web? To her surprise

Ursula herself opened the door. Then she remembered that Ursula had said that they would be alone.

'Come in, come in, my darling little Emma. How well you look – and how pretty!' She might have been talking to a close woman friend, not to someone she normally treated as a mere servant.

Emma was lulled by this exceptionally friendly reception into thinking that it was going to be fun taunting Ursula about her new conquest – without of course letting on that it had really been a complete failure.

'Come on in, my little baby. Come, my little Emma. We have missed you. Now you must tell me about all the fun you have been having whilst I have been away. Have you been a good girl, Emma?'

Initially, Emma said nothing. But Ursula was adept at getting information out of her.

The fact that Emma had suddenly stopped making her little daily reports to Rafaela had aroused Ursula's suspicions. Although Emma may not have realised it, they were an excellent way of ensuring that Emma still regarded herself as her submissive slave. If they stopped, then it was a clear signal the girl might be trying to break away.

'Well my little Emma, I suppose you haven't had any fun whilst I was away? The poor little thing has had no one to play with! Poor little girl!'

Emma fell into the trap.

'No one to play with!' she exclaimed angrily. 'Well if you call going to bed with the most loveliest girl in the world having "no fun", then perhaps you're right, but personally I'm finding it very exciting. She's such a beautiful little creature – and so obedient and loving.'

Ursula's face had changed completely as Emma talked. It was now pinched and twisted with fury, and her normally hazel green eyes had changed to a dark green and were flickering.

She had suspected that perhaps Emma had been having a mild flirtation with some gormless young man. But to be having an affair with another woman, and behind her back, was unbelievable. Emma was her slave! To have this chit of a girl boasting that she had a girl of her own was just incredible.

'You've been doing *what*?' she screamed.

'Oh, yes!' laughed Emma, enjoying every moment of this scene. 'Do you know Sonia Richards, Ursula? She's gorgeous! Oh, it's been wonderful making love to her!'

Ursula could not stand this another moment.

'Get upstairs to my room!' she screamed, grabbing Emma by the hair and dragging her to the staircase.

'You're jealous!' cried Emma happily as she went up the stairs. 'You're jealous!'

If only Emma had known what was about to be happen she would not have taunted Ursula so mercilessly.

Ursula followed the laughing Emma into her bedroom. 'Get your clothes off!' she screeched.

'No!' said Emma.

'I said get your clothes off, you ungrateful bitch,' repeated Ursula in a quiet menacing voice.

Emma stood quite still and made a face at Ursula, just like a naughty child. Oh what fun this is, she thought. Then, suddenly before she knew what had happened, Ursula slapped her across the face.

The shock had Emma almost in tears, such was its strength and speed.

'Please don't hit me,' she cried. 'Please stop.'

'If you don't have all your clothes off within one minute, you'll know all about it!' was the angry reply.

Emma made a last attempt at standing up to Ursula. Pouting, she very slowly started to take off her stockings.

Ursula was further enraged by this show of dumb insolence. She grabbed Emma's little hands with one of her own strong ones, and with the other she reached up Emma's legs and tore off her panties.

'Who gave you permission to come to my house wearing panties?' she shouted. 'You know very well you have to be naked under your dress. I can see you've got all sorts of ideas above your station. First you stop making your daily reports, then you come here, bold as brass with some cock and bull story about having a girl of your own. A girl of your own indeed! I'll soon show you that you just have a mistress – *me*!'

Viciously she slapped Emma again across the face then threw her sobbing to the floor.

Emma heard her walk to a chest of drawers and pull open a drawer. She heard the clink of chains. She recognised the humming noise of one of Ursula's little machines. Then to her horror she heard a swishing noise and a thump as Ursula brought her cane hard down on a cushion. She came over to where Emma lay huddled on the floor. Punctuating her words with terrifying stokes of the cane on the cushion, she spoke slowly and deliberately.

'I'll teach you to think you can do what you like. You're my girl, don't you understand? My girl! And don't dare to even think about making love to anyone except me. You're going to learn your lesson the hard way, my girl! Now get on the bed!'

She paused and then, speaking slowly again, said: 'No! Perhaps the floor is the proper place for a little bitch like you.' She brought her cane down with another crash onto the cushion. 'Now get the rest of your clothes off quickly! Little dogs don't wear clothes when they are being punished!'

Emma was already tearing off her clothes, terrified at what Ursula might do next. There was another crash of the cane onto the cushion.

'Please let me go,' she sobbed.

'Let you go!' laughed Ursula. 'My God, you come here boasting of some girl you've been playing with behind my back, and you think I'll let you go! You're going to learn that you are nothing without me. Nothing! If I had a dog I wouldn't even demean him by mating you with him. And don't think that you're going to get off with a mere caning!'

Emma felt the freezing cold chains on her ankles, fastening them together, and then on her wrists, tying them behind her back.

'Now lie on your back!' Ursula ordered. 'And stop snivelling. Get your knees up – and spread them wide apart. Show yourself like the bitch on heat you've been acting as whilst I was away! Now get your legs right up in the air.'

With her hands chained behind her back, this was very difficult for poor Emma. 'Oh, please, Ursula,' she pleaded, 'I can't get them up with my hands and ankle chains.'

'Don't you call me Ursula, you impertinent little dog.'

There was a swishing noise and this time the cane came down across the back of Emma's thighs, making her cry out with pain. 'You'll soon learn, my girl, that when your mistress tells you to get your legs up, you damn well get them up . . . at once.'

Poor Emma, shivering with the cold chains against her naked body, struggled madly and finally got her legs right up. Such is the power of the cane in the hands of a strong-minded woman!

'And keep your knees wide apart too,' she was ordered.

I hate you, Ursula, Emma thought, I hate you!

But worse was to follow. She saw Ursula bend down behind her legs. Suddenly, without any preliminaries, she felt Ursula's little machine being thrust up inside her. It should have hurt! But the awful thing was that she knew she was excited and ready for it. She felt it penetrating. Then she felt it suddenly vibrating inside her. She heard the now muffled humming sound coming from deep inside her. Desperately she tried to reach it with her tied hands, but found she could not do so. Desperately she wriggled and writhed to try and eject it, but it was too deep inside her now. Horrified, she began to feel her body responding to it . . .

Ursula stood watching the chained figure lying moaning and twisting on the floor. Finally, she gave a satisfied smile and strode out of room, locking the door behind her.

# 12    LOCKED AGAIN INTO THE GILDED CAGE

Two hours later, Emma still lay helpless on the floor of Ursula's bedroom, her hands chained behind her back and her ankles chained together.

The awful humming noise was still coming from deep inside her. She had given up trying to reach the dreadful little machine thrust up inside her or even to try and expel it. For two hours it had kept her in a high state of arousal. But with her hands chained behind her back she had been quite unable to get to her beauty bud to give herself the relief that the horrible machine was making her body cry out for.

She had longed to climb up onto the comfort of Ursula's soft bed. But one of the chains was looped round the leg of the bed, making this impossible – she was forced to remain lying on the hard floor.

Over and over again she had cursed herself for having fallen into Ursula's trap, for taunting her about making love to Sonia – especially as in fact the whole episode had ended in failure.

What a fool she had been! She should have known that far from treating her with respect and as an equal because she had claimed to have a girl of her own, Ursula would have regarded such behaviour as quite inadmissible in a girl she enjoyed treating as her lady's maid.

Emma saw that outside it was already starting to get dark.

Suddenly she heard the noise of distant voices. She recognised Ursula's laugh. But there was also the laugh of another woman. Who was she? Were they laughing at her plight, Emma wondered. Was Ursula describing how stupid Emma had been in telling Ursula about Sonia?

She remembered that Ursula had said that they would be

alone in the house this evening. Had she, perhaps, specially rung a friend to come over and help her punish Emma? She gave a little shiver when she remembered Ursula saying that she would not get away with just a caning.

Nervously she wondered who the friend might be. She knew that Ursula enjoyed watching her being thrashed by another woman. She remembered how on their very first weekend together, at the health farm, Ursula had watched the strict Miss Perkins beat her. Oh, please let it not be Miss Perkins!

But who else might it be? Might it be the horrible fat Helga?

What should she do? She hesitated at first about calling out, for she did not want this unknown friend of Ursula to see her in such a shameful state.

By now it was getting dark in the bedroom too. Emma was feeling very hungry. She had not eaten since breakfast, since Ursula always insisted on her arriving with an empty stomach so that she could, if she so decided, feed her like a baby. The voices were getting more animated. She felt that she had now nothing to lose.

'Help! Help' she called out weakly. But the voices paid no attention. No one could hear her.

She decided that if she banged her feet on the floor, then, despite their being chained together, the noise should attract attention downstairs.

She kept this up for several minutes, until suddenly she heard the rattle of a key in the locked door which was then flung open and the lights switched on. She blinked in the sudden bright light.

There standing in the doorway was a grim-faced Ursula. Her cane was in her hand. Emma caught her breath with fright.

Behind her was a younger but equally tall and well groomed woman. She was smiling as if enjoying the scene.

'Look, Jennifer,' she heard Ursula say, 'this is the little slut who got ideas above her station. She actually thought that she could kick over the traces and have a girl of her own behind my back! The little tart! She's just nothing! Just one of my bitch pack!'

'Bitch pack?' said Jennifer.

'Instead of a pack of hounds, I have a pack of bitches.'

Jennifer laughed. 'Oh, you are clever, Ursula! What a way to describe them! Can we have a look at your bitch?'

She walked over to Emma and stood looking down at her with disgust. 'Are there any more? I don't think much of this one. It's an ugly little brute.'

'Well, you little bitch,' said Ursula, 'as you see, my friend is an expert at denigrating little girls who get too big for their boots. And later she might want to enjoy you. So you'd better show yourself to her properly and hope she finds at least that part of your body attractive. So get your legs up again. And bend your knees more. Well, Jennifer, do you think you'd like to take this little creature?'

'Ugh! No thank you!'

But Ursula now began to resent Jennifer's tone. She did not like any of her girls being criticised by anyone except herself. That was her right and hers alone. So to spite Jennifer she started being protective towards Emma.

'Oh Emma, Jennifer simply hasn't seen what a pretty little lady's maid you can be. So you're going to dress up and be our maid. We shall want you nicely powdered all over. Then you'll show Jennifer what an obedient little maid you are. You'll like that, won't you, Emma?'

Emma felt that she had no alternative. Unless she played the role she risked more of Jennifer's scathing tongue. She also knew that Ursula could be extremely vindictive if she did not properly play the part that Ursula might suddenly decide on.

'Now little Emma, show yourself prettily again to Jennifer. Knees wide apart. That's better. Are you an excited little maid? Let's have a look.'

Horrified, Emma saw, through her parted knees, that Ursula had put down her cane and bent down to examine her. She felt very humiliated, especially with Jennifer present and especially since she knew that with the awful machine vibrating away inside her she was indeed highly aroused.

'Oh, yes, you certainly are excited! And all just by the thought of being our little maid!' Ursula laughed, knowing that Emma's arousal was really involuntary and had nothing to do with the prospect of having to be their maid. 'So the excited little maid is now going to be able to give Jennifer and me some of her

122

moisture! Then when you've done that properly we'll take your chains off.'

Ursula slowly removed the dripping little machine. She pulled Emma to her feet and made her stand up on a table. Her loins were now level with Ursula's face.

'Stand up straight, head up, look straight ahead and don't look down! Knees apart! Wider! Now thrust your belly forward and offer yourself like a good little girl. Um! Um! It's delicious, Jennifer! Come and taste it.'

Emma felt utterly degraded, standing there helplessly with her hands chained behind her back, having to offer Ursula the juices of her intimate arousal. It was bad enough having to offer them to Ursula, but to have to do so to Jennifer, a stranger, was too much.

'No! Not her! Not her! Please!' Emma cried.

'Jennifer, hand me my cane!' Ursula's voice was very angry.

'Oh no, please don't beat me!' pleaded Emma.

'You impertinent young girl! How dare you insult my friend! And how dare you speak without permission!' screamed Ursula. 'I don't want to hear one more word from you. Now, head up, knees wide apart and strain your belly right forward in the proper position to offer your juices to Jennifer. And hold that position whilst you offer them to her. And to make certain you do, I'm going to give you two strokes across that pouting little belly for insulting a friend of mine.'

Ursula took the cane from Jennifer. Emma was trembling with fear, but she did not dare break position, nor open her mouth. She gritted her teeth as Ursula brought the cane down twice across her soft little belly.

'That'll teach you to argue the toss with me, you little bitch. Whatever I tell you to do, you damn well do it – at once and without any argument. And just remember that the cane will be waiting for you again at the first sign of hesitation – or if you dare to say one word!

Poor Emma could hardly have felt more humiliated as she stood there in silence, straining to let her juices down onto Jennifer's tongue, whilst Ursula tapped her cane warningly against her bottom to ensure that she thrust her belly right forward.

123

Ursula could hardly have asserted her domination more degradingly, Emma realised. How could she have ever dreamt that Ursula would treat her as an equal or let her have a girl of her own!

But worse was to follow.

'I think I'll use my Polaroid camera to take some photographs of you offering your juices to Jennifer. And if you don't behave well, Emma, I might even send them on to your friend Sonia. That'll show her your real position in life!'

That would be too awful! Emma wanted to protest, but she did not dare to open her mouth. She knew she would just have to be very very good.

So it was that the rest of the scene of Emma abjectly offering her juices to Jennifer was illuminated by the flashes of Ursula's camera. Finally Jennifer raised her head. She licked her lips in satisfaction and nodded to Ursula.

'Now run downstairs to the maid's room, and wash and get dressed,' ordered Ursula. 'When I ring for you, you damn well come running back here dressed in your maid's uniform with nothing on underneath. You're to bathe and attend on Jennifer as well as me. Just remember that you are her maid this evening as well as mine. Now go!'

Down in the bare little maid's room, Emma felt so ashamed by all that had happened, that she decided to cheer herself up, and impress Ursula and Jennifer, by really making herself look really beautiful. Having had a quick bath, she made herself up carefully, rouging her cheeks, putting plenty of eye shadow on her eyelids, and mascara on her eyelashes. She even decided to shock them by painting her beauty lips. Then she powdered herself all over and put on the humiliating little uniform with its short skirt, white cap and apron, and black stockings and shoes.

Just as she finished, the bell rang imperiously.

In a flurry of scent, powder and general excitement, Emma rushed upstairs. She knocked on the door and went in.

'You rang, madam? Your little servant girl is here!'

But the room was empty.

To Emma's horror, she found Ursula and Jennifer in the bath together, playing with each other's nipples. This was a real shock. She knew, of course, that Ursula had other girls but to find her naked in the bath with Jennifer was too ghastly for words.

'I'm not bathing *her*!' Emma cried in a fit of temper and jealousy.

'How dare you!' said Ursula. 'Jennifer, did you hear that? What shall we do with this ungrateful little wretch? When I think of all that I've done for her, a mere servant girl. Now, Emma! Are you going to behave properly?'

Emma nodded contritely. She knew she had no alternative but to do what she was told. She felt disgusted, however. She really hated both these women with all her heart.

'Very well,' said Ursula. 'Now scrub our backs. Yes . . . There's a good little maid. Then you'll dry one at a time, starting with me now. Later Jennifer will tell you what she wants you to do.'

Jennifer giggled. 'What do you mean?' she said coyly.

'You know very well!' replied Ursula as, gripping Emma's proffered arm, she stepped out of the bath and then stood for Emma to dry her. 'Jennifer, you said you liked playing with little maids. I want you to feel free to play with mine.'

She paused whilst Emma carefully dried every inch of her body as if her very life depended on it. Emma could not get the Polaroid photographs out of her mind.

'Then in a few minutes time I want to use Emma to put on a little show for my amusement.' Ursula laughed as she felt the horrified Emma's hand shake at hearing these words.

'Now, Emma, hand me my wrap. I'm just going to get my video camera ready and then sit on my bed and watch the show. And just remember, Emma, that if you don't do just exactly what Jennifer tells you, then I'll lock you up in the maid's room for three whole days with a bowl of water and a crust of bread. I want a perfect video tape to send to your little friend Sonia, along with the Polaroid photographs. Now go and dry Jennifer!'

Emma felt that the whole situation was getting out of hand, but she was too scared of Ursula's cane to say a word. But the thought of being shut up for three days scared the living daylights out of her, especially as she knew that Ursula really meant it. And the threat of Sonia being sent a video featuring her in a key role really frightened her.

Jennifer was hard but very attractive; the idea of performing with her in front of Ursula repelled Emma. Jennifer might like enjoying little maids, but she could probably be quite brutal in the way she did so.

But Emma knew she had a task to do. It would be just a job she had been ordered to do by her mistress.

'Come on!' called Ursula from the bedroom.

'I like my maids to crawl,' said Jennifer. 'Just crawl in after me. Just crawl, little maid! Crawl, you little bitch!'

Emma did as she was told.

Ursula loved the spectacle. 'Clever, Jennifer!' she cried. 'I like your little maid! This is going to make excellent video.'

Jennifer made Emma crawl all round the room and then towards Ursula's bed, making her keep back a little so that Ursula and her video camera would not miss anything.

Poor Emma, still on all fours, was hating every moment of it.

'I don't like this girl's ugly little face,' said Jennifer. Clearly she had planned this. 'Let's hide it behind something nicer. What have you got, Ursula? A chimpanzee mask, perhaps? No? Well, let me see what I have brought with me. Ah yes, a pretty little dog mask! That'll make her look like a real little bitch!'

Emma looked into the mirror in dismay as the realistic rubber dog's head was slipped over her own. She saw through the little eye holes what seemed to be a real dog with the body of a woman dressed as a maid.

Suddenly she heard the well-known hum of Ursula's horrible little machine. Still kneeling on the floor, her bottom scarcely covered by the very short maid's skirt, she felt Jennifer thrusting it up her backside.

Horrified and almost screaming with pain, she could not help calling out from under the mask.

'No! Not there!'

'Little dogs don't talk – they bark to show their appreciation of their mistress' kindness,' said Jennifer, bringing Ursula's cane down across Emma's exposed bottom. 'Now bark, little bitch, bark!'

'Woof! Woof!' cried Emma, in pain and desperately humiliated, but too scared of the cane to do anything else.

'Look! She's beginning to like it,' cried Jennifer, clearly getting very excited herself and pushing Emma's head down to the floor so that Ursula could get an even better view of her raised hindquarters, which were now pointing towards her.

'She's just like a real bitch on heat. Now bark to show your arousal, little bitch. Bark, or you'll get the cane.'

'Woof! Woof!'

Ursula was also getting excited at the sight. She put down her video camera and beckoned to Jennifer. Leaving Emma kneeling on all fours on the floor, and not daring to remove the horrible machine which, in truth, was indeed now arousing her again. The two women started to feel and touch one another.

'Now crawl round the room, little dog,' called out Ursula. 'Keep your head and bottom up and your back arched downwards! Thrust your belly down towards the floor!'

The sight of the crawling Emma, her face hidden by the dog mask, and her bottom wriggling with the pain and excitement of the little machine, was driving them wild.

Ursula put her hand on her mouth to taste Jennifer's juices. It was too much! They both climaxed, whilst Emma was left there watching them from behind her mask as she continued to crawl round the room. She was hating them both and wondering how Ursula could have been so cruel as to do this to her.

'I think our little maid has been a good little girl' said Ursula. She was always in a softer mood once she had climaxed. 'Shall we let her crawl into our bed, Jennifer?'

Emma started to crawl up onto the bed. But it was difficult with the awful little machine still vibrating up her backside. It was also difficult to see through the little eye holes of the dog mask.

Gently daring, she begged them to remove them.

'You can take out the vibrator,' Ursula said to Jennifer, 'but I certainly want her still wearing her dog mask and her maid's uniform in my bed. That'll be much more exciting! And I certainly don't want her touching my body with her dirty little paws.' She pulled a pair of white gloves from a drawer in their bedside table. 'So put these on her.'

Two minutes later a humiliated Emma climbed under the bedclothes. Despite the gloves she could feel the dampness of the women's arousal on the sheets. Through the mask she detected its characteristic odour. To her shame, she could feel herself being further aroused by this combination. What animals we women are, she thought, realising that it was not only the sight and smell of her own arousal that had so turned on the other two, but also the degrading, and yet exciting, sight of the dog mask that they had made her wear.

Emma had never experienced being between two women before. After all the previous humiliations, she now found this terribly exciting. Whilst Jennifer reached down to touch her where she had only recently thrust in the little machine, Ursula took hold of her beauty bud and then wrapped her mouth around it. Emma climaxed as she had never done before in her whole life.

It was the most extraordinary sensation, like being taken from the front and back simultaneously by two burly men. It drove all the sad thoughts of her failure with Sonia right out of her mind.

It also drove out all ideas of wanting to be Ursula's equal. If this was what would sometimes happen to her as Ursula's servant, then she did not wish for anything better! Exhausted the three women fell asleep.

Early next morning, Ursula kicked Emma out of bed with orders to report to Rafaela, Ursula's housekeeper, who would by now have returned after her day off. Emma was to resume her duties as Ursula's maid and bring them breakfast in bed.

Rafaela greeted Emma in her usual surly way. She insisted on Emma leaving the bathroom open, and came in to scrub her all over with a stiff scrubbing brush, laughing as she saw the marks of the cane. She even inspected Emma's hands and nails before giving her the heavy tray to carry upstairs.

It was therefore a well-washed and freshly groomed Emma, who, wearing a fresh maid's uniform, brought breakfast to the two sleeping women and drew back the curtains.

First, feeling deeply embarrassed, she had to accompany each of them to the bathroom and then serve breakfast. She felt very jealous of the delicious grapefruit, coffee and fresh croissants. All that Rafaela had allowed her was a glass of water and some hard biscuits.

Then she had to help the women to dress.

Emma was surprised at how anxious to please she was, and how she enjoyed serving them. It was almost as if she really was a natural servant.

After Jennifer had left, Ursula told Rafaela that she was going to visit a gallery out in the country to arrange an exhibition, and that Emma was to act as her chauffeuse. Humiliatingly, as if Emma were a little girl who could not be relied on to do anything without being supervised, Ursula told Rafaela that Emma was to wear a special chauffeuse's uniform with nothing on underneath. The uniform, which included a cap rather like that of an airline hostess, was intended to make clear that the status of the wearer was that of a servant. Emma had to allow Rafaela to dress her. Looking in the mirror, she saw that she now indeed looked like a paid chauffeuse. She had not even been allowed to put on any make-up and her hair had been swept up under her cap.

Ursula sat in the back of her expensive looking car, busy with papers, as Emma drove in silence, not daring to disturb her mistress. Arriving at the gallery, Emma jumped out to open the door for Ursula, just as she had been taught to do.

Ursula swept into the gallery, leaving Emma sitting in the car in the car park at the back of the gallery.

Emma knew that Ursula would be enjoying a delicious lunch with the directors of the gallery. She herself felt very hungry, but did not dare to leave the car for Ursula had warned her that she might call her on the car telephone at any moment to bring the car round to the front entrance.

It was therefore a rather sad little Emma who sat all by herself in the car. She could not even listen to the car radio, for Ursula had locked the controls saying that chauffeuses should not waste their mistress' batteries by listening to foolish programmes on the radio.

After an hour, a girl came out and handed Emma a bag saying that Miss de Freville had asked her to take this out to her young bitch dog that she had left in the car.

Eagerly, Emma looked inside the bag. It contained a bowl of chopped up dog food and biscuits. Ducking down in the car, so that no one would see, Emma eagerly gobbled up the strong smelling food.

As she chewed the biscuits, Emma thought back on the events of the past week. When she had finished, she looked despondently into the bag. She was still hungry. She picked out a piece of dog meat in her fingers and put into her mouth. It seemed to drive home her status as Ursula's girl, her servant. It seemed to drive home that the bars of the gilded cage had firmly closed behind her again.

Suddenly the telephone rang.

'Emma! Bring my car round straight away.'

'Yes, madam, at once!'

# 13 'THE BRUTE': HENRY REAPPEARS

Emma sat in the sun in the square in Bruges – sunlight dancing on the pavement, loud Belgian music playing in the bandstand, and the belfry ringing out its recorded chimes as she reflected on her last meeting with Ursula.

For several weeks after her recent very chastening experiences, Emma had been the very image of an obedient and submissive lesbian lover. She had humiliatingly reported by telephone to Ursula, or to her housekeeper, Rafaela, after each meal and again after going to the bathroom in the morning. She had hastened to come up to London whenever Ursula summoned her. She had behaved dutifully in whatever role Ursula ordered her to assume: baby girl, little girl, teenage niece or lady's maid.

She had hardly spoken to a single man except for John, and had certainly not looked a man in the face, never mind, as she repeatedly had to assure Ursula, made eyes at one.

Ursula for once seemed satisfied with her submissiveness and she herself had revelled in the way Ursula seemed to control every minute of her life.

Then two things had happened. Firstly, John's elder sister had asked her to step into the breach and take her young teenage son and one of his school friends to Bruges for a few days holiday. It would only be for a few days and the boys would be going off on their own to see Brussels, Amsterdam and other local sights, so it would not be very exhausting for Emma. John had accepted for her, saying that as he would be away, she would have nothing else to do – leaving Emma wondering how on earth she was going to get Ursula's permission to go.

Then, suddenly, Henry surfaced again. He had heard from her sister-in-law that she was going to be in Bruges for a few days and proposed to join her there. To avoid complications with the boys, he would be staying at a different hotel. However, he said, doubtlessly they could arrange to spend a good deal of time together!

Emma's heart was in her mouth as she listened to his persuasive voice. He had apparently ignored the letter that she had written to him under Ursula's supervision saying that she never wanted to see or hear from him again. Emma was at first terrified, remembering how Ursula had made her promise never to see him again. But how could she put him off? And anyway did she really want to do so? With Ursula left behind in London, surely she could do what she liked in Bruges with no chance of Ursula ever learning the truth?

So she had agreed!

Now, sitting in the square in Bruges, she could not help laughing as she remembered Ursula's jealous face the night before she left. Ursula had simply refused to believe that she was innocently going away with two schoolboys.

'Two randy young schoolboys! Two adolescents!' she had shouted. 'And what are you going to get up to with them, you little slut? So it's boys now, is it? What next, you little slut?'

Emma had tried to explain that she was merely taking her nephew and a school friend on a little educational holiday. But Ursula was obsessed with being in complete control of Emma and furious that she had agreed to this trip without first asking her permission. She simply would not listen to reason.

For Ursula there was always the threat that perhaps 'The Brute', as she derisively called Henry, might, reappear on the scene. She had, she thought, put enough pressure on Emma to make sure that she never dared to see him again. Even so, she was still haunted by the idea that little Emma might return to this horrible man, who at one stage seemed to have had more influence over Emma than she had. 'The Brute!' she thought. God, how she hated him! She would, she had declared, ruin his precious manhood for ever if, one day, she ever met him. She would make him scream with pain, she had confidently told Emma.

But now Emma sat alone in the market square in Bruges, sipping a cold lemonade. She was looking bronzed and lovely without, it seemed, a care in the world. The two boys had been attentive and well-mannered, carrying her bags, bringing her drinks and pastries, and amusing themselves for almost the whole day.

She looked up at the church tower clock. Henry would be arriving in only six hours time! What a nerve she had, she thought, to see him again after all that had happened last time! Would Ursula have had her followed? Ursula had actually told her that she was going to be followed to Victoria to see if her story of catching the boat train was really true. But that would have been harmless; Ursula would have been told by her private detectives that Emma had indeed caught the train and was travelling with two boys.

But now, this was something very different. What a chance she was taking! If only 'The Brute' knew the appalling risk she was running in agreeing to meet him.

Emma gave a little shiver. But was it a shiver of sheer fear, or of fear mixed with excitement?

The hours went quickly for Emma. She knew she had prepared herself for 'The Brute'. Her mind was in a fever of anticipation. She thought of the horrible letter that Ursula had forced her to write to him. Would he want to punish her for writing it? She remembered how Ursula had thrashed her until, mad with pain, she had promised to get rid of him. And now here she was secretly meeting him again behind Ursula's back.

Of course, thought Emma, when it came to men, Ursula was just insane with hatred, contempt and jealousy. Of course she knew that 'The Brute' had controlled Emma. It was this above all that really angered her most. She had to be Emma's 'Controller' and no one else. She would not share this control with anyone and certainly not a man! The very idea! Ursula's girls did what she said and no one else!

Yet now Emma found herself at the station, almost unable to contain her excitement at the thought of meeting this man again!

Indeed she was so excited by the idea of this clandestine meeting that she had gone there two hours before his train from Brussels was due to arrive lest his plane might have been early and he had caught an earlier train. Only the good Lord knew how many cups of coffee she drunk as she waited desperate with impatience and anticipation, or how many times she went over to the information desk, or how many times she walked round the station booking hall or how many times she eagerly rushed to meet a crowd of passengers coming through the barrier. She felt like a schoolgirl meeting her first boyfriend. Would she ever feel like this when meeting Ursula?

Suddenly there he was!

He was looking as cool as ever. Clearly he had no idea of the pain and anguish that he had caused the last time they had met and no idea of the fear running through her mind this time. He was as charming, and yet commanding as ever, as she took him to her hotel – before the boys got back.

He made her bathe him and caress him. But, the swine, he allowed her no relief. She would have to wait, he told her, until the next day. She could not believe him. She had been so looking forward to this romantic meeting, she was so excited, so aroused – and here he was not merely denying her any relief but positively ordering her to keep herself pure for his use on the following day!

But keeping her waiting did not stop him from enjoying his predilection, as he called it, for taking her from behind as a way of asserting his masculine superiority over her. It was something she always hated. It was both painful and uncomfortable – and the physical pleasure seemed minimal. But, as Henry intended, it filled her with the realisation of her utter submissiveness and obedience to him as her master. As he thrust up inside her, he ordered her to cry out: 'Master! My Master! Your little slave is offering herself to her master!'

As she did so, she could not help thinking how horrified Ursula would be at her calling a man, any man, 'master'. And as to offering her backside to one – well the idea would drive Ursula mad with rage. Thank heavens she would never learn about it!

So it was that when the two boys arrived back from a day's visit to Amsterdam, and joined them for dinner, Emma was still in a state of scarcely suppressed arousal. It was a state that continued even more frustratingly after the boys had gone to bed, and Henry took her to one of Bruges' many bar-discotheques.

There was, she knew, a method in his madness. Older than her, he had learnt long ago that the most appreciated things in life are those that are awaited with eager, better still frantic, anticipation. In her state, Henry had little difficulty in getting her talking. He even got a glimmering of her relationship with Ursula, of what had happened to her after they had last met and what risks she was running in meeting him now. She begged him to forgive her for the nasty letter she had sent him, and hinted at the duress she had been under when she wrote it. She even told him that it had been posted by Ursula.

All this Henry found very amusing and diverting. He found it difficult, though, to take it all very seriously. How could any red-blooded girl like Emma really want to make love to an older woman? It was all a mere passing phase and meanwhile they should forget it and make the best of their weekend together.

He would, he told her mysteriously, give her a visiting card before he left for her to show Ursula what a real brute he was. Meanwhile, he added, Emma was to go back to her hotel and promise to keep herself pure and eager for his attention the following day.

After tossing and turning in her frustration and excitement all night, Emma was so eager that she turned up at Henry's hotel whilst he was still having breakfast in the dining room. She had been terrified lest he might go off on his own. Infuriatingly the boys could not agree where they wanted to go that day, and even talked of spending the day with her in Bruges! But at last she managed to get rid of them, and invited Henry up to the suite that she shared with them.

Their lovemaking was all that she desired. Henry was masterful and strong. He put her through her paces like a circus ringmaster – even making her bark her pleasure like a little dog when he finally allowed her to yield to him.

It was wonderful, and afterwards as they sat drinking on the little terrace of her room, she felt that she was indeed in heaven.

Henry ordered her to look lovingly and adoringly at him all day – and it was an order she had little difficulty in obeying. He ordered her take his hand and skip along beside him in the street like a little girl out with her favourite uncle. He ordered her to put her hand shyly in his under the table when they sat out at a café. He ordered her to lift her skirt when she sat down so that her soft little bottom, secretly bare under her skirt, would feel the cold metal of the chair. He made her run like a little girl across the square to fetch him a newspaper. He made her wait, thirsty in the heat, until he had drunk his cool drink, before allowing her to take a sip. All this she did willingly and happily, and all thoughts of Ursula were banished from her mind.

That evening, she was again in a seventh heaven as she was again allowed to bark her pleasure. What a man he was, she felt.

The next morning was to be their last. At midday, she would have to leave with the two boys for Ostend where they would take the ferry back to England.

She came early to his hotel. She knelt down at his feet, her hands busy pleasing him. She slipped out of her dress under which, in accordance with Henry's orders, she was naked.

Henry made her lie down on her front. He told her to put a pillow under her belly to throw up her bottom. Oh no, she thought, not his predilection again! But it was not his manhood that she felt a second later, as he gripped her neck to hold her down. It was a stroke from his belt. A stroke that was followed by another and by another, each one placed carefully below the previous one so as to leave a well whipped pattern on her buttocks as she cried and protested. A mild beating could be very exciting, but this was really too hard. At last it was over. He looked down admiringly at his handiwork and stroked her. She looked back up at him resentfully. He had really hurt her!

Then he took her.

Not until she was dressing to rush back to her hotel to pick up the boys and leave for the station, did she look in the mirror. The weals looked red and angry. They would not disappear for a couple of days, she realised. And she had promised to meet Ursula that evening as soon as she got back to London and got rid of the boys! What was she to do? What an awful position she was in!

With a cry of dismay, she turned to the smiling Henry.

'My God! What have you done to me?' she said, looking at herself in the mirror.

'Merely my visiting card,' said Henry innocently.

There was no time to say anything more, or she would miss the train. She kissed Henry with a strange feeling of respect and fled.

The rest of the day passed very quickly, leaving Emma with no real opportunity to think about what she should do, and an aching void in her stomach at having had to leave Henry just when they were having such fun together. She picked up the boys and caught the train by the skin of her teeth. The ferry was crowded and they had to queue for ages, first for something to drink and then for something to eat. Then there was a panic about whether the boat train was going to arrive late in London and whether her nephew's friend would catch his train home from Waterloo and finally the discovery that he hadn't got enough money for his ticket. Boys! thought Emma, as finally she dropped her nephew off at the home of another friend with whom he was due to stay.

What with one thing and another it was already late when Emma at last arrived at Ursula's – or rather as she felt, reported for duty to her mistress.

She had half wondered about calling it off and going straight home where she would ring Ursula with some excuse about being taken ill, which would solve any problem over Henry's wretched visiting card. But Ursula, perhaps anticipating that she might try to cancel her visit, had made her leave both keys to the cottage with her. So, as her husband was away, Emma couldn't go home without Ursula's permission even if she wanted to. All her friends in London were away. She realised that she simply had nowhere to go except to Ursula's. What a dreadful level of control Ursula seemed to have over her!

Ursula opened the door. She was in an exceptionally good mood and obviously delighted that Emma had turned up, just as she had told her to do.

'Ah, my little sweetie, my little baby girl,' she murmured with unaccustomed gentleness. 'Shall we put you into your little cot tonight? Is the little girl tired after her long journey? Does she need Rafaela to wash and powder her – and then let Ursula excite her? Is she longing for her mistress after her little absence? First we shall have to have a little inspection!'

Ursula put her arm around Emma. She was still unusually kind and affectionate. She took Emma's face in her hands and looked down into her eyes.

'Come along, my little baby, come straight upstairs. We'll have a little drink – rather I shall have a drink and the little baby will have a glass of milk! My little baby looks gorgeous tonight – how I'm going to enjoy myself with her!'

Emma began to tremble with fear. She decided to pretend that it was the wrong time of the month – this normally kept Ursula at bay. But she had forgotten that Ursula kept a record of all her bodily functions.

'Nonsense!' said Ursula, checking with her pocket book. 'Don't be silly.'

'But I'm so tired and I'm feeling a little ill – so do you mind if I go off to bed alone?'

'Go off to bed alone!' screamed Ursula. 'Certainly not! I haven't summoned you here, my girl, merely so that you can slip off to bed!'

Her voice was steely. She's as hard as nails, Emma thought. She just has no feelings or consideration for other people. I'm just one of her playthings and she makes me feel it.

Ursula's tone made Emma so cross that she suddenly decided she would turn the tables on her. The fun and games with Henry had left her feeling very self-confident. Yes, she decided, she would not try to hide the marks on her bottom – on the contrary she would actually show them off!

She would put on the catsuit that Ursula had bought for her and which she often made Emma wear to heighten her amusement and pleasure. It was very realistic with paws and claws, and a tail which Emma had to learn to swish with flicks of her bottom. But the hindquarters and lower belly of the suit had been cut out, leaving Emma's bottom and body lips quite bare. It was all rather humiliating for Emma, which was just what aroused and amused Ursula. But this time, Emma smiled to herself, Ursula would be laughing on the other side of her face when she saw the marks on the little cat's naked bottom!

Emma persuaded Ursula to let her slip away to bath and change. She promised to be very quick. Ursula clearly could not wait to get her hands on her.

In the bathroom Emma noticed that the marks were still there. She did not put on any powder to hide them. Instead, revelling in her new-found self-confidence, she left them looking red and raw.

She put on the daintily cut catsuit. She pulled down the hood that just left her eyes and mouth visible. She flicked her tail suggestively, and looking in the mirror, she saw a very pretty little size $8^1/_2$ girlish figure being well displayed with her breasts, belly and bottom quite bare. She knew that the front view alone would arouse Ursula, and she suddenly found herself getting enormously excited herself at the thought of Ursula's fury when she turned round, and Ursula realised from the marks that Emma had been playing in someone else's yard!

The answer came a few minutes later when Emma, clad in her catsuit, crawled across the floor of Ursula's spacious bedroom towards the chaise longue on which Ursula reclined.

'Meow, meow,' purred the cat.

Ursula had her little whippy cane, Sambo, in her hand. Behind her face mask, Emma could not help eyeing it with dread, her former courage now evaporating fast. Had she been a fool to tempt providence – and Ursula's temper in this way?

'What little tricks is my little minx going to perform tonight?' cried Ursula, tapping her cane against the palm of her hand. She barked a series of orders: 'Up! Stand up straight! Hands to your sides! Now, wiggle your tail! Now, part your legs. Close your eyes and think of pleasing your mistress. I want to see those body lips starting to glisten with excitement.'

There was a long pause. Emma could feel her juices beginning to run.

'That's better, you little minx!' Emma heard Ursula's harsh voice. 'Now keep your eyes shut, and start playing with your nipples.' Emma shrank back as she felt the cane tapping her breasts. 'Stand still! Don't you dare back away. Harder!'

There was the sound of the cane giving her a smart stroke across her naked belly.

'Harder! That's better. I want two really ripe little cherries being offered to me – as well as a succulent little peach lower down!'

Ursula was licking her lips in eager anticipation. Her eyes

were bulging with passion. Emma was going to have to perform tonight as she had never performed before, Ursula decided. She would beat the silly little creature into utter submissiveness. She fancied tying the little cat down on the bed to keep her really helpless.

Ursula glanced at her watch. Francoise would be arriving any minute now. She was a well known French lesbian who was over in London for a few days. Ursula had boasted to her about her new submissive slave, and Francoise had asked to see her.

'I can do better than that, darling,' Ursula had laughed. 'Come over and help me enjoy her tonight!'

This was why she had been so angry when Emma had asked to go to bed. How galling it would have been to have to tell Francoise that she had allowed the girl to go off to bed as she was feeling a little tired! Francoise would, she knew, particularly enjoy both the sight and the feel of the little slut nicely tied up and wearing her catsuit. The feel of the fur and the way in which the girl was dehumanised behind her mask all made it so much more exciting, and it was so worthwhile sharing with a real connoisseur of girls like Francoise. Between the two of them they would certainly put Emma through her paces tonight!

'Turn around,' she suddenly screamed 'Turn round, you teasing little minx!'

Emma felt frightened. She had almost lost her nerve. Then she thought of the sheer pleasure she had shared with Henry that afternoon. Why should she be made to feel ashamed? Ursula did not own her! Her self-confidence returned. With a shrug of her shoulders she turned and flaunted her freshly marked bottom at Ursula.

There was another long silence. Emma longed to turn round and look at Ursula's face, but could not pluck up enough courage to do so. She could hear Ursula catching her breath. Suddenly she heard her get up. She grasped Emma by the waist.

'Bend over!' she ordered.

Emma felt Ursula running her steely nails over the marks. She felt her tracing the weals carefully and slowly as if seeing just how each stroke had been applied.

'My God!' she finally exploded. 'I want to know exactly how you got these, you filthy, unfaithful little slut.'

140

'Please, madam, I slipped and fell trying to get a taxi to come here. My train was late and I was afraid you would be angry,' sobbed Emma behind her mask.

'You little liar!' screamed Ursula. She pulled the cat's face mask back off Emma's head. Then she smacked her hard across the face, twice, before thrusting her away in disgust.

# 14  MORE RETRIBUTION

Terrified by Ursula's display of temper, Emma stood there petrified. She watched Ursula slowly walk over to the table. She helped herself to a cigarette. She put it into one of the long holders and lit it. She came back to Emma. Again, with one hand she gripped Emma by the hair.

'I'm going to really hurt you! That'll stop you behaving like a bitch on heat looking around for the nearest male.'

She lowered the cigarette holder to Emma's body lips. She now held Emma firmly. Emma felt the heat of the cigarette. My God! she thought, Ursula really meant it. She started to scream.

'No! No! Please no! Please . . . I'm sorry!'

'Sorry!' yelled Ursula. 'You come here, cool as a cucumber, with those marks on your backside and all you can say is your sorry? You're going to say a lot more tonight before I've finished with you, my girl!'

Furious, she shook Emma by the hair.

'For a start you can tell me, you filthy little slut, just who did this. Who?

Emma stood there, paralysed with fright, unable to move and unable to speak.

Could she tell Ursula the truth, Emma wondered desperately? And if she did, what would happen to her?

Her frantic thoughts were interrupted by the ringing of the front door bell. Ursula went over to the intercom.

'Who is it?' Emma heard Ursula say impatiently. 'Ah, Francoise, come up at once!'

Ursula pressed the button that unlocked the front door. Moments later a very French-looking slim dark-haired woman of about thirty-five entered the room. She gave the appearance of being exceptionally strong physically and there was something unusually cruel about her eyes. She had in fact been a trapeze artist and animal trainer in a circus until she found that it was more profitable training the girlfriends of rich lesbians in Paris to put on little circus-type displays. It was at one such discreet performance, given in the chateau of one of her friends, that Ursula had first met Francoise.

The two women embraced tenderly, exchanging little compliments.

'So this is your new little girl!' laughed the French woman in fluent if accented English, eyeing Emma in her catsuit. 'She would make a fine circus animal if you are interested in having her trained to perform in the ring.'

Emma stood still, too terrified to speak or move, wondering who this frightening woman was.

'She's certainly very attractive, *ma cherie*,' the woman continued. 'I must congratulate you on catching such a pretty little fish! And she's not, I think, a natural lesbian like you or me. All the better! The reluctant ones are so much more fun to catch and train! And I like the complete absence of hair – it gives her such little girl look!' She pointed down to where the catsuit was cut away between the legs. She stood back admiringly and then went behind Emma.

'*Mon Dieu!*' she cried. 'She must have been a very naughty little girl.'

Ursula explained that, on the contrary, she herself had only just discovered the marks, only moments before Francoise's arrival. 'So you've come at just the right moment to help me get the truth out of this ungrateful slut.' Ursula's voice was grim. 'She asked me if she could take her nephew and another young boy to Belgium for a few days. Reluctantly I gave my permission. And now she's come back with those marks on her! Someone's been thrashing her. Thrashing my slave! I want the truth even if I have to kill her to get it out of her. And if she's been betraying me, then she's going to wish she had never been born!'

She threw a strip of elastic cord to Francoise. 'Tie her hands!'

Ursula watched as Francoise very efficiently tied Emma's wrists together with elastic. She could still hardly believe the evidence before her eyes. How dare anyone else take control of Emma! How dare they!

Francoise, of course, was delighted. She had certainly arrived at just the right moment. It was a situation with which she was well familiar. Indeed it was one in which she had often been called in to help: a girl had been caught being unfaithful to her mistress with other woman – or worse still with a man. It was a traumatic moment for both the girl and her mistress. Ursula would be very grateful for her help, and would reward her well. They would also probably have a little fun together – at the expense of the wretched girl who had betrayed her mistress. She would, she decided, take advantage of Ursula's intense anger to ingratiate herself into her good books. Ursula was after all a wealthy woman!

'Please, not too tight,' whispered Emma. But Francoise merely made a face at her, pinched her hard, and tied the elastic so tight that Emma felt almost faint with the pain – though she knew from experience that the elastic would gradually ease.

As she fastened the knot, Francoise glanced at Ursula. She saw that she was getting hot and excited as well as angry. All the better, she thought, Ursula would certainly want her help. She herself was also getting excited. Tying up and punishing a young woman was what she enjoyed most of all – after, of course, training them to perform little tricks in a circus ring or in a cage with a wild beast. Making a petrified girl perch naked on a stool in a lion's cage along side a real lion had probably been the most exciting experience of her life. But she felt that what was going to happen to Emma would run a good second.

Francoise also had another and more secret interest in the very strained relationship between Ursula and Emma. She acted as the agent for the directress of a very special school in France – a school where inmates were usually young women sent there by their mistresses for disciplining. The fees at this so-called school were astronomical – to match the personal attention that was given to the individual pupil. The commission that Francoise could earn by persuading a woman to send her girl there was also very large.

Francoise had heard rumours that Ursula had had difficulties with her latest girl, and it was for this reason that she had asked Ursula if she might see her, not thinking that she would arrive at such a critical moment. She now decided to wait and see how things develop᭴ and then perhaps suggest to Ursula that she might like to have a word with the directress of a school which specialised in dealing with naughty and recalcitrant young women. Luckily the directress also happened to be in London visiting other potential clients that Francoise had recruited for her. So . . .

If she played her cards right, thought Francoise, she would almost certainly have found another client!

'Well, Francoise, which is to be? Shall we put her over the table, or would the little wretch mark my good table with her struggles? Perhaps it would be better to use the kitchen table.'

Francoise made Emma stretch across the big solid table. Carefully, she fastened Emma's tied wrists to the far end of the table, leaving Emma bent over the other end with her toes just touching the ground. She was still wearing her catsuit with the cut-away bottom and her buttocks were well displayed.

'Now listen you dirty little slut. I want to know who gave you that thrashing, and what you have been up to in Belgium. Francoise is going to give you five strokes with the cane and then you are going to tell me what I want to know. And if you hesitate at all in answering then you will get another five strokes and so on. Right, Francoise, give the slut her first five strokes.'

Emma was terrified. Her bottom was still very sore from Henry's beating with his belt. The thought of being beaten again, this time with the cane, was terrifying. All her resolve to be brave went by the board.

'No, don't beat me,' she screamed, 'I'll tell you. I'll tell you everything.'

'Yes, you will,' shouted Ursula angrily, 'but to make certain, you'll still have the first five strokes now. Go on, Francoise, go on! But make it nice and slow – I want to enjoy this.

Tantalisingly slowly, Francoise touched Emma's bottom with the cane. She ran it up over the existing weals, making Emma groan with pain and fear. She paused and then she brought the cane down hard just below one of the existing marks. Emma gave a scream.

'Please don't beat me any more, I'll tell you everything.'

But Ursula was implacable. She was also becoming aroused by the spectacle. Not until the fifth stroke had been painfully delivered did she ask: 'Well who was it?' She went to the end of the table and reached down to pull Emma's head up by her hair. She looked down into Emma's eyes. 'Look up at me, girl. Now who was it?'

Emma looked up at Ursula's blazing eyes. She had never seen Ursula look so angry. She was terrified.

'It was Henry, madam,' she cried.

'Henry!' exploded Ursula, throwing Emma's head back down onto the table in disgust. 'That awful man, the brute you swore you would never, never see or talk to again!'

There was a long pause as Ursula assimilated the degree of betrayal that she felt that Emma had committed. Her voice was quieter now and even more menacing.

'Francoise is going to give you another five strokes and then you're going to tell me whether you had planned to meet him in Belgium before you even left London. Go on, Francoise, and make it really hard this time.'

'Yes,' Emma was screaming as the well separ:ed strokes were applied. 'Yes, I arranged to meet him before I left, but please don't beat me again. Oh . . . Oh!'

'And why did he beat you?' came Ursula's insistent voice.

'I don't know. He said he was leaving his visiting card for you to see.'

'What?' screamed Ursula. 'You mean he deliberately beat you so that I would see the marks? When did he do this?'

'This morning,' wept Emma, 'just before we parted.'

'You mean you were in his bed this morning, knowing that you were coming here this evening! You were in a man's bed, deliberately betraying me, behind my back, and with a man you had promised never to see again?'

'Yes,' said Emma in a very contrite little voice. 'I'm sorry, madam.'

'Sorry! You betray me. You lie to me. You deceive me. You are unfaithful to me – and with a man. It's unforgivable. I'll make you sorry, you betraying little slut.'

Francoise came slowly over to the raging Ursula. She put her hand on her shoulder.

'She's not worth getting angry about. Let's just enjoy a little revenge. Why don't you enjoy watching me giving her another

146

five strokes – and then we'll kiss and plan more revenge.' She touched Ursula's breasts.

'Yes, you're right. I'm going to enjoy my revenge. Go on, beat her!'

Emma turned her head in dismay to see Francoise raising the cane high in the air. Then to her horror, she also saw that Ursula was exciting herself as she watched the next five strokes being slowly administered.

'That was lovely!' Ursula murmured, her eyes now blazing with excitement rather than with rage. Francoise came over and gently bit Ursula's ear. Then the two of them were kissing each other passionately on the mouth. Ursula put her tongue into Francoise's mouth and they both rocked to and fro for a few minutes. They were now in a very aroused state, whilst poor Emma was still crying from the pain of her beating.

'Tears!' sneered Ursula, breaking away from Francoise's embrace. 'I'll give you something more to cry about. Turn her over, Francoise. Let's have her breasts quite bare. Tear the catsuit back . . . That's it. Now hand me that little dog whip. You can use the other one. We'll both give her strokes simultaneously across her breasts. That'll teach the slut to betray her mistress!'

Emma now lay tied helplessly on her back, scarcely able to move a muscle.

The catsuit had been torn back to expose her breasts. As Francoise had bared her breasts she had made mocking, and horribly degrading remarks, but Emma was almost past caring now – until both the women simultaneously brought their dog whips down across her breasts. This really seemed to turn Francoise on and she was clearly delighted to see a well-educated young woman getting her comeuppance. She even wondered if she would now replace Emma in Ursula's affections. Slyly, she started to flatter her, hoping to win her approbation.

'How clever you are the way you use your whips and cane on the girl. What an experienced mistress you are! You've certainly brought this disobedient slut to heel quickly enough. How about making this little cat purr prettily whilst we enjoy ourselves and make love?'

'Why not?' replied Ursula. She could feel her juices flowing. Emma looked on shocked as Ursula removed her smartly cut trousers to reveal nothing underneath.

Francoise knew exactly what was required. Quickly she undressed. Then, kneeling, she touched Ursula's ankles. She moved her hands up her calves and thighs, then put her hand up to Ursula's throbbing bud. Ursula loved it all.

'Purr like a little cat,' she screamed at Emma, raising her dog whip menacingly. As the two women became even more aroused, they screamed more and more abuse at Emma.

'Purr louder, louder,' ordered Ursula as she felt her climax approaching. Both women soon fell exhausted onto Emma's body.

Emma could feel their wetness as they collapsed on her. She could smell them. She was disgusted. Ursula had done again what she had so often threatened to do and what Emma always dreaded – to make love to another woman in front of her, and to enjoy it all the more because Emma was helpless to intervene.

The two women were still pulsating on top of her. Suddenly Emma could feel that Ursula was about to reach her climax again. Clearly she found a threesome exceptionally thrilling – particularly since Emma was not being allowed to enjoy the orgy.

'Shall we take the little wretch,' Emma heard Ursula whisper to Francoise, 'or isn't she worth having?'

Francoise nodded enthusiastically. She was game for anything. She was also very experienced. She helped Ursula mount Emma. Then kneeling to one side, she pinched Emma to make her wriggle to give pleasure to her mistress.

'Get off me, please,' cried Emma.

'Who gave you permission to talk?' screamed Ursula. 'How dare you speak to your mistress without permission. Beat her, Francoise, beat her again and keep her wriggling. Yes, like that . . .'

Once more Francoise's dog whip was in command! Emma could hear Ursula's heavy sexy breathing becoming faster. The weight of Ursula's body pressing down on her made her poor whipped breasts and sore bottom ache like mad. But Francoise saw to it that she kept wriggling quite delightfully under Ursula, and when Ursula rolled off Emma, satiated for the time being, Francoise took her place . . .

Half-an-hour later Emma lay frightened and scared in the half dark of Ursula's dressing room. Her hands were still tied. She wanted to lie on her tummy to ease the pain of her buttocks, but that only made the pain in her breasts worse. All the feeling of bravado and self-confidence which made her flaunt Henry's visiting card to Ursula had now completely gone – whipped out of her by the combination of the cane on her bottom and the dog whips on her breasts. She felt like a whipped cur.

What a fool she had been to think that Ursula might have laughed off the visiting card. Would she never learn that Ursula would not accept anything less than complete and continuous control over her? Not only over her sex life, but also over what she did, who she saw, what she thought and even over her natural functions. Ursula would not tolerate anything less than a hundred per cent control, and she was clearly still bent on teaching that lesson to Emma. Francoise and Ursula were planning something in the room next door. She could hear their whispers. She heard them make a telephone call. What more were they planning to do to her?

Francoise came into the little room. She switched on the light. She looked down at the cringing Emma.

'So now that we all know what you've been up to, you little slut, do you know what we do with little madams who get above themselves? We teach them a lesson that they won't forget as long as they live! And not only by corporal punishment. You think you've been a clever little bitch. You thought you could fool your mistress, didn't you? Well now we are really going to show you.'

Emma had never come across Francoise before. She did not know what connection she had with Ursula. She was, it seemed, new to the scene, and yet here she was talking as if she were Ursula's close confidante. How humiliating it was to be spoken to like that by a stranger. How humiliating it had been to have been beaten by her at Ursula's order. She felt jealous of Francoise's closeness to Ursula.

'Well, Francoise, I'm not going to tolerate Emma having it off with anyone else.' Ursula turned to Emma. 'You are under my control, you little wretch, do you hear – my control, and now you're really going to understand what I mean when I say, under my control. I'm going to take you out and teach you a lesson.'

It was already midnight. Where, wondered Emma, more scared than ever, would they take her at this time of night – and for what purpose?

Emma was blindfolded tightly and given a wrap to put round herself. She felt more frightened than ever. Up to now, in Ursula's house, she had felt moderately safe, but now they were dragging her downstairs to take her out.

'Please, be careful of my sore bottom,' she cried out as they pulled her by her hair, bumping her down the stairs. 'Please, you're hurting me dreadfully.'

She heard Ursula and Francoise laugh contemptuously. 'That'll teach you to have visiting cards left on your bottom, you slut,' answered Ursula as they continued to pull her painfully down the stairs, knowing that with her hands still tied she could do nothing to protect herself. At last Emma realised that they had reached the bottom of the staircase, which led to the private underground car park. She heard the door being unlocked.

'Let her crawl to the car,' she heard Ursula say. She felt Francoise fasten a cord round her neck and give it a tug. Awkwardly, with her hands bound and unable to see anything, she crawled behind Francoise. She was very conscious of what she must look like with her bare well-beaten bottom being displayed by the catsuit, and her whipped breasts hanging down below her. She was bundled into the car . . .

The car was going very fast. Emma could see nothing, and with her hands tied she was helpless as she sat slumped alone in the back. She thought of those two carefree days in Bruges with Henry, of the fun she had in the discotheque, of cycling around the town with the two boys before Henry arrived and above all of the sheer physical and mental delight that she had experienced after he arrived. And now here she was, bound, blindfolded and miserable, being driven to an unknown place for something unknown to be done to her. Could Henry have had any idea of what would be the result of his light-hearted prank? Had he done it specially so that she would be punished so fiercely by Ursula? Why had she allowed herself to be manipulated in this way? She had been so strong at times before she had met Ursula. Now she was just a helpless little animal, Ursula's terrified slave.

She heard Ursula talking fast in German on the car phone. She could not understand a word. Then she heard Ursula speaking in French to Francoise – too fast for her schoolgirl French.

The car was gathering speed. Emma presumed that they must be out of London now. She had no idea how long she had been in the car. Later she heard the screeching of tyres as they turned down a side road and then gathered speed again.

'We will be arriving in ten minutes. Have the gates open,' she heard Ursula say on the car phone in English. Then the phone went dead.

It was shortly after this that Emma was dragged out of the car. She had no idea where she was. She could hear a waterfall in the distance. They made her walk barefooted over wet grass and mud for a long way. She heard a door being unlocked. She was pushed inside. It was cold, damp, and smelt of fish.

'We'll leave her locked up safely for the night,' she heard Ursula say, 'but I want to leave my visiting card on her in case a fisherman comes in the morning and finds her. Knowing what a glutton for men she is, perhaps she'll ask him to leave his card as well, but somehow I doubt it! Now let's see if there is a suitable cane in this hut . . . ah, yes. This will do excellently. This time, I'm going to give her five strokes whilst she counts them and you hold her nicely bent over.'

Shocked and appalled at the thought of another beating, and of possibly being found in her present condition in the morning, Emma allowed herself to be bent over. Francoise was apparently holding a torch so that Ursula could see to beat Emma. She had already had fifteen strokes of the cane on her bottom. Now she was to have another five. Twenty strokes of the cane! And this was not counting Henry's belt, nor the thrashing of her breasts. It was certainly a thrashing she would never forget. And Francoise had said that her punishment would not only be corporal!

'Now start counting,' ordered Ursula. 'One!'

'One!' whimpered Emma . . .

It was nearly five minutes later when the two women left. She heard a key being turned in a padlock. She heard them laughing as they walked away, leaving Emma even more scared and in great pain from the last beating. She longed to rub her bottom to ease the pain, but with her hands tied in front of her this was impossible.

'Oh my God!' she cried out in utter despair. 'What's going to happen to me? Where am I?'

She managed after a struggle to get the blindfold off. In the darkness she could just make out that she was in a small hut. Fishing tackle was hanging on the walls, together with the bamboo cane with which she must have been beaten. There was no electric light. The door was firmly locked. There was a little window, too small to climb out of. She shrunk back as her hands touched a mass of spider webs. She heard a rustling sound in the rafters above the ceiling and gasped in fright. Rats!

She was desperate. She wondered about calling out for help. But she could not see any other building through the window. The hut seemed quite isolated, and who would hear her cries at this time of night?

She began to cry. Oh what a fool she had been! Exhausted with all that had happened during this long day, she slumped onto the hard wooden floor . . .

Gradually she could see daylight coming. Soon it was light enough to look out through the filthy little window. She saw a river and a rowing boat moored outside. So it was a fisherman's hut! But there was no sign of anybody. In the distance she could see a large house.

She longed to relieve herself, but there was no sign of anything suitable in the little hut. She held out for as long as she could, but eventually with her nerves in such a state of fright, she had to let it flow. The floor was filthy and in no time at all she was in the middle of a disgusting swamp. She felt relief but also nausea. The ghastliness of it all, and the sheer unreality, made her realise yet again just what she had let herself in for. How could women be so cruel? They were far worse than men.

As it became lighter, Emma was feeling more degraded by the minute. She was scared lest an early morning fisherman might come and find this strange looking creature in the hut. He might even report what he saw to the police. The disgrace that would then ensue! How could she ever explain it all to John and his family? She could feel her heart thumping. She was still feeling sick, sick with fright. To be sick whilst locked in this tiny hut would be too awful. And tears were no help. She remembered what Francoise and Ursula had said about teaching her a lesson. She felt she had truly learnt it.

She soon began to feel both hungry and thirsty. She had not eaten anything since the sandwich on board the ferry the previous day. She looked around. There was no sign of food. Then she saw, lying in the corner of the hut where it had been thrown away, the remains of a small half-chewed ham sandwich. Eagerly she ate it. She had, she thought, been brought down to the level of a scavenging dog.

But there was no sign of anything to drink. How long would Ursula leave her locked up in this hut? It might be for days. Perhaps she and Francoise had gone off together. She shivered with fear. She remembered stories of prisoners having to lap up their own urine to keep alive. Perhaps even that, she thought, was better than having to lie in her own wastes like an animal.

The degradation of it all!


Up in the big house, Ursula and Francoise ate a hearty breakfast. They had both slept well after their work earlier on during the night and had then made love again. The kedgeree and coffee were delicious.

The discovery of Emma's second betrayal with that man Henry had come as a terrible shock, but revenge was sweet. Ursula thought of the now terrified and very penitent Emma locked up in that small, smelly, dirty little hut. It was all she was fit for! The contrast with her own comfortable warm room made her revenge even sweeter.

'Shall we go and see whether we caught anything in our nets during the night?' laughed Francoise. 'Perhaps we should see how our little catch is getting on! Perhaps it might need a little attention.'

'Oh, I don't think we need hurry about that,' smiled Ursula. 'It won't get away and the longer it is left in suspense the better. But I think this particular honeybee will soon be ready for a little taste of nectar!'

It was quite late in the morning before they eventually strolled down to the hut. They peered in through the cobweb-covered windows and made out a slumped wet body.

'Perhaps we should leave her to stew in her own juice for a little longer,' said Ursula angrily.

Francoise was a little taken back by Ursula's harshness. She began to feel a little sorry for Emma. She persuaded Ursula to unlock the padlock on the door.

'So has the slut learned her lesson yet?' demanded Ursula. 'Get up! You damn well stand in the presence of your mistress. I'd have thought you would have learned respect by now, but if not, by God!'

Emma saw that Ursula was reaching for the bamboo cane with which she had already been beaten. With a gasp she quickly forced herself to her feet. Automatically she stood at attention with her tied hands still behind her back, now desperately anxious to placate Ursula.

The two women looked her up and down. Francoise felt something stirring inside her. The sight of this humbled wretch, with all the marks of her beatings showing well, aroused her. She remembered Ursula's remark at breakfast about nectar. She looked around and saw a fisherman's stool in the corner of the hut, brought it over and place it at Emma's feet. She looked across at Ursula, who nodded, smiling.

'Legs wide apart, little slut!' Ursula ordered. She picked up the bamboo cane as if to reinforce her order. 'Keep your head up and don't look down!'

Francoise sat down on the little stool, Emma's thighs now spread wide apart in front of her. A moment later Emma felt Francoise's hand. She felt disgusted. She was in no mood for this now after all that had happened and in the dirty, unwashed, state she was in.

Horrified she looked across at Ursula as if to seek help, but none was forthcoming. On the contrary, Emma saw that Ursula's nostrils were flaring with desire.

'Keep quite still, you slut!' warned Ursula, tapping the bamboo cane across the palm of one hand as if she could hardly wait to use it again.

For two whole minutes there was complete silence. Emma, to her disgust, was powerless to prevent her body from responding to Francoise's experienced attentions. She was even more powerless when she felt the hand being replaced by a soft tongue. She began to moan. She wanted to back away, but was too frightened of the bamboo cane in Ursula's hands to make any resistance. She felt Francoise's hand now gripping her thighs as her tongue became busier and busier. Emma felt her juices beginning to run. A few moments later, Francoise stood up and wiped her mouth with the back of her hand.

'She's ready for you now,' she said to Ursula, who silently handed her the cane and took her place on the stool. 'Now you give your mistress a nice little taste of nectar or you'll be sorry,' she said.

# 15    IN THRALL TO HER
        MISTRESS

The boot was slammed shut, leaving Emma curled up on the hard rubber lining in the dark. Her hands were tied again – this time behind her back so that she was even more helpless, even more frightened.

She heard the two laughing women get into the car. She heard the doors shut and then the noise of the engine being started. She was jerked and thrown around as the car went over the rough tracks that led away from the fisherman's hut.

'I'm not going to have that filthy animal in the back of my car,' Ursula had screamed as Francoise had led Emma out of the hut, dirty, wet and dishevelled still wearing the remains of the catsuit, her feet bare. 'Put her in the boot! Quite apart from spoiling the upholstery, I don't want to smell her all the way back to London. You'd better tie her hands; we don't want her getting up to any little tricks in the boot.'

A few moments later the strong arms of Francoise lifted her up and dropped her unceremoniously into the boot, where she lay shivering. She was wet, tired and miserable. She could hear Ursula and Francoise giggling and laughing all the way on what seemed to be an interminable journey.

Suddenly the car stopped and the engine was switched off. Emma heard the women's voices, much louder now as they got out, slamming the doors behind them. The boot was suddenly opened and Emma blinked in the sudden bright light as Francoise's hand came down and gripped her hair, pulling her violently to her feet and out of the boot. She saw that they were back in Ursula's private basement garage.

'She crawled to the car here last night and she can damn well crawl out of it now,' said Ursula harshly to Francoise.

Francoise gave Emma a push. With her tied hands she was

powerless to prevent herself from falling to the floor. Francoise bent down and untied her hands.

'Now crawl behind your mistress!' she ordered, giving Emma a kick to encourage her towards the door that led to the rest of the house. She crawled across the hard concrete floor towards it. The door was locked behind her. Still crawling, she followed the two women up the stairs.

'Get cleaned up, you disgusting bitch,' Ursula yelled at her as she herself sat down in a comfortable chair and helped herself to a cigarette and a glass of sherry. 'Francoise has a French friend coming round to have a good look at you. It's a lucky thing that she happens to be over here and Francoise was able to contact her. You may be seeing quite a lot more of her soon, so smarten yourself up! I don't want you looking a wreck. I shall want you on parade in half an hour.'

From the way that Ursula was smiling at Francoise as she spoke, it was clear to Emma that Francoise was now very much in Ursula's good books. Presumably she was grateful to the French woman for her help in disciplining Emma so effectively during the night. What new devilry were they cooking up?

Emma hated the dreadful Francoise after all the ghastly things she had done to her. Now she was also jealous of her close relationship with Ursula. Who was she anyway? How dare she have so much influence over Ursula that she could invite some friend of hers round for a late lunch? Emma had never dared to suggest inviting any of her friends to Ursula's, even when she too had been in Ursula's good books. She knew that she was far superior in every way to this common French woman, and yet here she was being treated by Ursula as if she was the lowest form of animal. And all because of Henry! Learning about him had made Ursula behave with such incredible cruelty! Emma felt she was in unknown territory – the outcome could be anything. She gave a little shiver of fear.

But Emma was still too exhausted, wet and devastated by all that had happened since the previous evening to think properly. She just longed to slip into a nice hot bath and then go to bed and sleep!

She ran the bath in Ursula's bathroom, got into it, and lay there relaxing.

Suddenly Francoise, that demon of a woman, stormed into the bathroom with a long handled stiff scrubbing brush in one hand and a pumice stone in the other.

'Why aren't you out of the bath, you idle slut? Good heavens, you haven't even washed yourself yet. Don't you realise you've got to serve my friend at lunch shortly? Look at yourself, you filthy hussy, your hair's still a mess and your body still looks disgusting. I'll show you what happens to lazy sluts who can't even be bothered to clean themselves up for their mistresses!'

With that she started to belt poor Emma alternately with the flat side of the long handled brush and then with the bristles. She held Emma's head under the water whilst she scrubbed her hair, until Emma thought that she was going to drown. Then she set about Emma with the pumice stone.

There was a shout from Ursula, still sitting in her comfortable chair outside in the bedroom.

'Good God, Francoise, can't the idle slut even wash herself? Shall I come and help?'

'Get out of the bath,' screamed Francoise.

Francoise stood back and looked at Emma's now clean but dripping wet little body. She rather liked what she saw. She thought that Ursula would enjoy it even more!

'She's nearly ready now,' she called out to Ursula. 'Come and have a look at her!'

Ursula was greeted by the sight of a shivering Emma, her body covered in horrid red marks from Francoise's recent beating with the scrubbing brush.

'Bend over the bath for further punishment,' ordered Francoise. It was a sight that really excited Ursula.

'Beat her again, and this time make it harder,' she cried to Francoise.

Francoise gripped Emma by the hair and pulled her down so that she was bent over even more tightly.

'Bend over more, you little bitch,' she ordered.

Ursula was loving every moment of the scene. She saw that the marks that the hated Henry had left on Emma had just about gone, and instead there were the marks of the scrubbing brush, becoming redder and redder with every stroke from Francoise's arm.

158

Ursula simply could not resist what she saw. She forgot that Emma was being punished for being unfaithful to her. She just wanted her. She started to lick the trickles of wetness off Emma. Emma began to moan.

'Well, Francoise,' she said, 'do you think she's worth having?'

Francoise was feeling equally turned on, partly because she knew now that she had replaced Emma as Ursula's favourite bed-mate, partly because she also enjoyed dominating Emma, and partly because she had, during the drive back to London, persuaded Ursula to consider sending Emma to the special girls' school near Paris, something which would increase her own bank balance handsomely.

So it was that before long, whilst Ursula was licking away at Emma from behind as the latter was still bending over the bath, Francoise was licking away at Ursula. She could feel Ursula becoming more and more excited just as she herself was also becoming highly aroused.

Only Emma received no pleasure. Indeed, Emma was near to collapse, due to the heat of the bathroom and the degrading position she was made to hold – still bent over the bath. She could see Ursula's face in the mirror; all around the bathroom were mirrors. Normally, Emma loved the reflections of what she saw, but not now. She saw a tired, sore, and weary young woman covered in the marks of the beating that Francoise had given her. Her degradation was complete when Ursula stood up and actually congratulated Francoise on having done such a fine job on 'that wretch Emma'.

'Dry yourself,' screamed Ursula, 'and then get dressed in your maid's outfit and report to Rafaela. I shall want you to serve lunch.'

A quarter of an hour later it was a very pretty maid, in a black dress that opened down the front, with a white pinafore and cap, who opened the door to a well dressed and beautifully groomed woman. She led her upstairs, and Francoise introduced her friend to Ursula. Emma served them drinks and soon they sat down to lunch, again served by Emma.

Emma could not follow the conversation properly for it was in voluble French. But from the way the guest kept looking at her, she guessed that they were talking about her. She was horrified when she heard Ursula say several times in a bitter tone the word 'Henry'. When she also heard the words '*tromper*', '*infidelité*' and '*punir*', even her schoolgirl French was good enough to make her realise that the guest was being told that Emma had been unfaithful to Ursula with Henry and that she had been punished for her infidelity. She felt madly embarrssed.

She felt even more embarrassed when Ursula told her, just as they were finishing the meal, to take off her pinafore and unbutton the front of her dress. Shyly Emma complied, but she could not bring herself to open the dress and show the stranger her hairless body lips and the marks of her beatings. Francoise, however, quickly got up, held Emma's hands behind her back, and pulled her dress back over her shoulders. Then, pushing her forward, she displayed the blushing Emma's bare body.

The other French woman drew her long nails slowly down over Emma's breasts. She lifted them in a knowledgeable way. Her fingers went down to Emma's waist and then on down. Emma tried to wriggle away, but Francoise held her still. She felt like an animal being checked over. At last the humiliating examination was over. The woman nodded to Francoise and turned smiling to Ursula, as if to reassure her about something. Emma was left to button up her dress again and to go on serving as if nothing had happened.

At last the elegant French woman rose to leave. Emma saw Ursula go to her desk, write out a cheque and hand it to her. Emma wondered what on earth it could be for. But she also knew that it was none of her business, even if, as she suspected, it had something to do with her.

After the woman had left, Ursula and Francoise amused themselves watching the now naked Emma, kneeling with her hands on the floor, desperately licking their plates clean. That was her lunch!

The sight of Emma being debased in this way excited both women. They embraced and kissed and then went off to the bathroom to undress, leaving Emma kneeling on the floor outside Ursula's bedroom.

Ursula and Francoise left the bathroom and climbed into

Ursula's large bed. Emma, too scared to move, heard them making passionate love.

For the first time in years, Ursula was being dominated by another woman, Francoise, and was clearly thoroughly enjoying the new experience! Francoise was so full of new ideas!

When Francoise knew that Ursula was well on her way to her second orgasm, she clapped her hands for Emma to crawl naked into the bedroom.

'Look up, you little tart,' she shouted at the crawling girl.

Emma looked up. She saw Ursula with her legs wide apart, with Francoise's head lowered between her thighs, bringing her again to a fever pitch of excitement. Emma was disgusted, but before she could say a word, Francoise screamed at her coarsely: 'Get to my arse with your lips, you trollop.'

But Emma just could not bring herself to please this horrible woman. Meanwhile Ursula was beseeching Francoise to let her come for the third time. But Francoise was too cunning for that. She was getting increasingly frustrated whilst Ursula had all the fun. She wanted some too!

'Ursula!' Francoise cried out, infuriated by Emma's hesitation. 'Get up and beat Emma!'

Poor Emma gave a cry of despair. She could see that Ursula was livid at being denied her further fun. But she was also clearly enjoying being bossed about by Francoise. Ursula quickly got up and fetched her cane. Hastily Emma applied herself to pleasing the kneeling Francoise under the watchful eye of Ursula, who did not hesitate to use her cane to encourage her to further efforts – efforts which culimated in Francoise giving a cry of joy and collapsing on the bed.

'What do you want me to do now, Francoise?' Ursula asked.

'Tie her to the bed,'

Emma was forced to kneel on all fours while Ursula tied her wrists and ankles to the sides of the bed. A large leather cushion was put under her belly to keep her high up on all fours. With breasts hanging down below her she felt like a cow, like a helpless animal. The comparison with a cow also occurred to Francoise.

'O.K. Ursula,' said Francoise, smacking her lips with anticipation. 'You crawl under the cow's udders and take them in your mouth. Meanwhile I'm going to borrow Duet and mount her from behind.'

'You're hurting me,' cried Emma.

'Good!' cried Francoise as she drove Duet slowly further and further up.

For several minutes Ursula and Francoise worked on Emma. Tied down as she was, she was quite unable to prevent Francoise's painful penetration, whilst Ursula's bites and pinching of her nipples kept her bottom wriggling attractively for Francoise as she rode the bucking girl, gripping her tightly by the waist to hold on to her. Emma could feel herself becoming aroused, but she hated it. Both women were becoming frenzied, using Emma for their amusement and ignoring her cries.

'Come back here, Ursula,' cried Francoise, slipping Duet down off her hips. She went up to the top of the bed where she seized Emma by the hair and bent her head back to force her to please her with her tongue. 'Keep her moving, Ursula! Use your fingers and tongue where Duet's just been.'

Soon Emma could feel her little wetness going into Ursula's mouth. Then Ursula strapped Duet onto herself and continued where Francoise had left off, something that brought Ursula to new heights of excitement, whilst Francoise still gripped Emma's hair and held her to her.

The two women looked at each other as they forced Emma to please them in different ways. Their passion was rising fast. Suddenly Ursula slipped out of Duet. Francoise reached forward and pulled away the big leather cushion from under Emma's belly. She collapsed onto the bed, as she did so the two women collapsed onto her, kissing each other passionately, and crying out in their ecstasy.

Emma could feel their sweat and their juices running down her body. It made her feel like the lowest form of animal life. She would never forget this. Ursula had finally destroyed her. She broke down and sobbed herself to sleep.

She wasn't sure if she had passed out or what, but when she awoke hours later, all was silent. She could hear nothing. She could move about the bed. Her hands were free now. She was still in Ursula's bed, but there was no sign of Ursula – nor of Francoise, thank God.

Emma got out of bed. She soaked herself in a hot bath, then sneaked down to the empty kitchen and made herself a quick snack, hoping that Rafaela would not notice what she had taken. She was so hungry! She took the sandwich up to the little cot in Ursula's dressing room.

There was still no sign of anyone. She wondered if she could get away. She tried the front and back doors. They were both locked as was the window she had used to escape after Henry's first appearance. She was securely locked in!

She wondered if she could telephone for help. She found that the telephones had all been unplugged and locked away. She was a complete prisoner.

She went back to the cot in despair, and soon fell asleep again.

Goodness knows how long she slept this time. She was awakened by Ursula's voice on the intercom.

'How's the little baby today?' came the voice.

Ursula wanted her little Emma to come to her. But Emma now hated Ursula too much. How could Ursula talk to her like that after all that had happened?

'Come along, little Emma,' went on Ursula in a soft voice. 'Come and have little lullabies from Ursula!'

But Emma knew Ursula's sudden soft voice of old. She wasn't going to be fooled again! Anyway, she wasn't in the mood to respond to it.

'Now that nasty big Francoise has gone, little Emma can come to Ursula!'

Francoise had gone! It seemed too good to be true. Reluctantly, Emma now went in to the bedroom.

'Come into my bed, little Emma,' said Ursula gently. 'But first have a look at the little present kind Ursula has bought for her little girl. Ursula's bought you a lovely new baby doll nightie! Look under the tissue on that chair! Aren't you a lucky girl?'

Emma could feel her resistance crumbling. She loved presents just like a real little baby girl.

'Now put on your baby powder, all over! Then put on your exciting little nightie and tell your mistress that you want to be a good little girl!'

After all the horrible things that had been done to her, after the way the disgusting Francoise had been allowed to use her, and after all the whippings, how could Ursula expect her to respond as she used to when Ursula wanted her to play mothers and daughters? But Ursula's voice was as hypnotic as ever.

Emma found herself meekly behaving just like a real seven-year-old girl. She put baby powder on her sore little bottom and down between her legs and on her sore nipples. She tied little bows in her hair. She put on the absurd baby doll nightie and went up to the bedroom.

'Yes, yes, mistress, this little girl will do as she is told,' Emma lisped, knowing that she had capitulated totally.

'Good little girl,' purred Ursula, her eyes gleaming. She knew she could make Emma do whatever she wanted. 'Good little girl! And as a special reward for being good, you can have a little chocolate.'

Eagerly Emma took the chocolate. Ursula did not normally allow her to have any sweets, not even at home. It was delicious, she thought. She looked up at Ursula with gratitude.

'There, there, little girl,' murmured Ursula, putting her hands affectionately round Emma's neck.

Emma could hardly believe it. How could she let Ursula come near her? But she did! She was now responding to Ursula like an affectionate little girl! All the cruelty and whippings had made her so meek. Perhaps that was to be expected, she thought. But she was amazed and thrilled that after her terrifying harshness, here was Ursula now being her old self agan. She felt so happy.

Then doubts began to torture her mind. Could their relationship ever be the same again? Hadn't Francoise spoilt everything?

Initially these doubts made Emma hesitant to play Ursula's intense mother and daughter games. But slowly, slowly, they started. It was a dutiful little daughter who obeyed her beautiful mother's order to shut the bedroom door . . .

It was 4.30 in the afternoon when they thought about lunch!

Ursula said she had to leave. An exhibition of her paintings was opening outside London the following day. She had promised to be there.

'But can't I come too?' wailed Emma, once again helplessly in love with Ursula. 'I promise I'll be good.'

'Yes, perhaps it would be a good idea if you did come,' answered Ursula slowly. 'Then I'd be able to keep a close eye on you. We don't want you getting up to any mischief, do we?'

Emma was delighted. 'I'll be a good girl, I really will,' she cried jumping up and down with excitement just like a child, thought Ursula.

'You will stay in my room,' said Ursula in her old decisive voice. 'Then I shall know where you are. I've booked a suite and there's a child's bedroom as well. And when I go out, if I don't take you with me, I shall lock you in it. And at the gallery I shall expect you to make yourself useful as my personal assistant, or you will feel the cane again when we get back to the hotel.'

'Oh I shall, I shall, I promise,' cried Emma still overjoyed.

'Well I don't expect you will want to run off with a man again in a hurry, my girl!' laughed Ursula.

'Oh, no madam,' whispered Emma fervently, 'oh no, madam! Not a man!'

Ursula wondered if she really meant it. She would soon be taking certain steps that would make it of little concern whether she did or did not. Meanwhile it would do no harm if she made certain arrangements for a close eye to be kept on Emma after they got back from the exhibition.

Two days later, Emma caught the train back to her home. It had been a busy time at the exhibition and Ursula had never let Emma out of her sight. Now at last, Emma thought, she would be free again – free to do what she liked.

But would she ever dare to contact Henry again? She longed to do so, but she shivered at the thought of what might happen to her if she did. Ursula had certainly shown that she could be quite ruthless and utterly cruel in making sure that a girl who she regarded as hers, remained hers and was used exclusively by her. The next time, Emma thought, she would have to be much more discreet, and certainly not boast of her exploits to Ursula.

Ursula had sent her to the station in a private hire car with

Rafaela as an escort to make sure she did not stop off on the way or speak to any men.

Rafaela bought her a first-class ticket and took her to a reserved compartment. It was empty except for two large men wearing blue suits. They looked, Emma thought, like retired policemen. Indeed this was just what they were – retired policemen now turned private detectives, and hired by Ursula to keep and eye on Emma until further arrangements could be finalised.

Emma saw that the men exchanged nods with Rafaela, but nothing was said and Rafaela waited until the train started whilst the men silently read their newspapers.

When the train did start, Emma got up and went along the corridor to go to the buffet. One of the men followed her. On the way back she slipped into one of the train toilets. When she came out, the man was waiting outside. Emma gave a little gasp. She really was under surveillance!

When the train stopped at a station, a pleasant young man got into the compartment. Emma smiled at him, but he was told by the two men, in a gruff tone, that all the seats were reserved.

Emma felt like a prisoner being escorted from one prison to another. But at least, she thought, she would soon be home again. Doubtless these horrible men, their task completed, would then return to London, leaving her free.

She was therefore surprised when, arriving at her station, the men also got out. She saw that another blue-suited man was waiting for them. They all got into a yellow van. To a casual observer, it might have been a British Telecom repair van.

Emma picked up her own car and headed home. Her heart began to sing. She was free again! The awful experiences in the fishing hut and with Francoise were forgotten. She was free!

Then, after a mile, she saw in the driving mirror that she was being followed by the yellow van. 'Oh no,' she cried, 'Oh no!'

She pressed hard on the accelerator. But the van seemed to have no difficulty in keeping up with her. Clearly she was not going to shake them off.

When she turned down the deserted lane that led to her house, the van stopped by a telegraph pole. Emma realised that from there the men inside the van would be able to see everyone who came or left her house.

An hour later Emma saw from her bedroom window that the van was still parked at the end of the lane. She gave a little shiver. She did not know whether to be frightened by the precautions that Ursula was clearly taking to ensure that she did not slip away again to meet Henry, or excited that she should be the cause of so much expensive and elaborate activity. Ursula must really love her, she thought, to have gone to so much trouble.

She rang her husband's office. John sounded delighted that she was back. He even sounded amorous. It had been a long time, he said meaningfully. Would she dare respond, Emma wondered? She remembered Ursula's explicit instructions forbidding her to make love with her husband. But she need never know, she thought. Nor would those horrible men in the van know. At least they could not see into her bedroom!

Two hours later John returned. Emma was waiting for him in the bedroom, dressed in her slinkiest negligée – a cast-off that Ursula had given her. They embraced passionately. Breathlessly Emma told him to go off and shave and bathe and then return.

Suddenly the telephone rang. It was Ursula!

'No, Emma,' came an angry voice, 'you will not do any such thing! You will go and remind your husband about what my lady doctor said to you: no sex with your husband, and certainly not behind my back, you little slut. Do you understand?'

'Yes, madam,' Emma answered contritely. Goodness, she thought, she's even had my bedroom bugged. That's what the van is doing parked at the end of the lane. Perhaps they have even tapped her telephone as well. Shamefacedly she went to tell her husband that she was sorry, but . . .

The next day when she went to work at her office, the van followed her car all the way. Several times when she looked out of the window she saw a blue-suited man watching the office entrance. The van followed her home again. All Emma's high hopes of being free again when she went home had turned to dust. She now felt as much under Ursula's domination as she did when in Ursula's own house. It was a horrible feeling – and yet strangely exciting too.

When she had first returned home, she had found a letter inviting her to a preview of a local exhibition of sporting paintings. It would, she knew, be a big social event. All her friends would be there, male and female. She longed to go, but was frightened to do so without Ursula's permission. For a whole day she tried to pluck up sufficient courage to ask Ursula.

'Of course, little girl, you can go to the exhibition,' came the unexpectedly friendly reply. 'You know I like my girls to improve their minds. Just make certain that you keep your eyes on the pictures!'

The next day Emma put on her prettiest dress, again another cast-off from Ursula, and set off for the preview. All her friends were there. In no time she was gossiping with her girl friends and flirting outrageously with several men. Several had made passes and she was seriously toying with the idea of taking up the suggestions of the very attractive man to whom she was talking excitedly.

Then suddenly she was stopped dead in her tracks. There in a corner of the room, watching her closely, a sneer on her face, was Francoise!

Emma's mouth fell open. Ursula must have sent Francoise to spy on her, to make sure that she did not talk or flirt with any men. How much had she seen? What report would she take back to Ursula? Had she heard her conversation?

Desperately, she smiled ingratiatingly at the French woman, but all she got back was an inscrutable stare.

Emma felt her former happy-go-lucky feeling turning to ashes. She broke away from the attractive man and lowered her eyes to the floor. She went over to the pictures, which she had previously virtually ignored, and started to study them intently, getting herself ready to answer Ursula's inevitable questions. She looked around carefully. Francoise had followed her and was again watching her with an expressionless look on her face.

Emma's mind raced. She remembered all the awful things that this woman had done to her. She remembered the pain she had enjoyed inflicting on her. She remembered the way in which she had enjoyed poisoning Ursula against her. She felt very frightened.

Shortly afterwards she crept, mouse-like, out of the preview with its champagne, its beautifully dressed and amusing women, and its handsome men. For her it had all been ruined by the watching presence of the terrifying Francoise, just as, she thought, Ursula had intended it to be. It was a lesson for her. It was a reminder that she was now in thrall to her mistress.

# 16 A FRENCH SCHOOL FOR YOUNG LADIES

For several days after the shock of seeing Francoise at the exhibition, Emma hung around the house waiting for the phone to ring. She hardly dared go out, lest Ursula ring, summoning her back to London, perhaps to be punished for flirting with men at the exhibition. She did not dare to ring Ursula. She had been given a new number on which to make her thrice daily humiliating reports. This number was always answered by Ursula's housekeeper, Rafaela, and never by Ursula herself. Rafaela was always brisk and curt on the phone as she wrote down the degrading reports, saying simply that she would pass them on to Ursula. Emma longed to ask Rafaela to give Ursula some personal message but did not dare to do so. Nor did she dare to ring Ursula herself. Like one of the concubines in a sheik's harem, she must merely wait to be summoned.

She now felt deeply ashamed at the way she had dared to betray Ursula with Henry on two separate occasions. She felt she thoroughly deserved her terrible punishments, but, as Ursula intended, was resolved never ever to risk them being repeated. She was now, she realised, completely controlled by Ursula, and she was too frightened of the consequences to even contemplate any alternative. Never, never, would she kick over the traces again. Never? Well, perhaps!

She was becoming increasingly morose and moody as the days passed without the telephone ringing. She was too frightened to go out and enjoy herself lest Ursula was having her followed again. Increasingly frustrated, she longed to share again the bed of her husband, but was too scared to do so lest their house was still bugged. So she continued the charade that Ursula had insisted on, of saying that the lady doctor still did not consider that she was fit to carry out her conjugal duties and had again written to repeat this. Poor John, denied pleasure with his wife, was also becoming increasingly fed up with her moods and general tetchiness. It did not help matters when he kept innocently enquiring about Emma's attractive and highly intelligent artist friend in London.

Then one day, as he was having breakfast before leaving for his office, he put down his paper.

'Oh, Emma, I forgot to tell you. That interesting artist friend of yours rang me in my office yesterday. She wanted to know if I would object if she sent you off to Paris for a month for what she called an arts appreciation course. It would be at her expense and, she said, it would enable you to be more useful to her and would provide you with a good training in her line of business. What's it all about?'

'Well . . . I think . . . It's a . . . sort of . . .' stammered Emma, caught on the hop and wondering what on earth she should say. She was also secretly delighted at Ursula's revived interest in her, but mortified that Ursula should have discussed her training course with John first without bothering to tell her, making it clear that she considered Emma's views to be of no consequence, and that she was simply to do what she was told.

'Anyway,' continued John, 'I said that of course I had no objection and that it was very good of her to have asked me first. It sounds a wonderful chance for you, Emma. I gather that she wants you to go next week. I shall be going away myself. But you'll be back a month or two before I leave – this time to the Pacific for three or four months. I'm glad you'll be in good hands while I'm away, with plenty to keep you busy. Now, I must dash, or I'll be late for the office. Oh, by the way, she wants you to ring her. I nearly forgot to tell you. Bye-bye!'

Cursing John for not having told her sooner and delighted that he would soon be going on a long trip, Emma excitedly dialled Ursula's number. Please, God, she silently prayed, let her be there. Her prayer was answered.

'Hello, little Emma,' said the slow well known voice. 'And how's my favourite little girl?'

Emma caught her breath with excitement. 'I thought I wasn't your favourite any longer?'

'Oh, Emma, you really do take everything so seriously. Of

course a woman like me enjoys a change from time to time. But you are definitely one of my favourites. There now, does that make you feel happier?'

'Yes,' whispered Emma, feeling so happy that she could have thrown her heart over the moon.

'Yes, what?' Ursula's voice had suddenly become harsh.

'Yes, madam,' cried Emma happily.

'That's better! That's a good little girl. Do you still love your mistress?'

There was a long pause. Then all Emma's pent-up passion burst out.

'Oh, yes, madam, I do love you. I do love you. I adore you, madam. I can't think about anything else. And I've been so unhappy thinking you had lost interest in me.'

'Oh no, Emma, I haven't lost interest in you at all. On the contary, I've got great plans for you. But you're still a little headstrong. I want you really obedient and submissive. So if you want to go on seeing me, then you'll have to agree to go away and be properly trained in pleasing a woman and learning to obey orders instantly. Do you understand, Emma?'

'Yes, madam,' breathed Emma happily. She would cheerfully go on umpteen courses if they meant she could keep Ursula's interest, and remain Ursula's little girl.

'It's really just like sending a young dog off to be properly trained as a gun dog,' said Ursula calmly. 'A dog may have the instinct to retrieve or to put up birds, but to be of use to her master she must be sent off to a professional dog trainer. It's the same with you. You've got the instinct to please, but you need to be sent off to a proper trainer. Do you still understand, Emma?'

'Yes, madam,' whispered Emma unhappily. The comparison with a dog had really humiliated her.

'I spoke to that booby of a husband of yours, and he agrees that you would benefit from a month's course of intensive instruction in what he imagines will be the arts. So I've booked you in. I want you up here tomorrow morning so that I can drop you off at the school on my way to Morocco.'

'School?' queried Emma. 'Back to school?'

'Of course,' snapped Ursula angrily. 'Where do you expect

172

teaching to be done? Just wear your schoolgirl clothes. You won't need anything else. And bring your passport. Just remember, Emma, that I'm spending a lot of money having you trained for my pleasure, and I shall expect good value for my money when I pick you up again on my return. So you must work really hard to improve whilst you are there.'

'But where is this school? And who runs it?' It all sounded rather mysterious and frightening.

'Emma! I've told you several times I don't like curiosity in a girl. You'll learn about it all in good time. Your forwarding address will be care of Rafaela here in London. Oh, and don't forget I want you naked under your school clothes.'

'Yes, madam,' said Emma, thinking of the short skirt. At least a blazer would hide her nipples, pressing against her thin blouse. But she would have to sit terribly carefully in the train with nothing under that little blue pleated skirt. Of course, she thought, that's why Ursula had given her that order – to make her realise all the time that she was completely under Ursula's control no matter what she was doing or where she was. It was very exciting, but terribly embarrassing.

It was in the early afternoon of the following day that a chauffeur-driven car approached the closed gates of a large secluded house outside Paris. The chauffeur got out and spoke into a security microphone. Moments later the gate swung open to allow the car to pass and then close behind it.

'I'm glad to see that security is so tight,' murmured Ursula, sitting in the back of the car with Emma. Emma eyed the high walls and gave a little shiver. She was dressed and made up as a teenage schoolgirl, wearing the same blue skirt and blazer that she had worn when Ursula had taken her to the health farm.

They had flown to Paris in the morning, and the school had sent this car to meet them. Ursula had been busy with her business papers both on the plane and in the car, virtually ignoring Emma who had been bursting to ask where she was being taken. Naked under her blouse and skirt she had been treated as a complete child. Ursula had taken charge of her passport, her ticket and even the small amount of money she had brought with her. Indeed, like her passport, Ursula had also confiscated Emma's credit cards and cheque book. 'I don't want you having any ideas of running away from school, Emma,' she had said firmly.

Emma spoke only a little schoolgirl French and did not know her way around Paris. She had, therefore, little or no idea where they were going. Ursula, on the contrary, spoke fluent French, knew Paris well and, putting down her papers, had chatted, incomprehensibly to Emma, to the huge chauffeur. They must have been discussing her, thought Emma uneasily, for she saw the chauffeur eye her in the driving mirror and give an ugly laugh. He looked tough and brutal.

Now the car stopped before the house itself. Emma noticed that there was another drive out of the grounds. Although she did not realise it at the time this was to allow visitors to leave discreetly without the risk of being seen by others arriving. Indeed, discretion and privacy were the keystones of the whole house.

The door was opened for them by a man wearing a black butler's coat. Evidently he had been alerted by the call from the chauffeur. Clearly visitors who were expected were not kept waiting outside for one moment. The black butler, who seemed to be as big and burly as the black chauffeur, and equally frightening with tribal scars on his cheeks, led them into a spacious office, furnished with typical French elegant gilt-edged chairs and a large desk.

A well dressed and beautifully groomed woman rose from behind the desk and greeted Ursula effusively in French. With a shock, Emma recognised her as the French woman who had so mysteriously come to lunch, and examined her, the day after Ursula had learned the truth about Henry.

The French woman motioned Ursula to a chair in front of her desk, leaving Emma standing awkwardly, shyly twisting her hands like a real schoolgirl, embarrassed at being discussed by her elders and betters.

She would have been even more embarrassed and shy had she understood the rest of the conversation, which was in French. She was, however, shocked to see that the woman, presumably the directress of the school, now held in her hand the little black loose-leaf notebook, marked 'Emma' in which Ursula had filed her monthly records: all the records of her

174

weights and measurements, her diet and, she suspected, a record of her punishments and the occasions on which Ursula had allowed her, or instructed her, to yield.

'Thank you, mademoiselle,' said the directress, 'for sending me the details of our little pupil. It saves so much time. This seems a fairly straightforward case. A married woman, unused to the subtleties of arousing and caressing a woman, and not always as submissive as we would like. Moreover she has twice betrayed you with a man despite severe punishment. With such a girl we use the short sharp shock system for the first few days and then when we feel she is sufficiently submissive she joins our morning classes to receive instruction of – what shall we say? – a most explicit nature. She then has to demonstrate with her fellow pupils that she has been paying attention to the instructors. Then she will start being offered to our visitors for their private use, so that she can practise what she has been taught – knowing that the slightest complaint about her performance will result in a most painful experience.' She nodded to a glass cabinet behind Emma in which half-a-dozen canes were hanging. 'Of course, as you know, our visitors always wear a mask to protect their identity. In this way we ensure complete anonymity and prevent our pupils from forming an emotional attachment to any lady whom they might particularly please, instead of remaining the creature of the mistress who has paid to have her trained here. That would never do.'

'Indeed not,' agreed Ursula. 'It is not so much the masked visitors that I am really worried about – indeed I must confess that I would very much enjoy being one myself – but the instructresses. Girls seem to form so easily what the English call a crush on a woman who is their superior and who is teaching them the most intimate ways of giving pleasure to a woman.'

'Yes, I agree. It is something that worries us too. So, we have introduced a new system of instruction that not only eliminates the risk of the girl transferring her passions from her mistress to her instructress, but also breaks any residual attraction she might have towards the male sex – something which usually concerns our clients as regards their young ladies.'

Ursula laughed. 'Really? How clever of you, madame. What is your system?'

'We have merely taken a leaf out of the book of our Moslem friends. They may not tolerate our particular feminine preferences and usages, but for centuries in their harems they have had a most effective method of instructing young women in the arts of giving pleasure and of ensuring utter submissiveness and obedience.'

'You mean . . .' began Ursula, intrigued.

'Yes, the use of male slaves – not always eunuchs. The girls' masters are happy to leave them in the hands of these cruel and repulsive creatures, knowing that not only are they expert instructors but also that the young women concerned would be so repelled by the physical appearance of these savage and brutal men that they would turn to even the most ugly master with relief and adoration.'

'I see,' said Ursula. 'Yes indeed. One could not be the least bit jealous or concerned about such creatures as the chauffeur who drove us here, or the butler who announced us.'

'It is Achmet, the chauffeur, whom I have earmarked to be Emma's principal instructor,' said the directress with a smile. 'Girls seem to find him particularly repulsive. I think he will put your girl off men for life!'

'Yes, I can see that,' laughed Ursula, 'but does he know what to teach?'

'For ten years he was in charge of the European girls held against their will in a high-class Tunisian brothel. In particular he was responsible for the exhibitions that the girls were forced to put on for the amusement of the clientele. There is nothing he cannot make the most reluctant woman do and no aspect of giving pleasure with which he is not familiar. You will find your little Emma transformed.'

'But will he not want to . . .' asked Ursula anxiously.

'No, like many such men, he prefers boys, and we keep him and the other servants here well supplied.'

Ursula laughed again. 'I can see that you have it all planned out. Poor little Emma! She has no idea what she is in for.'

'We'll give her drugged tea now. It will put her out quickly and when she awakes she will be chained naked in a dungeon, under the orders of Achmet. But mademoiselle, are you in a great hurry? May I offer you the services of the house? There are ten other girls here, trained or under training, and available to my visitors.' She handed Ursula a photograph album. 'Choose the one that catches your eye and then you can have a closer look at her. Later on, on the screen, we will be able to take a peak at your little Emma enjoying the beginning of her short, sharp shock.'

Emma felt very jealous as she saw Ursula looking at the book of photographs of naked girls. She felt even more jealous when Ursula pointed to a particularly pretty girl and when she saw the directress pick up the phone on her desk and say something that Emma recognised as 'Prepare number six'. Emma couldn't believe what she had seen and heard. Was Ursula really going to enjoy another girl before she left her here?

Her thoughts were interrupted by the awful butler offering her a cup of tea. It tasted bitter, but she was so upset that she did not notice. She swallowed it all hastily. Ursula and the directress were talking again in French. They seemed to be talking about her again. They kept looking at her. Suddenly the room seemed to go round. She staggered. She felt herself slipping to the floor – and then nothing more.

The directress smiled. She pressed a button on her desk. The man who had driven Ursula and Emma from the airport came into the room and, without a word, picked up the unconscious Emma, slung her over his shoulder and left the room.

'Now, mademoiselle,' said the directress to Ursula, 'perhaps you would like to come and look at the girl you chose.'

An hour and a half later, Ursula was back in the directress' office. She had a contented smile, like a cat who had swallowed the cream.

'I hope, mademoiselle, that the girl proved satisfactory. She will be punished if she was in any way disobedient.'

'No, no,' said Ursula, 'I must congratulate you on her degree of submissiveness and her desperate eagerness to please in a very expert way. Clearly she has been very well trained. I just hope that you can do the same with Emma.'

'Oh, I'm sure we can,' laughed the directress, glancing at the canes in the glass-fronted cupboard. 'The one you just had is for sale, you might be interested to know.'

'Really?'

'Yes. I originally trained her for her mistress a year ago. She was very pleased with her, but a couple of weeks ago she brought her back. She wanted to leave her here whilst she went off on holiday with another girl I had supplied and whom she wanted to try out properly. She wrote to me today, saying that she has decided to keep the new girl, and to help pay for her, she wants me to sell this one. But I expect she will be insisting on selling her to a Saudi lady.'

'A Saudi lady?' said Ursula astonished.

'Yes, I'm doing quite a lot of business with them. They have plenty of money and really enjoy having a white girl as their personal slave. It gives them a certain status in the eyes of their friends. And their former mistresses here also like the idea.'

'Oh?' queried Ursula.

'Yes, you see it's an ideal way of disposing of an unwanted girl. She just disappears for ever into the harem of her new mistress' husband and is never seen again. Many distinguished women here are frightened that a discarded girl will try and make a scandal by telling the press about her former mistress, or talk indiscreetly to her new mistress. The Saudi solution eliminates that risk completely. There's also the point that many women don't like the idea of a former girl of theirs enjoying men again. However, once her new Saudi mistress has her back in the harem, she will never again see a man face to face – except her new mistress' husband, of course.'

'How ingenious!' cried Ursula. 'How very clever.'

'Well, it's not quite true,' admitted the directress with a smile. 'Some of my Saudi lady clients have told me that they have used a girl they have bought from me as a wet nurse for their own children, having had her mate with a male servant in front of their friends. Others have told me that they have used their girls as a way of getting their husbands into their own beds, and away from his other wives and concubines. Having such a well-trained and beautiful European girl in her bed with her acts as a powerful magnet for her husband. But, of course, she makes certain that the girl merely gives pleasure to her husband and that it is she herself who receives it.'

'Yes, indeed,' said Ursula.

'Perhaps, before you go back to the airport to catch your plane for Morocco, you might have time, just for a second, to see how Emma's training has started? You must realise that she is just starting her training.'

The directress switched on a large television screen.

It showed Emma crouching, terrified, in a corner of what seemed to be a stone walled dungeon. There was straw on the floor. She was stark naked.

The directress moved a switch, training the television camera round towards the object of Emma's terror. The screen now showed a huge, half-naked man. His body glistened with oil. His face was covered with tribal scars. In his hand he held a whip. His only garment was a bulging loincloth. He was shouting orders at Emma. Ursula recognised him as the chauffeur who had picked them up earlier.

The directress switched off the set.

'They seem to be making a satisfactory start,' she said with a smile. 'I think you'll find her very compliant when you return. She will feel that anything is better than that man! And she will be capable of giving pleasure with her mouth or tongue for hours on end . . . Now I really must not stop you catching your plane.'

# 17   EMMA STARTS HER TRAINING

Days later, Emma knelt down on the hard cobbled floor of the dungeon. She longed to put some straw under her knees, but she knew that she was not allowed to do so. She had been beaten by Achmet for doing so. The straw had to remain beautifully clean and fresh-looking for the directress' inspection.

Once she had made the mistake of thinking that she could lie down on the straw – and had been beaten for that too. She knew now that she had to push back the straw and lie down on the cobbles.

Once she had similarly made the mistake of assuming that she was intended to relieve herself onto the straw. She would not quickly forget Achmet's anger when he discovered what she had done. Nor would she easily forget the humiliation of being taught by a repulsive man how she was always, and only with his prior permission and under his personal supervision, to perform into a bowl as he stood over her, his dog whip in his hand.

'Go on! Hurry!' he would scream, raising his whip, until she had learnt to perform to his satisfaction.

As she now knelt, she put her mouth over the strange little rubber teat at the bottom of a special plastic container that hung on the wall. It contained a sticky liquid with a strange taste. It was no good, she had learnt, just sucking the teat. The thick liquid had first to be coaxed down into the teat and then out of it by a mixture of heating it with her mouth and tongue and then sucking it hard through the tiny hole at the end of the teat.

It was all very tiring and exhausting, but she knew that she simply had to empty the container, drop by drop, before the timer rang. She glanced at the timer – one hour to go. She looked up at the container – it still looked so full. The graduations on the side still showed ten. That would mean ten strokes from the awful bamboo carpet beater that Achmet used for more formal beatings.

Desperately she applied herself to the task of licking and sucking each little drop of the sticky liquid out of the container. She knew that Achmet would sweep into the room as soon as the timer rang, the carpet beater in his hand. He would glance at the amount of the liquid remaining and then take her out into the passage to be beaten with the same number of strokes as shown on the graduation.

She longed to use her hands to squeeze the wretched stuff down into the teat and onto the floor. However, she knew that the internal television camera in the corner of the dungeon would be trained on her. If Achmet, perhaps alerted by one of his colleagues watching on a remote screen, saw her cheat by using her hands, he would, she knew from bitter and painful experience, drag her out into the passage for an extra beating.

Each time she was beaten she had to stretch out over a special table in the passage. Achmet would quickly secure her ankles wide apart to two of the table legs, and then make her reach forward so that her wrists could be fastened to the tops of the legs on the far side of the table. The table top was polished from the wriggling of innumerbale girlish bellies as they writhed under their trainers chosen instrument.

Through a slit in the door of her dungeon she had seen some very pretty young women from the adjacent dungeons being flogged as she waited her turn. With the slit closed she had also heard many more floggings. She did not know which was more terrifying – watching a poor girl being thrashed or having to listen to it. Each brought her to a new peak of fear and panic.

She had seen how some of the other huge trainers used a carpet beater, like Achmet, whilst others preferred a wide rubber paddle. Both left no clear weals, just generally reddened areas. In both cases, she knew only too well, having the girl strapped down over the table put her into the ideal position for chastisement. The man could readily apply his carpet beater or paddle to the girl's bottom, to her back, or to the lower part of her thighs.

Emma had lost all sense of time. She had no idea how long it was since she had awoken to find herself locked naked in the cellar. She had no idea whether it was day or night, for there were no windows in the dungeon and the electric light, controlled from the passage, was never switched off – just as the television camera's little red light never ceased to flash, showing that it was switched on and watching her.

All she knew was that every four hours, the wretched timer would ring and Achmet, or, if he was sleeping, one of his equally cruel colleagues, could come in and check the plastic container, before frogmarching her out to be beaten.

She had learnt to keep her eyes lowered to the ground in the presence of the trainers. Once she had dared to raise her eyes to Achmet's in a furious gesture of defiance. Immediately she had been taken out and flogged yet again. Now she kept her eyes demurely down at all times. She did not even dare to raise her eyes to the television camera.

If she slept between Achmet's inspections, then she risked being beaten for not emptying the plastic container of its sticky contents. However her tongue and lips were now becoming more adept and she found it less tiring to use them for an hour or more at a stretch. Indeed, she found that she could now empty the wretched container in about two hours, and then, keeping a close eye on the timer hanging on the wall, snatch a little sleep.

Periodically, all the girls were taken out of their dungeons and made to line up for feeding time. Emma longed to speak to them, but if a girl said one word to another girl she earned a beating there and then. So Emma had no idea who the other young women were. Indeed, she was not supposed to know, for security at the so-called school was very tight. They all seemed very pretty, and like her, had been reduced by their trainers to a state of utter abasement. There were usually three or four girls in all, but new ones would be periodically added and others disappeared never to return.

They had to stand in line, their eyes dutifully lowered, while the trainers inspected the naked bodies in each other's charge, calling out lewd comparisons. She had felt utterly degraded from Achmet's callous and appallingly intimate handling. But to be prodded and felt by his colleagues was even worse. She was, she realised, being reduced by fear and shame to a new level of submissiveness and obedience. She could not believe that Ursula, her beloved Ursula, could have condemned her to such a terrifying regime. Was it because of Henry?

When a gong was rung, the line of girls would have to run across the passage, kneel down on all fours, with their hands flat on the floor, and thrust their heads deep down into a trough containing a sort of watery porridge. Any girl who did not put her face into the horrible mixture, had her head pushed down by the trainer, and got a stroke or two across her back or bottom from his dog whip.

They had to stay like that motionless, scarcely able to breath. Then when the trainers were satisfied with their submissiveness, the gong would be struck again. This was the signal for feeding time to start. As this was all the food that they were given, Emma soon learnt to guzzle and gobble hastily, and get as much of the tasteless mixture down her throat as she could before the gong was rung again, marking the end of feeding time. They would then have to kneel up instantly. Occasionally the gong was rung for the third time because a girl had been seen to raise her hands off the floor to try surreptitiously to scoop more food into her mouth to ease her hunger. As Emma had learned the punishment for this was to be immediately fastened across the table and given a dozen strokes. She now slurped and guzzled like the other girls and kept her hands prominently flat on the floor.

When the gong rang again, the girls had to crawl back to their dungeons, trying as they went to clean the horrible sticky porridge off their faces and out of their hair. They knew that to use the clean straw for this would bring down the wrath of their trainers, yet again.

Emma now had no bodily secrets whatsoever from Achmet. When he came into the dungeon she immediately had to assume the position of what she learnt he called 'presentation' – lying on her back with her hands down between her raised knees, and gripping the outside of her ankles. It was impossible for her to close her legs in this position and it was, perhaps, the most humiliating position that a woman can be ordered to take up. He would then kneel down and inspect her. If he thought, rightly or wrongly, that he had found the slightest sign of her having touched herself, then she would be immediately ordered out to lie over the table, and be given ten strokes.

Ursula could not have known, she told herself, just what appalling things they would do to her in this school. She simply could not have had any idea, she kept telling herself. But then the nagging doubts kept coming back. Supposing it was all being done on purpose - to put her off men for life, and ensure her faithfulness to Ursula?

She was now far more submissive and obedient than before. The awful degrading beatings by Achmet, the constant fear of another and of hearing her companions constantly being dragged out of their dungeons to be beaten in the corridor, stretched over the same table as she had been stretched, had made her far more humble and servile. She would do anything to avoid another beating, she kept telling herself, as she degradingly presented herself, lying on her back with her legs parted and raised, as soon as she heard Achmet's key in the door. Had Ursula sent her here, she wondered, to have any sign of recalcitrance beaten out of her for ever? Was this all part of what Ursula and her cruel woman friend had so laughingly referred to as having her 'professionally trained'? Would it enable her to keep Ursula's interest? If so, then she did not mind so much. Certainly Achmet had put her right off all men!

It was all indeed part of what the directress had described to Ursula as a short, sharp, shock. It lasted only a week, but to Emma it seemed like months. Months of degrading humiliation. Months of sucking and licking at the ghastly teat until her tongue and jaw ached and ached, as she drove herself to empty the container - or at least get it nearly empty before the timer announced Achmet's return.

Unknown to Emma, Achmet, pleased by the degree of obedience and submissiveness that he had succeeded in instilling into her, had recommended to the directress that she was now ready for the next stage of her training - a recommendation in which the directress, who had been monitoring Emma's progress on her television screen, concurred.

Suddenly and unexpectedly, the door of Emma's dungeon was flung open by Achmet. He stood there in the doorway - a

184

terrifying figure, impatiently tapping his dog whip against the palm of his hand. He was now smartly dressed, Emma was astonished to see, in a well-cut blazer and white trousers. The incongruity with her own abject nakedness was even more humiliating than when he had just worn that dreadful loincloth. Hastily, Emma flung herself onto her back on the floor in the degrading 'presentation position', hoping to assuage the fearsome man's temper by this show of complete subservience. What had she done, she wondered? Had the television showed her touching herself for a brief second? She was shivering with apprehension as she gripped her ankles and displayed herself, like a bitch on heat, to the huge man.

'Up,' he barked. 'Inspection!'

She jumped up and stood in front of him in the second position he had taught her: hands straight down to her sides, fingers straining downwards, shoulders back, legs apart, knees bent, pelvis thrust forward, chin raised, head straining right backwards and eyes fixed on the ceiling. It was the position in which he and his colleagues had often kept her, whilst sitting comfortably in front of her as they examined her, or compared her with one of the other girls, when they were ordered to stand in silence and in the same position alongside each other. It was a position in which the girl had to strain every muscle. She tried to stop herself from shivering at the thought of more strokes from the ruthless trainer, as she stared up at the ceiling whilst he slowly walked round her.

Then suddenly she felt a canvas hood being thrust over her head. She could see nothing. She felt a rubber ball, all part of the hood, being thrust into her mouth. It must have had a strap attached to it at the front of the hood for she felt it being buckled behind her neck and then seconds later another strap, closing the bottom of the hood, was also fastened round her neck. She was in complete darkness. Terrified, she raised her hands as if to pull the hood off. Instantly, Achmet gripped her wrists and she felt him slip manacles onto her wrists. They seemed to be joined by eighteen inches of chain. She could no longer reach the front of her body. Now she was terrified of suffocating. But there were two little holes below her nostrils and she found that she could breathe quite easily.

185

She was then frogmarched out of the dungeon and along the passageway. Her naked feet felt the stone floor giving way to a carpet. She heard the noise of a heavy door being opened and shut again. She heard several men calling out to Achmet. They were making obscene remarks about her naked body. She felt herself being pushed into a lift and then being taken down a passageway with a linoleum floor. She was stopped. There was the noise of something metal being lifted. She was made to step up onto a platform and then kneel down on all fours.

Then she was thrust into something. There was the metallic crash of something being closed behind her. She felt a hand reach for her and turn her round, then her own hands being released. She felt Achmet's hands busy with the fastenings behind her neck. She felt him pulling the combined hood and gag off her.

Suddenly the hood was off. She could see! She saw Achmet's hand withdrawing as it gripped the canvas hood. It was withdrawing through some widely spaced iron bars right in front of her. Indeed through the bars she saw Achmet's face only inches away. He was standing in a passageway. She saw him slide what looked like a double-glazed window in front of the bars. She heard it close with a click. She found herself gripping the thick bars – her fingers could touch the double glazing just a couple of inches beyond, strong and unbreakable. Achmet's grinning face was now at the other side of the glass.

She looked round. She was in a little cage. It seemed to be one of a line of cages on a raised platform. There was a similar cage on each side of her. In each cage there was another naked girl. Excited at having contact with another female she turned to put her hand through the bars at the side of the cage to reach out and touch her neighbour. But there was another strip of double glazing between the bars of the two cages. She called out. She saw the mouth of the pretty girl, kneeling in the next cage, open and close. She could hear nothing. She looked up at the top of the cage, some four feet above the floor. Beyond the bars was more double glazing. It was like being in a fish tank – an hermetically sealed fish tank. In the back of the cage, some three feet from the front, was a little ventilation blower and a grill to let out the air. Otherwise, she realised, she was indeed in a sealed cage.

The cage's length along the passage was only some five feet. Its depth back from the passageway was only three feet, so that she would have to lie down curled up. Otherwise, as it was only four feet high, she would have to remain kneeling or crawling on all fours. She looked down. She was, she saw, kneeling on a piece of thick rubber, underneath which she could feel the bars that formed the floor of the cage.

In one corner, adjacent to the passageway, were two hinged plastic bowls. Being hinged, she realised, they could both be refilled, when the double glazing was slid back, without the need to open the small barred central door to the cage. One of the bowls contained water, the other just a few coloured dog biscuits. Anything, she thought, was better than that awful porridge, even dog biscuits, and she could certainly use the water to clean herself up.

In the opposite front corner of the cage, the thick rubber mat had been cut back to disclose a sand-covered tray under the thick bars that formed the base of the cage. The tray could be readily slid out from under the bars from the passage, when necessary, by simply sliding back the double glazing. The sand covered tray reminded Emma of similar trays that were used by well-trained cats. She blushed as she realised its purpose. Achmet would be able to check her droppings daily.

'Look!' suddenly she heard Achmet's voice. The double glazing had been closed and the voice came from a little speaker attached to the bars across the top of the cage. She saw that Achmet had been speaking into a microphone on the front of the cage, in the passageway.

Achmet now moved to the front of the cage on her right. It held a pretty girl with lovely long black hair. She saw Achmet switch on the microphone in front of her cage. She saw his mouth opening and closing, but she could not, of course, hear through the double glazing that sealed her own cage. But immediately the girl crawled over to the mirror hanging down from the side of her cage. On a shelf below it was a hairbrush, a comb, lipstick, powder, eye make-up, and a set of rouge.

As Emma watched, the girl began to wash and comb her hair and then to make up her face.

Emma had noticed a similar mirror and make-up shelf in her own cage. After the complete absence in the dungeon of even a comb, she was thrilled. Eagerly following the example of the girl in the next cage she reached towards the shelf. It had everything she needed, even soap. Hesitating, she glanced through the bars of her cage towards Achmet. She did not now dare do anything without his prior approval. She saw that he was smiling at her instinct to make herself look as attractive as possible. He nodded his head in approval.

Delighted, Emma washed her body and her hair, powdered herself all over and made up her face. Achmet watched her as she did so. It was humiliating, but she knew that she had no bodily secrets from this terrible man. Twice his voice on the little loudspeaker interrupted her.

'Look!' he said simply. She followed with her eyes as he strode to the next cage door. She saw his mouth open to give an order. The pretty kneeling girl turned towards Emma's cage. She held up her breasts. Emma saw that her nipples were painted the same shade of red as her lipstick. Ursula had often made her do the same. But that was not all. The whole aureola of her nipple had been outlined in black. It gave a bizarre and erotic look.

The man smiled again in approval as Emma painted her nipples scarlet and outlined them in black.

The second time he called out 'Look!' the girl had tried to kneel up in her cage with her legs wide apart, facing Emma. But the cage was too low and she went back onto all fours and turned so that her buttocks were facing Emma. Apparently at a word of command from the man she parted her legs. Emma saw that the girl's body lips were painted bright scarlet too. This was also something that Ursula had made her do. But what was new was that the whole of the girl's mound, like her nipples, had been outlined in black.

Again the man smiled in approval as Emma copied the girl next door. The cage being too low to enable her to kneel up properly, she had to do it awkwardly lying on her back with raised knees, and using the mirror to guide her hand.

She had noticed that the girl in the next cage had the number '16' painted in black on her forehead and on her right breast. She had seen the number '10' on her bowl. Was that her number, she wondered? Was she just number ten?

As if he knew what was going through Emma's mind, Achmet now slid back the double glazing on the front of Emma's cage. He beckoned her to crawl forward. He made her press right up against the iron bars. Emma saw that he had a black waterproof marking pen in his hand. She was going to be marked with her number! She shivered with fear. He made her press her forehead against the wide gap in the bars. She felt him writing something carefully on her skin. Then he made her thrust her right breast through the bars. He lifted it up with one hand, held it steady and then carefully wrote on the skin above the nipple.

Then he roughly pushed her back and closed the double glazing. Shocked by the suddenness of it all, Emma glanced in the mirror. There on her forehead and on her breast was the number '10'. It made her feel like an animal.

Nevertheless, thought Emma, even though she was locked in a cage like an animal with her most intimate bodily functions closely and degradingly watched and controlled by a hideous brutal man, and she may just be number ten, but, thanks to a wash and make-up, she felt a new woman. Indeed she could not help thinking what an excitingly pretty girl was staring back at her in the mirror, with her painted face, nipples, body lips and number. She could not help thinking that if Ursula could only see her now, painted like a whore and with a new submissive look in her downcast eyes, she would be quite unable to keep her hands off her. She blushed at the thought. Perhaps this awful training was worthwhile after all. She would go through anything, she knew, just to keep Ursula's interest.

Although no word of explanation was given to Emma, she was in fact now in the second phase of her training. The short, sharp, shock was over. She would, however, sleep, eat, rest and defecate in her cage, like an animal. The degradation and humiliation that that entailed was calculated to ensure that she remained submissive and obedient throughout her training.

Emma was now going to spend several days under intensive training, getting herself ready to be offered to the rich female clients who used the school as a discreet lesbian brothel. She would be used to supplement the girls that the directress kept permanently on offer. Masked to hide their identities, the large number of these clients and the wide variety of their sensual demands combined to form an essential part of the training offered to those clients who, like Ursula, sent a girl here for 'professional training'.

Achmet was looking forward to the generous tips that a well-trained and properly humble Emma would soon be earning him from delighted clients – quite apart from a share of the high fees that the directress would charge clients for her use.

Indeed, it was only a few minutes after Emma had been marked with her brothel number, that the directress herself came to inspect the inmates of the cages. Emma recognised her and longed to scream at her, protesting that Ursula would never have agreed to the horrors that her little girl was being made to suffer. But with each cage hermetically sealed against sound, what was the point? She saw that as the directress and Achmet and several other trainers paused before each cage, the girl inside would start crawling round and then brazenly display herself in the position of 'presentation'. She saw that the directress, like the men, also carried a dog whip which she used to point out to the trainers those parts of the anatomies of the caged women which pleased or annoyed her.

By the time the directress arrived at her cage Emma was a bundle of fear, all thoughts of protest completely banished from her mind. Instead, all she wanted to do was to please this strict woman dressed in a long black gown who so impatiently tapped her dog whip against the palm of her hand as she gave orders to the trainers regarding each girl – orders which of course, thanks to the double glazing, the girls could not hear.

Hastily Emma showed off her beautifully slimmed down and sleek body crawling round the tiny cage, and then, as she had seen the other girls do, she raised her breasts with her hands through the bars of her cage so that the painted nipples touched the glass of the double glazing. Then she lay back and degradingly offered her prettily painted body lips in the position of 'presentation'. She knew she must hold this position until the directress moved off to the next cage.

Emma saw that the unsmiling directress was gesticulating towards her with her dog whip as she discussed Emma with Achmet, who was nodding his head respectfully. It was indeed probably fortunate that Emma could not hear their conversation. Even though she could not understand voluble French, she might have followed enough of the gist of what was said to have given her sleepless nights.

'Well, Achmet, I must congratulate you on the degree of submissiveness you already seem to have instilled into this girl. Her mistress will be delighted.'

'My people have a saying, madame,' smiled Achmet, pleased at his employer's praise, ' "Control a girl's natural functions and you control the girl, but do not spare the whip". It is the mixture of these two that has broken the girl's independence of spirit. Now all that she thinks of is instant obedience, unthinking and unquestioning obedience to whatever order is given to her, just like a well-trained soldier.'

'That's just what her mistress wants. That is what she is paying for – in addition, of course, to the expertise which we will now start teaching her. Has she learnt to suck and lick for long periods, Achmet?'

'Indeed, madame, she can now lick and suck for hours on end!'

'Her mistress mentioned two other points. Firstly, the girl is used to playing with herself, and her mistress wanted us to try and stop this. Secondly, she wanted us to get her figure down to that of a young girl whilst keeping her breasts well developed, of course.'

'Madame,' replied Achmet obsequiously, 'her intake of solids has been greatly reduced and provided she is not allowed to get at food during the remainder of her time here, then I think your client will be pleased with the result.'

'But those dog biscuits, what about them?' asked the directress pointing to the half-dozen remaining dog biscuits of different colours in Emma's food bowl. Emma had already snatched a couple of them. She felt half starved after only being fed on the watery porridge when in the dungeon.

'They're just to make sure she gets some vitamins and a little protein,' replied the man knowledgeably. It was not for nothing that he had been in charge of the women used for putting on exhibitions in a nightclub come brothel. 'They are really intended for bitches feeding their puppies, but they are also excellent for keeping a woman's breasts nice and plump whilst she is losing weight.'

'Achmet,' laughed the directress for once, 'you know so much about women's bodies!'

'And as regards her mistress's other requirement – that we make her frightened of masturbating when alone,' said Achmet with a smile, 'should I start introducing her to the frustrating delights of our electrified belt and gloves?'

'Yes,' agreed the directress. 'But of course only when she is in her cage and alone. There is no need for her to wear them during her training sessions.'

'Of course, madame,' bowed Achmet. He enjoyed using this technique on a sensual and passionate girl like Emma, especially since so much of her training would arouse her and make her long to seek relief once she was back in her cage.

'You can have her all day for another few days, Achmet,' said the directress in an authoritative tone. 'After that she'll only be on instruction in the mornings. In the afternoons she will start being available to my clients, and again in the evenings. She'll sleep in her cage of course – unless the client spends the night here and wants to keep her with her. But I discourage this; it tends to give the girl ideas above her station and to undo all our good work. It's much better for a girl, when she's being made to behave like a whore, to be sent back to her cage after she's been used by a woman.'

She looked down at the prettily pouting body lips that Emma, lying on her back, was now so degradingly displaying.

'I presume you will be starting to exercise those now. A girl needs a lot of practice if she is to be capable of pleasing her mistress for a long time with both her face and body lips. I know you've already made a good start on her face lips, but a woman likes to feel her girl's juices against her own lips for a long period – even if she does not allow the girl to climax.'

'Madame, number ten's special training will be starting immediately.'

'Excellent,' said the directress, passing on to the next cage.

'Now this other girl was found by her mistress actually kissing a young man. She was thoroughly thrashed, of course, but she's been sent here by her outraged mistress not only to make men repulsive to her, but also to make her look repulsive to men. So not only must you treat her as degradingly as possible, but you are also to shave her head completely and keep it shaved. Her mistress wants her to be completely bald with a shiny pate. She'll be just as effective between her mistress's thighs, but she won't find so many men keen to kiss her in future!'

Ten minutes later a horrified Emma saw the pretty girl in the next cage being made to put her head through the bars of her cage. Achmet put a piece of wood behind her neck to stop her from trying to pull her head back again. Then slowly and methodically he cut off all the girl's beautiful long black hair with a pair of scissors whilst the girl was weeping with despair. Then he ran some electric clippers over her head and finally settled down to shave her whole head very carefully. To match the bizarre effect, he shaved off the girl's eyebrows as well and polished her bald cranium with saddle soap. When the wretched girl saw her shiny bald head and absence of eyebrows in the mirror of her cage, she screamed and screamed.

But, of course, no one heard her behind the double glazing of her cage.

# 18 EMMA'S TRAINING CONTINUES

Emma was pulled to the post, facing it. A heavy belt with a ring at the back was fastened tightly round her belly. A loose strap was then passed round the smooth well-worn post and fastened through the ring at the back of her belt. Then Achmet fastened her hands behind her back. She could now move easily round the post, but could not move her belly more than six inches away from it.

A ring was painted round the post level with her hips and another just above her knees. Her task was to use her beauty lips to oil all round the post, between the two red circles, and then polish it with her belly. But no oil or polish was supplied. She would, she knew, have to use her own oily juices.

She knew from experience that she could reach the top ring by standing on the tips of her toes as she inched her way round the post. To reach the lower ring she would have to bend her knees until she was in a crouching position.

The worst part was getting her juices running so publicly, for not only was Achmet watching her performance closely, but four other girls were similarly being made to polish other posts on the little raised platform. The embarrassed girls' bellies were level with Achmet's eyes as they strained and wriggled against their posts. Only by a mixture of wriggling against the post and thinking of Ursula, or Henry, did Emma think she'd become sufficiently wet. But then, to her horror, she found that the most effective stimulus was Achmet's little dog whip. It did not have to be applied very hard for her to be ready to start rubbing her oils into the smooth wood.

Perhaps most humiliating of all, Achmet had shown her how to get her oils onto the wood so that she could then start rubbing them in. She had learnt to lean right back in her harness and to raise her feet around the post, so that her body lips were in direct touch with it. This would enable her to deposit a little of her oil into the wood so that she could start spreading it over and around the post, repeating her little trick again and again to deposit another few drops onto the dry wood. It was a long and tedious process to ensure that all the wood between the rings had been covered properly with her oil – and before Achmet was satisfied that she had done a good job.

Then came the equally long and tiring process of polishing the oil well into the wood, so that it all shone beautifully.

'Gently, Number 10,' ordered Achmet in his heavily accented English. 'You just rub it round and round with lower belly, very gently until the wood begins to shine. Round and round and up and down, and thrust your belly in and out, in and out.'

Like the other girls, Emma had learnt to do a sort of belly dance, or Hawaiian hula-hula dance, her hips and buttocks thrusting and shaking wildly in a completely uninhibited way, as she desperately tried to spread the oil and polish the wood.

'You pretend post is your mistress, Number Ten,' encouraged Achmet, his dog whip raised menacingly to drive home his point. 'You pretend you trying to give pleasure to mistress with your beauty lips. Then you polish post very nicely. You try and make post cry out with pleasure – just like mistress. And you keep going on and on, until I satisfied. You not rest until then. You keep going on and on. You frightened of whip. You not dare stop for one second, no matter how tired. Your belly muscles getting ready to give pleasure to mistress for long, long time.'

There was a long pause whilst Emma continued to cavort and press her lower belly against the post, slipping up and down as she alternately bent her knees and moved her feet a little forward so that she could grip the post more tightly between her thighs.

'Wood too dry here, Number Ten!' It was the remark that she most dreaded. She felt his hand come down over her bottom and between her legs, checking whether she needed the stimulus of his dog whip to produce more oil. 'You beg me beat you.'

'Please, sir. Please beat me again,' came the shamed voice of Emma.

Three times the dog whip descended. Then the huge man's hand again examined her. She was soaking wet! It was extraordinary how a beating never failed to have that effect, thought Achmet. It was something deeply inbred into women, he thought. Secretly, he knew, they longed for the whip. And he made sure they got it!

'Now up! And spread it!' he ordered.

Obediently, the now deeply blushing Emma lent back in her harness, and fastened her legs round the post, giving little wriggles of excitement as she felt her oil dripping, drop by drop, onto the wood.

'Ten more minutes!' came the voice of Achmet as he proudly strode up and down the line of horribly ashamed young women, each wriggling in a mixture of delight, fear and concentration on the task in hand. It was just the sort of mixture that would most appeal to Ursula, a steady mixture of continual wriggles, writhes and what American striptease artists would recognise as good, old-fashioned grinds. 'Ten more minutes and then we see which girl has polished her post best and which deserve a beating for not trying hard enough.'

That was enough to provoke gasps of fear from the four girls as they each applied themselves even more frantically to their task.

This was the first exercise that they had to do in each morning, afternoon and evening training period.

'Next!' called out the huge trainer. He snapped his fingers.

Emma ran prettily towards him, her eyes downcast, her arms straight and swaying, her fingers outstretched. She ran on tiptoe. Gracefully she fell to her knees by his feet. 'I only exist to please you,' she whispered as she licked his feet, inserting her tongue between his toes.

'Again!' he ordered angrily. He smacked her face hard. 'And this time I want to see you really submissive.'

Emma wiped away her tears. She rose to her feet, facing him, head down and backed away for exactly six paces. He snapped his fingers. Again she ran up to him and fell on her knees.

'I only exist to please you,' she whispered huskily in a voice full of humbleness.

There was a long pause. Emma held her breath in terror.

'Better!' he said. 'Next!'

'Well done, Number Ten,' he said. 'You bring the whip well.' He took it from Emma's teeth.

Emma flashed him a smile of gratitude. Praise from Achmet was praise indeed.

'Next!' he called.

'No two mistresses are the same,' said Achmet to the class, first in fluent French and then with more difficulty in English. Was she the only English-speaking girl, wondered Emma, glancing at the rest of the class. None of them had dared to exchange one word with each other.

They all knelt facing him, their buttocks against the wall of the training room. The palms of each girl's hands were flat on the floor at her sides and her legs were tucked prettily under her.

'You must therefore strive to serve and please each mistress in the way that she particularly desires. It is a challenge for you to find out what it is that she really wants on that particular occasion. You must learn to read a mistress' innermost thoughts. You must be sensitive to her moods and their changes. Find out what she wants from you and then see that you give it to her, utterly and completely, and beyond her wildest dreams. Make her realise that you exist only for her pleasure and to serve her in the most degrading way that she can imagine. Then you will keep the attention of your mistress.'

'Gently, Number Ten, you are not rubbing down a rhinoceros.'

'Yes, sir,' said Emma.

'Use the sponge well,' he said. 'Remember that it must not clean but caress. Do not forget to fondle and kiss your mistress, humbly and lovingly.'

Emma put her hand down under the water. The girl, one of the class, gave a little whimper of delight. Emma kissed her cheek. It would be her turn next to play the part of the mistress being bathed by her girl.

'Remember sometimes to press your body against that of

197

your mistress, as if by accident. Brush her lips with your nipples. If she parts her lips, press it more to her, begging.'

'Good, Number Sixteen,' said the trainer. 'That is exactly how to remove a woman's nightdress. Make it a sensuous experience for her in which you show her your submissiveness and your eagerness to serve her and only her – or her lady friends.'

The strange-looking bald-headed girl nodded. There was not a single hair on her well-oiled shiny head.

'Rub your little bald head against her belly as you open up her nightdress. She will enjoy gripping it between her thighs. And the rest of you, just remember that many mistresses like to see a slippery shiny bald head kneeling between their legs. It is much less cumbersome there than a full head of hair. And many also feel that it is more amusing in that they can make a girl change her personality by wearing a different coloured wig without being reminded that the girl is not really a redhead or a brunette. She is nothing. She has no hair. She is whatever her mistress makes her.'

Number Sixteen smiled contentedly for the first time since her head was shaved by order of her absent mistress.

Emma shivered. Could Ursula ever really have that done to her? To have her transformed into a living shop-window model?

Emma carried the heavy tray round to the left side of the man seated at the table. Achmet was watching her carefully from the other side of the table.

The tip of her naked breast touched the top of the scalding hot coffee pot as she bent over to serve him. She wanted to drop the dish and scream with the pain, but somehow she held her position and kept silent. Her breast was still hurting, but she knew she must not show any sign of pain. Trying hard to smile, she went back to the seated man. Somehow she smilingly continued to hold the tray as he slowly helped himself to milk and sugar.

'Serving a table silently and correctly is an important part of a girl's life in the service of her mistress,' said the big trainer. 'No matter what happens, she must never open her mouth. She is there only to serve her mistress's guests, and to be shown off by her mistress to them.

'Now listen you girls,' Achmet was saying to the class sitting deferentially in front of him. 'Thanks to your training in the dungeon, your lips and your tongue are now far more capable of giving pleasure and for much longer. Equally, thanks to your training at the post, you are now capable of continuously wriggling and thrusting under your mistress when she comes down onto you. But what I want to feel is how sensitively you use your tongues, your lips and your body lips to give pleasure. So you will now line up and gently press each of those parts of your anatomies to the palm of my hand. I shall expect a high degree of expertise.'

'Inspection!' ordered the brutal man.

The class lined up on their toes, arms straight and held right back, fingers straight, eyes fixed on the ceiling. They were a pretty sight. Every muscle in their bodies seemed to be straining to hold the position.

'Remember, you must move from one position to another with grace and humbleness. A woman likes to see her girl obeying her every order. She also likes to show off her girls and their submissiveness to her lady friends. Your mistresses will be given a list of the words of command you have been taught to obey. Make sure you remember them. Now . . . Crab!'

Instantly the girls gracefully lowered themselves to the floor, lying on their backs for an instant and then their legs parted and their knees bent, and they raised their bodies so that only the soles of their feet, their shoulders and the palms of their hands were touching the floor.

Achmet, dog whip as ever in his hand, walked up the line of straining girls. It was a difficult position to maintain.

'I want to see your bodies in a perfect straight line from your knees to your neck, with hips and bellies well raised.'

He paused by Emma. He touched her inner thigh with his dog whip.

'Keep that belly up,' he ordered. 'Show yourself properly.'

Poor Emma blushed at the thought of what this horrible man

was seeing. Oh, how awful these lessons were! To be taught all these intimate things by a man was just too degrading for words. Never again, she thought, will I be able to look a man in the face. It was a thought that would have delighted Ursula greatly.

'Punishment!'

Gracefully and obediently, eyes humbly downcast, the line of girls rose to their feet and then bent over, their legs apart, their buttocks thrust back, their hands clasped behind their necks. It was a position that cried out for the use of a cane.

'Pointing!'

The girls again lay down on their backs, their left legs on the floor with toes pointing ahead. Their right legs were raised, with the knee bent, and the foot again pointing ahead. Their arms were raised and held straight, again pointing in the same direction. Their heads were back, their eyes fixed on the ceiling.

'Daisy chain!'

The girls, rose and then fell onto their hands and knees in a circle, their legs parted and their heads thrust forward, forming a perfect little daisy chain.

The more explicit part of their training was just beginning.

For Emma, and indeed for all the girls in her class, it was a desperately humiliating experience, made even more so by the fact that their instructor in these secret ways of amusing a woman was a man.

# 19    EMMA BECOMES A WHORE

'So Number Ten, your instructor tells me you are now ready
to put into practice what you have been taught.'

It was the voice of the directress. Emma was standing at
attention in front of her desk in her office. She was looking
straight ahead at the wall above the directress' head. She could
hear Achmet tapping his dog whip warningly behind her. She
felt very frightened.

She also felt like a whore – a very special whore, a woman's
whore. Not only had she been trained as a whore, but she was
also dressed and made up as one. No longer was she naked. She
now wore black stockings, a black suspender belt and white
high-heeled shoes. She even wore panties, but they were
completely transparent and through them glistened her heavily
painted body lips, outlined in heavy black. She also wore long
black gloves, a black choker round her neck and a big black
picture hat. Her bare breasts were heavily powdered with the
nipples painted scarlet, and again with the whole aureola outlined
in black. Her face was heavily rouged and her eyes and eyelids
heavily painted. Her lips were painted the same shade of scarlet
as her nipples and her body lips. Her hair was up.

'In the morning your lessons will continue as at present. But
starting now, every afternoon, and again in the evening, you
will be taken to a pretty bedroom to await any visiting client
who happens to have been taken by your photographs.'

Emma had seen the polaroid photographs that lay on the
directress's desk. They had been taken by Achmet as he put
her through the graceful routine of moving from one humiliating
position to another. They showed every little detail of her body.
They made her look appealing and submissive. The directress
put the photographs into the same album that Ursula had chosen
her girl from. It was all too humiliating for words.

'You will not touch the bed, nor the armchairs. They are for the client, not for you. You will keep yourself made up like a whore, just as you are now. When the warning buzzer goes, you will know that a prospective client is looking at you through the one-way mirror in the door. You will then parade around the room in the way that you have been taught and then go through the various positions you have been taught to show yourself off. If the client rejects you, you will be thrashed, so make certain you look as appealing as possible. If the locked door is opened by the client, you will greet her in the position of inspection, or on your hands and knees with your head to the floor. You will then do whatever she says. She will be masked and if you try to discover her identity you will be beaten. Just remember that before she leaves here, after using you for her pleasure, she will fill in a form marking your performance out of ten for obedience, appearance, submissiveness and pleasure given. At the end of the day you will line up outside my office with the other girls. You will be called in, one by one. Your marks will be read out to you. You will receive one stroke from Achmet for each shortfall from the maximum of ten marks under each heading, and from each client, less a stroke for each client you have attracted. So it will be in your own interest both to give maximum pleasure to each client, and to be chosen by as many clients as possible. Do you understand?'

'Yes, madame,' said Emma. Indeed, the terrifying Achmet, her trainer, had already instructed her in all this.

'You will only speak to the client when spoken to. And if you try and persuade her to take some message to the outside world, she will tell me and you will be beaten. And I warn you, don't think that you are now going to be able to ease your own little frustrations. Achmet has taught you how to give pleasure without the client having to be bothered to give you pleasure. Make sure you follow his instructions.' The directress turned to Achmet. 'Have you stopped her masturbating?'

The man nodded enthusiastically. Emma thought of the awful little belt that had been fastened over her body lips and of the special gloves. She had to put them on every time she was put back into her cage and she could not take them off. The belt was a sort of open metalwork and the gloves also had little strips of wire in the fingers. Achmet had showed her what happened when she put her fingers onto her body lips. She had received a violent and painful electric shock that left her feeling sick. In her cage, she had not dared to touch herself. She was too scared to do so. Masturbating was now something that she only dreamt about.

'Take her away, Achmet, and put her in the Blue Room,' ordered the directress.

Achmet took Emma by the arm. He lifted up the thick canvas hood and gag, ready to slip it over her head. Emma lowered her eyes dutifully.

'Oh, Number Ten, just before you go, take a look at the glass-fronted case in the corner,' said the directress smilingly.

Surprised, Emma looked up. She gave a little gasp as she saw the collection of beautifully oiled long bamboo canes of different thicknesses. Some she saw had silver curved handles and silver tips.

'These are what Achmet will use on you when you report here at the end of each session with my clients in the bedroom. Look at them carefully. Remember what they look like when you are tempted not to strain every nerve in your body to please one of my clients.'

Emma gave another little gasp. Then the hood was slipped down over her head. Roughly Achmet forced the gag into her mouth. She felt the straps being tightened behind her neck. She was in complete darkness again. She could only just make a little whimpering noise and even that was probably inaudible beyond the hood.

'Take her away,' ordered the directress . . .

Emma took a deep breath as the hood was lifted off, and blinked in the bright light. She was standing in a very pretty bedroom. After a week of dungeons and cages, interspersed only with visits to the bare training room, she was taken aback by the beautiful curtains, by the chintz-covered chairs, by the large bed and by the glimpse of a large bathroom. But she knew that the comfortable chairs, the inviting bed and the luxurious bathroom were not for her. Achmet pointed at an old blanket in the corner of the room and opening a cupboard showed her a simple combined sluice and washbasin. These were what she

would have to use. Over the sluice was a mirror and a shelf, jus
as in her cage, on which was a comb and a variety of make-up

'Make sure you look always like an attractive whore,' sai
the trainer. He went to the door. Emma saw that it had no handl
on this side – it could only be opened from the outside. Ther
was a telephone by the bedside to enable a satiated client t
ask for the door to be opened, or for the girl to be replaced.

'Remember,' he said, pointing to the mirror on the door, '
shall be watching you. You not use bed, chairs or bathroom
You just listen for buzzer telling you client is inspecting yo
through the mirror. Then you show yourself off prettily. An
do not dare draw curtain over mirror. That closed only whe
you performing here for a client.'

He turned, left the room and closed the door, leaving Emm
all alone in the now locked room. Eagerly she went to th
window. It just gave into a little well and there were bars acros
the windows. She could not escape her fate. She was now
whore.

Half an hour later Emma was sitting on the old blanket i
the corner of the room wondering what, if anything, was goin
to happen, when suddenly the buzzer sounded. Flustered an
blushing with embarrassment at the thought that an unknow
woman was watching her through the one-way mirror, Emm
hastily rose to her feet. Feeling rather foolish she went throug
the elaborate routine that Achmet had taught her, walking an
pirouetting round the room like a model at a dress show, wit
the big difference that she had no dress to show off – just he
own naked body. Then she went through the routine c
assuming the various positions that she had been taught; fir
the difficult crab – on her back with her weight taken only b
her feet and the palms of her hands, a highly embarrassin
position; then the provocative punishment position – bendin
over with her buttocks towards the unseen watching woma
then dropping gracefully onto her knees and then onto her bac
to assume first the pretty pointing position and then the utterl
degrading presentation position which she had had to assum
so often when in the dungeon. Then rising to her feet again sh
assumed the inspection position, straining every muscle as sh
forced her arms and head yet further back.

She held this position desperately as she wondered whether the unseen woman would open the door and come into the room. She remembered those awful canes in the cabinet in the directress's study. Had she been appealing enough? she asked herself. Had she shown herself off in a sufficiently submissive way?

The door remained closed. She heard footsteps, a woman's high shoes. They were going away, going further down the corridor, going to look, perhaps, at another girl in another room. She had been rejected! She would be thrashed!

Then suddenly she heard the footsteps returning. Quickly she resumed the proper inspection position, her eyes fixed on the ceiling.

She heard the lock in the door being turned. She heard the door being opened. She did not dare look down as the door was closed. She smelt a strong perfume. She was trembling with anticipation. She felt her loins suddenly become moist. Then her hair was gripped and her mouth pulled down to a masked face. It was a black mask that covered the woman's eyes and nose. Only when she felt the woman's tongue forcing its way into her mouth, did she try to twist away, but the woman was much stronger than her and held her tight, forcing her tongue deeper and deeper into Emma's mouth.

'Little slut,' she said, eventually pulling her head back and still holding Emma tightly, 'you're going to do things for me that you've never even dreamt about doing . . .'

Two hours later, it was indeed a shocked and ravaged Emma who watched the still masked woman being ushered out of the door by an obsequious Achmet, sure of being given an exceptionally large tip by the now satiated lady.

As her watch had been taken away, Emma had no idea of the time. But it was, in fact, past midnight when, her first evening session as a whore completed, a smiling Achmet, his wallet bulging with tips, hooded and gagged her again to take her down to join the line of other hooded and equally frightened girls waiting outside the directress's study. Still hooded and gagged, she could feel the half-naked bodies of other silent girls on either side of her, as she waited. She heard the noise of the door being opened, of a girl being thrust through it, of the directress's stern voice, of the swish of a cane, of little whimpering noises, of the door being opened again and of a girl being dragged out.

It was terrifying. She never knew when it would be her turn to be thrust through the door to be judged by the implacable directress. The suspense was awful as it was intended to be.

As she waited, her mind went over the events of the afternoon and evening. She had had to force herself to comply with the first woman's demands. The afternoon session had been completed by a petite but very cruel French woman. She had to admit that she had learnt a lot from having to please these two women. Then she had been taken back to the cage for a little rest, a few more dog biscuits and then her body and face beautifully dressed and made up again like a tart, she had been taken back to the bedroom for the evening session.

Her first client had been a huge and powerful German-sounding woman, rather reminding Emma of Ursula's fat friend Helga. She had crushed Emma beneath her, just as Emma had always feared that Helga longed to do. Then raising herself she had kept Emma wriggling like mad underneath her for what had seemed hours. Emma was grateful for the hours of practice at the post. Next, astonishingly, two masked women had come into her room. Dutifully she had had to undress and bathe both. Dutifully she had had to apply her newly learnt techniques of *Feuille de Rose*, or Rose Petals, and *Pas d'Araignée*, or Spider's Footsteps, to first one of the women and then the other as they writhed in each other's arms.

Emma's role had merely been a secondary one. Not once during the day, she thought ruefully, had she herself been allowed to climax. After giving pleasure to five women, she herself was as frustrated as she had been at the beginning of the day, but she realised, as a result, she was still fresh and eager.

She knew that Achmet would put that awful electric belt on her before putting her away in her kennel for the night. She would not dare even to touch herself, never mind masturbate properly. The electric shock was just too violent. She would still wake up screaming in her cage whenever in her sleep her hand had, as usual, slipped down between her legs. It was, however, happening less and less as her body and her mind learnt to re-adjust itself to the presence of the electric belt and its associated special gloves. In fact they were making her turn away in fear from the very idea of masturbation. The directress and Achmet had succeeded in a few days to do what the nuns at the convent school in Ireland had failed to do in six years of embarrassing sessions in the confessional, of penance and of continual lies. She had even lied to Ursula. Would the memory of this awful belt keep her pure for Ursula in future, she wondered? Would her body and her brain adjust themselves to only giving pleasure?

Suddenly it was her turn to go in.

She caught her breath under the cruel mask and gag, as she felt Achmet frogmarch her into the directress's study. Desperately seeking to placate the directress she assumed the position of inspection, her knees wide apart and bent, her arms and head strained back. She heard the directress slowly sort out some papers on her desk.

'So, Number Ten,' the hooded Emma now knew why her brothel number had been painted on her breast as well as on her forehead, 'your first client gave you only two out of five for obedience. You must learn to master any natural repugnance you may feel towards any woman who has bought the right to enjoy you. The same applies to your third client: the large lady. However, most of them gave you quite good marks for submissive deportment and pleasure given. Let's see . . . Yes there's a shortfall from the maximum possible marks of fifteen marks . . . Less five marks for each of your five clients. You were lucky that one was a double. That makes ten bad marks, that's ten strokes, Number Ten. Not a very good start. You'd better try far harder to please tomorrow.'

Emma, hidden behind her hood and unable to say a word behind her gag, had been listening to all this with mounting concern. It was all so unfair. She had tried hard – or fairly hard. My God, she wanted to scream, please don't beat me. I really will try harder tomorrow. I really will. But please don't beat me. Please.

But all that the directress heard was a few little whimpers. They might have been whimpers of repentance or whimpers of defiance.

'Punishment!' the directress ordered. Emma, sobbing under her hood, bent over and clasped her hands behind her neck, over the neck straps of the hood and gag.

'I like to beat a girl myself after her first day,' Emma heard the directress say. 'It makes it seem more personal – a personal bond between you and me. You won't forget this beating in a hurry, and you'll do your utmost to reduce the number of strokes for tomorrow and subsequent days. When you've earned no strokes at all for two days, then I shall know that you've become a good little whore – a real live woman's tart.'

Emma heard these words with mounting shock. A good little whore! A real live woman's tart! She wanted to protest, to cry out, but of course she could not say a word.

She heard the directress stride to the dreaded glass-covered case in the corner of the room. She heard the directress select a cane and give it a few practice swishes. She heard the directress coming back towards her. Suddenly she felt Achmet gripping her shoulders. She could not move. She was being held, bent over, for the cane. She heard a swishing sound. Her bottom was on fire! She screamed and screamed but the gag swallowed up all the noise. She tried to wriggle away, but she was held helpless. She tried to put her hands down to protect herself, but the huge Achmet held them in a grip of steel. She heard another swishing noise . . .

It was, reflected Emma tearfully as she was taken back to her cage, just as the directress had said. It was indeed a beating she would not forget in a hurry. Horrified as she was to find herself now a whore, she would, nevertheless, try desperately hard to be a good one.


A week later, Emma graduated to the Display Room in the evenings. In the mornings her humiliating training continued. In the afternoons she continued to be on offer in the bedroom, hastily changing the sheets on the bed and the towels in the bathroom between each client. But in the evenings she joined half-a-dozen other girls in the Display Room. They were allowed to wear a pretty negligée over their tart's costume. They were encouraged to smile at each other as they walked round the room, for there were no chairs. But they were gagged and could not talk. Being gagged also seemed to make them more attractive to the clients.

There was a large one-way mirror in the wall for clients to have a preliminary look at the girls on offer, without being seen themselves. There was no buzzer, as in the bedrooms, and so the girls never knew when they were being looked at.

But after the client had had her preliminary look, the girls were all summoned into a pretty furnished room next door. They had to take off their negligées and line up to be inspected. It was a highly competitive affair. Each girl, thinking of the directress' cane, would be doing her best to look submissive and appealing, and to out-do the other girls.

Sometimes with the girls all in inspection position, the client would pass slowly down the line, feeling each girl as she passed. Sometimes she would require them to be put through their paces before she would choose a girl: watching carefully as they went from the inspection position to crab, and onto all the others – finishing as usual with the degrading presentation position.

The chosen girl would then be taken off to her bedroom to await the client. Not one of them, not even Emma, could resist, when they were chosen, giving a little superior toss of the head towards the girls they had defeated in the selection process.

The days went past. Emma had no idea how long she had been at the so-called girls' school. All she could think of was of avoiding a beating in the study of the directress at the end of each day or at least of reducing the number of strokes, by attracting and then pleasing as many clients as possible. She was, she realised, now a real whore, though whether it was entirely a result of her fear of a beating, or partly because it was her natural inbred nature, was something she did not like to think about. Certainly she was now much more adept at giving exquisite pleasure to a woman.

As she lay in her tiny cage at night, exhausted after a long day of more and more practising under Achmet in the morning, of being on offer in the bedroom in the afternoon, of being in the Display Room for the evening until the early hours of the morning, followed by the terrifying and long drawn-out wait outside the directress's study, and then finally the caning

administered by Achmet at the order of the implacable directress, Emma would wonder if Ursula had forgotten her. Had
she found another girl? Had she simply told the directress to
keep her as one of the whores? Was her fate now to be kept
here for ever?

She longed to ask the directress, but of course, as she was
always gagged and hooded in her presence at the end of each
day, she was quite unable to do so. She just had to carry on
working as a whore and to live for each day, working hard to
avoid a severe beating at the end of it.

Then one day, the tall masked figure coming down the line
of girls, each straining to hold the position of inspection as
prettily and appealingly as she could as her breasts were
carefully felt, seemed somehow familiar. It couldn't be true! It
was! It really was Ursula!

Emma could hardly contain herself. Her beloved Ursula had
come back! Her Mistress was back! Her Mistress had come to
see what her girl had learnt. Oh, how she longed to show her.
Oh, how pleased she would be with her little girl's vastly
improved performance. Oh, how Emma longed to show off all
her newly learnt little tricks. Oh, how she longed to be taken
away from this school by Ursula. She wanted to cry out to
Ursula, but like all the girls in the Display Room she was, of
course, firmly gagged. She longed to look up and smile at
Ursula, but was too terrified of Achmet's dog whip to raise her
demurely lowered eyes. But anyway, she knew, Ursula would
of course choose her.

But she didn't! She just felt Emma's breasts and passed on
without any sign of recognition at all. Instead she chose another
girl, a horrible girl, who tossed her head in a horribly superior
way as she was led away, leaving Emma feeling utterly
downcast and madly jealous.

Several other clients came to inspect the girls, but, for once,
Emma was too sad and miserable to catch their eye.

Then suddenly, Ursula was back again, apparently seeking
yet more pleasure with yet another girl. This time she did choose
Emma.

'No talking, Emma,' Ursula ordered as she unfastened
Emma's gag in the pretty bedroom. 'I just want to see what

210

you have learnt and whether I shall have to leave you here for a longer period. I have told that fool of a husband of yours that you've got flu and may have to stay here longer. It's up to you to convince me that you are now ready to be taken away.'

To Ursula's command, Emma beautifully and gracefully went through all the positions she had learnt, arousing Ursula's sensuality as she did so.

Then she made Emma perform for three hours. For three hours Emma strained every nerve and muscle in her body to convince Ursula that she was now fully trained. She would do anything not to have to spend another day in this terrifying school.

Ursula was very pleased indeed with this new much more submissive and highly-trained Emma. What a success the training period had been! The girl could now use her tongue and her lips almost inexhaustibly. She could wriggle her hips incessantly in a variety of deliciously different ways. And she was so keen to show off all the submissive little tricks she had learnt. She was indeed now a delightfully obedient little plaything.

Ursula would take back to London a new toy which would be the envy of all her friends.

# 20    THE CHASTITY BELT

Emma was terrified almost out of her wits by Ursula's totally unexpected threat to leave her in the school for a further period of training. Desperately she concentrated on using all her newly acquired expertise to give Ursula the most exquisite and continual pleasure. She was determined to show her that she needed no more of the awful training. She did not dare say a word but just devoted herself to her task of submissively obeying Ursula's every instruction whether it was given verbally or by a gentle movement of her slim body.

When Ursula finally telephoned for Emma to be taken away and put back in her cage, Emma still had no idea of her fate.

Curled up in the small, iron-barred, glass-covered cage, she lay awake for hours unable to sleep and asking herself over and over again whether she had done enough to persuade Ursula to take her away from this hateful school.

Next day, Achmet, as usual, supervised her whilst she gobbled up her breakfast of a few high-protein dog biscuits. He watched her carefully as she washed herself, combed her hair, powdered and painted her body and made up her face. He checked the smooth softness of her hairless body lips and controlled the passing of her meagre wastes.

Then she was taken up with the other girls for her normal morning training session, commencing with the usual humiliating period at the post . . .

Poor Emma was feeling utterly despondent. Clearly she had failed to please her beloved mistress sufficiently. Clearly she had failed to display herself as a now completely submissive girl. Clearly she had failed to persuade Ursula that she was now sufficiently expert in the art of giving a woman pleasure. At best, she was being left for a period of further training. At worst, for she now knew that the so-called school also acted as a slave market or clearing house for young women trained in the lesbian arts, she was to be disposed off to another mistress.

She had not paid any attention when Achmet, in the hectic midst of carefully controlling a Daisy Chain of the crawling girls, had nonchalantly answered the internal telephone.

She had not understood when Achmet, having called in one of his equally brutal-looking colleagues, took her back to her cage to be washed, hooded and gagged.

Surprised, she had felt Achmet slipping some simple clothes over her, but had not understood their significance – not even when she felt him plaiting her hair into two little-girlish pigtails, each ornamented with a little bow, just as her hair had been done when she first arrived at the school.

Wondering what was going to happen, Emma had been led away by Achmet. It seemed as if she was being taken to the directress's study. Her heart fell. The directress's study was associated in her mind with pain and humiliation: with being caned either by the directress herself whilst Achmet held her bent over, or by being caned by Achmet whilst the directress watched.

Desperately she cast her mind back wondering what she had done wrong. Why was she going to be punished? Surely, after all her extra efforts to please, Ursula had not made a bad report on her?

Standing outside the study, hooded, gagged and trembling with fear, she heard Achmet knock on the door and say something. She heard the directress's voice speaking in French. Suddenly Achmet unfastened the hood and gag and slipped them over her head. She shook her hair and blinked in the bright light. She saw to her surprise that she was dressed in the same schoolgirl outfit in which she had arrived. Achmet gripped her arm and led her into the study.

There, tall and elegant as ever, was Ursula, talking to the directress in French. She handed the directress a cheque. In return the directress handed back to Ursula the little black loose-leaf notebook containing Emma's records which Ursula had sent to the directress before taking Emma there. Emma also saw, to her embarrassment, that the directress was handing to Ursula the notebook marked '10' in which Emma had seen

Achmet noting something down every time he had beaten her, supervised her wastes, inspected her and every time she had had a client visit her in the special bedroom. As usual she would have no secrets from her mistress. But all that was secondary compared with the excitement she felt at realising that Ursula had after all returned to the school to collect her, to take her away. She felt just as she had when her mother came to collect her at the end of term in her school days in Ireland.

'Well, madame,' said Ursula, abruptly switching into English, 'I think that concludes our business. I think that you and your staff,' she turned towards Achmet who was still standing behind Emma holding her by the arms, 'deserve to be congratulated on doing an excellent job.'

She smiled at the man and handed him an envelope. Achmet released Emma, bowed and took the envelope. It clearly contained another handsome tip.

'Come, girl,' Ursula said to Emma and swept out of the room. 'Get into the car.'

As the school gates closed behind the car, driven as before by one of the trainers on the staff, Emma turned to Ursula.

'Oh, madam, I am so pleased to get away from that awful school, so pleased to see you again, so happy . . .'

'Keep quiet, Emma, that school seems to have failed to teach you that little girls should be seen and not heard. I want to get down to my paperwork. And anyway never let me hear you ever again say one word of criticism about that school. It cost me a lot of money to send you there. You should be grateful to them for teaching you so much and for improving your character. I also hope to see a great improvement in your attitude to men in future.'

Indeed Emma found on the journey back to London that she was now shy and frightened of men. As she silently looked out of the window whilst Ursula read her papers on the way to the airport, she found that her whole attitude to men had changed. Before she had regarded men as exciting and stimulating, now she kept remembering the way that Achmet had treated her and the degrading things he had made her do. Every time at the airport when she saw a man looking at her, she found herself wondering if he too was asking himself whether it would be

214

amusing to degrade her. Whenever a man came close to her, she found herself lowering her eyes to the ground, bowing her shoulders and moving closer to Ursula, as if seeking protection. And once when a man approached she could not help seizing Ursula's arm in a sudden movement of sheer terror – a terror that aggravated her by knowing that she was naked under her dress.

'It's all right, little girl,' murmured Ursula, who had noticed Emma's new attitude to men with increasing satisfaction, 'your mistress is here.'

How right Helga had been, thought Ursula, to advise sending Emma for a little professional training. It had transformed her! It may have been expensive, but the result was a delightfully submissive, eager and highly adept young woman, who was now far too scared of men ever again to chase after them.

Emma had been dreading having to sit alone in the back of the plane in the economy class. She was therefore thrilled when Ursula told her that she could sit with her in first class.

'But it's this once,' said Ursula in a firm voice, 'just to help you adapt after the school. I don't want you getting any ideas above your station. In future you will always travel like a servant with the hoi-polloi.'

'Oh thank you, madam, thank you.'

She found herself silently kissing Ursula's hand in gratitude. It was so exciting being back with Ursula again. She might now be scared of men, but she was free again – at least as free as Ursula would allow.

Back to her house in London, Ursula lost no time in further asserting her authority over Emma.

'Go and tell Rafaela to undress you and put you into your new maid's uniform,' she ordered Emma.

Emma was highly embarrassed at being undressed by Rafaela, especially when she realised that Rafaela would see not only her hairless body lips, but also the marks of her beatings at the school and the figure '10' painted on her breast – Achmet had removed the figures painted on her forehead before taking her down to the directress' study for the last time. However she had to admit that the long candy striped dress, with its pretty pinafore and matching cap, looked very fetching. At the same time, however, it clearly indicated her status – that of a maid servant.

Ursula seemed very pleased when Rafaela brought the blushing Emma back.

'Yes, yes, that looks very nice on you, little Emma,' Ursula enthused, giving her a kiss. 'Now, from now on, unless I give you orders to the contrary, your role when you are in this house is always to be that of my maid servant. You will remain in the small maid's room next to Rafaela's large bed-sitting room until I ring for you. You will answer the door and show up my visitors. You will take their coats. You will serve them tea or offer them drinks. And when I ring for you again you will see them out. You've been trained in serving, and I shall expect you to serve them perfectly. Now you can start by getting me a gin and tonic. Now, girl, now!'

Emma, not quite sure whether she was appalled or secretly rather excited at the future roll that her mistress had outlined for her, jumped to obey the order. Remembering all that she had been made by Achmet to practise over and over again, she offered Ursula her drink in a way that made it clear that she was also offering herself.

'Right,' said Ursula as she sipped her drink, 'now go with Rafaela and put on your new maid's walking out dress. In future, when you are here, you will accompany me when I go out shopping or visiting friends. You will carry my parcels. You will walk a respectful pace behind me. If I stop to talk to a friend, you will stand still and make no attempt to speak to me or my friend. You will keep your eyes down and above all you will not look at any man, though I don't expect that will be difficult now after your treatment by Achmet! And you will wear the simple uniform that I have designed for you when you go out, and when you act as my chauffeur. And just as you will wear nothing under the maid's indoor uniform, so you will also wear nothing under your outdoor uniform. Rafaela! Take her away.

A few minutes later Emma was again standing awkwardly in front of Ursula whilst Rafaela looked on. This time she was wearing a long black dress that reached almost to her ankles and which buttoned down the front from the high collar that was tight round her throat down to just above her feet. It was rather a shapeless dress and clearly not intended to show off her figure. It was indeed rather an ugly dress that was simply intended to show that the wearer occupied an inferior position in society. With it went a rather shapeless bonnet, rather like a nurse maid's cap. For use when driving Ursula, there was a little peaked cap – a female version of a chauffeur's hat. Looking at herself in the mirror, Emma realised that anyone looking at her would see just a rather unattractively dressed servant.

Ursula was delighted at what she saw.

'I hope it is clearly understood that you will normally be dressed either in your pretty housemaid's dress or this one for when you go out of the house. But you will not go out without my express permission or command, and in my absence that of Rafaela.'

Rafaela gave a little smirk. She was not at all interested in girls, but it would be amusing to take this girl down a peg or two.

'And,' added Ursula, 'when you are here you will be responsible for scrubbing the kitchen floor, and keeping my bathroom and loo spotless – as well as the one you will share with Rafaela, always asking her permission to use it first. Is that clear?'

'Yes, madam,' murmured Emma rather taken aback. She did not like Rafaela and was rather frightened of her.

'Speak up, girl,' said Ursula sharply. 'And stand up properly when you speak to me. I don't like a girl to mumble or slouch.'

'Yes, madam,' said Emma quickly. She had seen Ursula's cane, the dreaded Sambo, lying by her bedside.

'I may, of course, require you at times to play the roll of a baby girl, or of a little girl of six, in the nursery, or I may want you to be my teenage niece again. But unless I do order you to play these roles, I shall simply expect you to act the role of my maid at all times, and to be subject, when you are downstairs, to the orders of Rafaela. Understood?'

'Yes, madam.'

'You will spend two days here before I allow you to go back

home. I have already told your husband that the training course has been extended. You can ring him this evening, but in my presence. You are to tell him how you have enjoyed the course, and how kind it was of me to send you on it. Remember, I shall be listening to every word with Sambo in my hand!'

Poor Emma gave a little shudder, but she had to admit that it was a shudder of excitement as well as fear.

'Now girl, go and fetch the black box that I brought back specially for you from Morocco. It's in my suitcase.'

Intrigued and thrilled that her mistress had bothered to bring back a present for her, she found the box and handed it respectfully to Ursula.

'Blindfold her, Rafaela,' ordered Ursula. Emma caught her breath – it must be jewellery, she thought, as Rafaela slipped a scarf over her eyes.

'Now undress her,' she heard Ursula order. She felt Rafaela's hands undoing the buttons down the front of her long dress. How she hated being undressed by Ursula's housekeeper.

'Open your legs and clasp your hands behind your neck, and keep them like that,' ordered Ursula. 'Now put it on, Rafaela.'

Astonished, Emma felt something being fastened over her body lips. She felt a cold metallic chain being put round her waist. She felt another metallic chain being passed between her legs and then pulled up tight. She heard a click, as if of a padlock, in the small of her back. She felt something long and sticky being fastened down across her lower belly.

'Let her look at herself now,' Emma heard Ursula say. She felt Rafaela remove the blindfold. 'Look at yourself in the mirror, little girl.'

Emma looked at herself in astonishment. Her first impression was that her body lips, the pouting red body lips of a grown woman, had been replaced by the pale pink, slit-like lips of a little girl. She gasped in disbelief.

'Touch them,' laughed Ursula.

Emma reached down. The artificial lips seemed to be made of a soft plastic material. They felt very realistic. Then through the slit she felt something hard underneath. She could feel another slit inside. It was only about an eighth of an inch wide – far too narrow, she discovered as Ursula stood watching her,

218

laughing, for even her little finger to penetrate. It was a slit in a heart shaped, flesh coloured, hard plastic shield that completely covered her own real lips and to which the artificial lips were attached. It was a little like the plastic cricketers box, that Henry had jokingly made her wear. She remembered how intrigued Ursula had been with that, as well as furious that a man should have made her wear it. Had she had an improved version made, Emma wondered?

Then she saw that the sides of the shield, which like Henry's cricketers box were padded for greater comfort, were joined to a two-inch wide strap of skin coloured film-like material that appeared to have been glued to her skin. This made it impossible for even her little finger to penetrate underneath the shield from the side or from above. It was impossible for her to touch herself either through the soft imitation lips or by lifting up the shield. Henry's little box had just been a joke for it could be lifted up a little to allow a naughty finger to pass underneath. Henry had intended it to be merely a psychological chastity belt. This was much more serious – a real purity belt.

Alarmed and yet intrigued, she pressed the shield against herself. She could feel nothing. The hard shield was also sufficiently raised to prevent herself from rubbing it against her little bud – just like Henry's cricketers box.

She looked down again and into the mirror. She saw that instead of the elastic that had kept Henry's belt fastened round her hips, this belt had a little strong stainless steel chain that went round her waist. It would, she saw with dismay, prevent a man, or indeed herself, from slipping this belt down over her hips, as she had been able to do with Henry's belt. Attached to this chain were two short chains that led down to rings on the two upper corners of the heart-shaped shield. Another little chain had been attached to the curved bottom of the shield, where it disappeared between her legs. This chain had been led up tightly to the small of her back, where, she saw in the mirror, a little padlock fastened it to the two ends of the chain that went round her waist. Even if the glue round the shield itself was melted she would still not be able to remove the belt, for the swell of her hips made it impossible for her to slip the chain down over them.

Henry's so-called chastity belt had merely been worn as a joke, a toy. This one was for real. Not only could no man penetrate her, but she could not give herself any relief either!

'Yes, I pride myself that it's very ingenious – and very effective,' laughed Ursula as she ran her hands over it. 'It will serve you right for giving me the idea in the first place!'

Her eyes glinted. She stroked the soft artificial body lips with their hard base underneath.

'And moreover these can be used by the girl, wriggling and writhing under her mistress' hips, to give almost as much pleasure to her as her real ones would have, but without the nuisance of the girl becoming aroused in the process.' She pressed her hand against the lips. 'The girl can feel nothing. She just gives her mistress pleasure. And that's what you're going to do, little Emma.'

She gave Emma a hug.

'Oh, it's going to be exciting having you completely under my control.'

She produced a little bottle from her handbag.

'And when I do want to feel your real lips, all I have to do is put a couple of drops of this special solvent onto the edge of the shield and the glue melts instantly. Then,' she produced a little key from her bag, 'I simply unlock the padlock, and, hey-presto, the little girl is back to her normal self again. Not that that will happen often, little Emma!'

Ursula laughed.

'And just remember that I and Rafaela are the only two people who have the key to the padlock and who have bottles of the special solvent and glue.'

She paused. She gave Emma another little hug and kissed her passionately. Emma was embarrassed at being kissed like that in front of the unsmiling Rafaela.

'Oh, it's going to be exciting,' went on Ursula, 'sleeping comfortably in my bed at night, knowing that you are curled up in your hard bunk in my dressing room, or locked in your maid's room, frustrated and unable to touch yourself.'

Ursula stepped back and looked Emma in the eyes.

'And it will be just the same even when you are back at your home. Instead of worrying myself sick about what you are getting up to, I shall know, as I enjoy myself with one of my other girlfriends, that my little Emma is safely tucked up in bed, or working in the garden, or reading a book, quite unable to be unfaithful to me with her husband or any other man – or even with her naughty little fingers!'

Ursula turned to Rafaela.

'Nor will we have to worry about her picking up strange men on the train or crossing London on the way here. So you won't have to meet the train and escort her here. Quite apart from now being scared of men, she'll also find that she'll be too shy to speak to them for fear that they discover her chastity belt. And if any man did try to take her, he'll find the entrance barred, just as her own fingers will also find.'

She turned back to Emma.

'Oh, yes, I can see that this is going to work splendidly. It will keep you fresh and pure for me. And sometimes, if you are a very good little girl and a satisfactory maid servant, then I might even slip off your chastity belt and let you yield yourself to me. You'd like that, wouldn't you, little Emma?'

'Oh, yes, madam,' cried Emma, now thrilled by the idea of the belt making her keep herself beautifully chaste for her mistress. 'Oh, yes!'

'Well, the directress told me that she had partly cured you of playing with yourself. But I'd rather be safe than sorry. You certainly won't be able to masturbate now. The Moroccans are very ingenious. For centuries they have been making chastity belts like this to keep girls chaste. Recently they have learned to add the little film at the side to keep them pure as well. And I suggested the addition of the very convincing little lips – though, of course, those strict Moslems do not approve of us lesbians and would never have agreed to my suggestion if they had realised the use I intended to put them to! I just persuaded them that although their traditional belts are very good, modern plastics now enable them to be even better. Of course, not only do they make young girls wear belts like yours, but also their boys, for some Moroccan men enjoy boys as well as girls!'

'So,' went on Ursula, 'you will now wear this chastity belt at all times, unless I or Rafaela remove it. When you first arrive here in future, you are to report to Rafaela who will remove it, supervise the removal of any hairs that might have grown under it, and then lock it up again.'

'But what happens when I want to . . .' wailed Emma, growing horrified at the idea of losing control of her own body.

'You'll find that you can spend a penny in the normal way after a little practice. And as for anything else, you'll soon find that the chain at the back is so small that it won't stop anything. Anyway you'll soon learn to hold it to one side. And you can wash the chain yourself. You'll soon learn that you can do anything whilst wearing the chastity belt – except misbehave!'

'But what happens when I go home?' asked Emma in a worried tone.

'You will continue to wear it. My doctor friend has written to your husband saying that you are still not fit for any sexual activity. And if he happens to see it, the booby will probably not notice any difference. Except for the retaining chains, it is very realistic! So you will be all mine in future. Now off you go with Rafaela and put on your maid's outfit. You must get ready to serve my dinner. And remember I shall want you naked under your dress, except for your new chastity belt of course.'

Emma served Ursula's delicious dinner, carefully cooked by Rafaela. Ursula was glad to see that Emma was now a well-trained parlour maid.

'Thank you, Emma,' she said, 'I can see that you have the makings of a very suitable maid servant. When you've brought me my coffee, you can go down and tell Rafaela that she has my permission to put the scraps off my plate into a bowl which you can bring up here and eat like a little dog on all fours.'

Emma's heart fell. She was feeling very hungry and even the scraps would be delicious, but to have to eat them out of a bowl at Ursula's feet! Still, it showed that Ursula was in a good temper. Greatly daring, Emma decided to broach a subject that had been on her mind for some time.

'May I ask you something, madam?' she asked.

'Yes, little Emma. What is it?'

'Can I have your permission to ring my office tomorrow morning? I must tell them that I shall be back in the office the day after tomorrow. I don't want to lose my job. They were very good about letting me off for the past months, but I must . . .'

'Don't worry, little girl,' cut in Ursula. 'I've told them that you will not be coming back and that you now have a new job.'

'A new job?' asked Emma, 'but I don't understand. And I do need the money.'

'You'll be working for me from now on, little girl.'

'Oh!' cried Emma, excited. 'But what as?'

Ursula leaned forward. Angrily she slapped Emma's face.

'What do you think, you stupid girl? As my slave, of course. Now get down onto your knees! Lick my shoes!'

She rose and stood over the crawling Emma. She put one foot firmly onto Emma's neck and pressed it down onto the floor in a highly symbolic gesture. Emma felt that it was the most exciting moment of her life. To be the slave of Ursula!

'Yes, little slut, you are now my slave. What are you? Say it!'

She pressed down harder onto Emma's neck.

'I'm your little slave,' gasped Emma choking. 'I'm your slut.'

'Yes, you are,' said Ursula, who was savouring every moment of this scene. She looked down gloatingly at the girl at her feet. 'From now on you will think of yourself as being owned by me, as being my property, to do with what I like, just like serfs in Russia only a little more than a hundred years ago. But you are a lucky girl, you will be a paid slave. I shall pay you just what I would pay a maid servant. You will find that it is double what you were getting before. But I shall not allow you to have control of such a large amount of money. I have arranged that your wages will be paid into a new special bank account. The account is in your name, but all cheques must be countersigned by me, or in my absence by Rafaela. I will give you a little pocket money and travelling money each week. But I don't want this spent on fattening sweets, so you will have to keep an account book to show how you have spent your pocket money. I shall inspect it regularly and it must be countersigned weekly by Rafaela. If you need anything in particular you are to ask me or Rafaela. As for your clothes, you are to wear only my old cast-offs.'

Emma's head swam as she realised that she would now indeed be Ursula's slave and utterly dependent on her financially.

'And as for your housekeeping money from your husband, you are to write a letter to your bank telling them to transfer your husband's payments to your new account as soon as they receive them. In this way I will be able to make sure that you are not cheating by using the money for yourself. Even your butcher's bill will have to be paid by a cheque countersigned by me. Oh! By the way, I have decided that I want you to be a vegetarian from now on. I eat meat, but you don't.'

Ursula paused to let what she had been saying sink into Emma's brain. Then she continued.

'So, you see that from now on you are going to be completely under my thumb. It's going to be such fun having my own little secret slave. Of course a nice little sum will be slowly building up in your bank account but, like the slave that you are, you will not be able to spend a penny of it without your mistress's permission. Oh, and meanwhile I have confiscated all your credit cards.

'You will in future be coming here for several nights a week, and sometimes at weekends. You will keep a bag packed and when I summon you, I will expect you on the next train. No more excuses about having to go to the office! When I call you, you will jump, whether I am summoning you by buzzer in this house, or by telephone when you are at home.'

'But what do I tell my husband?' asked Emma anxiously. He was very easy-going, but even so . . .

'You can tell him that you now have a well-paid job as my personal assistant. You can tell him that; however, you never know when I shall need you urgently and that you are completely at my beck and call. Understand?'

Emma nodded. She had certainly let herself in for it, she thought. But really it would be all rather exciting never knowing what Ursula would want her to do next. If only she did not have to wear that horrible chastity belt!

'And when you are in the country,' Ursula went on, 'you will report to me or Rafaela by telephone in the morning, after lunch and every evening. I shall want to know what you have just eaten, the state of your wastes and confirmation that your chastity belt is still properly in place. And I shall want to hear that my little slave passionately adores her strict mistress.'

Ursula pulled Emma up to her knees.

'Now go downstairs to your maid's room and put on a nightdress. I shall ring for you when I want you to come and give me my bath. Now run along. I want to read a book in peace and quiet.'

Silently, Emma slipped out of the room, her mind in a daze by everything that Ursula had been saying. It was certainly all unbelievably exciting. No man, she thought, would have bothered to establish such a degree of domination over a girl. It was so much more thrilling to be Ursula's slave, than that of a man.

An hour later she was still trying to assimilate what her future life would be like as she lay on the hard bunk in her maid's room, wearing only a short nightdress, embroidered on the right breast with Ursula's monogram 'U de F'. Not for one minute, she thought, would Ursula allow her to forget whose slave she was. Absent mindedly, as she thought about her new life, her hand was unsuccessfully trying to find a way of inserting a finger under the horrible chastity belt. It was quite impossible.

Suddenly the buzzer sounded. Blushing, she jerked her hand away and jumped off the bed, stumbling to find her servant's shoes. She heard Ursula's voice, harsh and commanding on the intercom.

'Emma! Come at once when I ring!'

# 21 A MERE FRUSTRATED SERVANT GIRL

After she had undressed Ursula, and put away her clothes, Emma had to accompany her to her beautifully decorated bathroom where Ursula took a shower, using Emma's soft little body as a living bar of soap. Emma had to rub her well soaped breasts all over Ursula's hard frame. It was a thrilling game for Ursula, but a desperately frustrating one for Emma – thanks to the efficiency of her chastity belt.

Both mistress and slave were soon highly aroused, and greatly daring Emma found herself begging Ursula to unfasten her chastity belt – a request that earned a slap across her face, and the promise of attention later from Sambo. She was also told to concentrate more on giving her mistress pleasure and to stop thinking about having pleasure herself.

Indeed a few minutes later, back in her bedroom, an angry but excited Ursula instructed Emma to bring her Sambo crawling on her knees, the cane gripped between her teeth. She then had to assume the punishment position she had learnt at the school and receive six carefully applied strokes as a lesson not to annoy her mistress again by imploring her to remove her chastity belt.

Ursula then lay on the bed, the cane still in her hand, whilst she made Emma use her fingers, her tongue, her mouth and, most frustrating of all, her new soft little plastic artificial body lips, to start giving Ursula the relief she so passionately sought. It was of course a relief equally passionately, but quite pointlessly, sought by Emma.

'I think it's time you met another of my little toys,' laughed Ursula. 'I call him Thruster and I think you'll soon realise why!'

She took something out of the drawer of her bedside table. Emma saw that it was a rubber manhood, but a manhood with

226

an electric lead connecting it with a small control box. Emma gave a little shiver of fright and apprehension. She saw Ursula apply a little vaseline to the tip of the rubber manhood.

'Bend over Emma,' she ordered. Ursula then pulled aside the little chain that ran up between the cheeks of Emma's backside. Emma gave a little moan of pain and shame as he felt the manhood press against her little bottom and then slide up inside her. It was a horrible shame-making feeling.

'One of the joys of Thruster is that it can still easily be used to control a girl even when she's wearing her chastity belt,' explained Ursula, as if such a thing was the most normal thing in the world.

Ursula moved a switch on the control box in her hand and Emma felt the manhood start to vibrate inside her. She gave another moan of fear. Then she saw Ursula move the switch again. Suddenly she felt the rubber dildo thrust up inside her. She cried out with pain as her hips gave a violent jump. There was a pause. She felt the dildo slightly withdraw and then after a couple of seconds thrust again.

'That's it Emma, just let yourself respond quite naturally to Thruster,' cried the delighted Ursula as she watched Emma's hips involuntarily jerk in time with the thrusts of the rubber dildo. 'Oh, you're going to give me such pleasure, little girl. Now I'm going to speed it up a little.'

Her hand moved on the control box and instantly Emma was jerked faster and faster. She tried to stop herself, but Ursula moved another switch and now with each thrust Emma felt a little electric shock inside her that made her hips keep jerking.

'Now let's see you thrust with your tongue in time to Thruster,' ordered Ursula. 'Do it properly, push your tongue right out with each thrust, or I'll make the electric shocks harder.'

She touched the red button on the control box. The next thrust was accompanied by a shock that made Emma jerk more violently than ever. It also served as a lesson to do exactly what she was ordered to do: to thrust her tongue out more. Ursula watched carefully as Emma jerked her hips and thrust out her tongue at various changing speeds. Finally she seemed satisfied with Emma's involuntary obedience to her new toy.

'Now kneel down between my legs, and let's feel your tongue.' She lay back and parted her legs to give Emma greater access to her own seat of pleasure, holding the control box in her hands, the cane now discarded as an unnecessary form of control. Thruster was much more accurate and effective.

At first she made Thruster, and hence Emma's soft little tongue, move only very slowly. Once she had to press the red button to keep Emma working properly. The shock was enough to ensure that Emma now concentrated madly on keeping her tongue moving in perfect unison with the thrusts inside her. She was, she realised, behaving like an automaton – a real living doll.

She felt the thrusts coming a little faster and then slow right down again, and she varied the speed of the thrusts of her tongue accordingly. She could feel and smell Ursula's arousal.

'Wonderful, little girl, quite wonderful,' she heard Ursula cry out as she varied the speed to maximise her own pleasure.

After a few minutes, the straining Emma suddenly felt the thrusts inside her stop. Gratefully she rested her tongue. She could never have kept her tongue going so long, had she not been made to practise using it for so long in the school in Paris.

'Now lie down beside me,' ordered Ursula, 'on your back, legs slightly apart.'

Ursula lay on top of Emma like a man, her body lips touching Emma's artificial ones. Suddenly Thruster started up again. Encouraged by a few shocks from the red button, Emma found herself jerking like mad under Ursula. She of course felt nothing under the chastity belt, but she realised that Ursula was getting intense pleasure as she once again varied the speed.

'Perfect!' cried Ursula. 'Just perfect! You're having to do just what Thruster makes you do, aren't you, little girl? But now keep quite still. I want to feel your tongue again.'

Emma was still lying on her back, and Ursula now knelt over her face, holding her body lips immediately above Emma's tongue. Thruster started up again. Emma reached up with her tongue to give her mistress pleasure – her tongue again moving exactly in time with the varying thrusts she felt inside her.

Ursula was soon crying out with her pleasure as she moved the controls to speed up the thrusts and thus make Emma bring her to the very edge of a climax and then slow down again for a moment, before increasing them again. Thanks to Thruster she could control Emma's tongue perfectly without having to say a word and without having to bother at all about Emma herself. She was now first thrusting herself down into Emma's face – half suffocating the girl, then making her reach right up with her tongue.

It was all unbelievably exciting, and the slightest sign of hesitation from Emma was instantly corrected by the pressing of the red button.

It was now time, Ursula decided, to reach a first real climax. She slipped down over Emma's still jerking body. Her body lips were once again pressed against the artificial jerking ones, her hard little breasts were crushing Emma's soft ones and her mouth was clamped to Emma's in a long and profound kiss. She reached for the control box to speed up the thrusts and hence the jerking of Emma's hips. She was almost there. She pressed the red button and kept on pressing it. She felt Emma's hips give the most wildly exciting jerk. There was another violent jerk underneath her and she exploded into her climax – the first of several.

Half-an-hour later, Ursula, clad in her beautifully cut satin pyjamas, lay satiated and fast asleep in her large soft bed. Emma, however, dressed only in her girlish short nightdress above her chastity belt, lay wide awake as she tossed and turned in the frustration of her aroused and unrelieved sensuality in the hard little bunk bed in Ursula's dressing room, off the bedroom.

Ursula had two bell pushes by her bed. One had rung the buzzer in Emma's room earlier on, the other rang a buzzer next to the bunk in which Emma was now lying. A series of short rings, Emma knew, was the signal for her to accompany the half asleep Ursula whilst she paid a short visit to the bathroom. A series of long rings, however, was the signal for her to insert Thruster inside her again and to crawl up under the bedclothes to start pleasing her mistress again, stroking her once again with her tongue in perfect time with Thruster.

The buzzer went three times during the night: once with a series of short rings but twice with a series of long ones. Ursula was clearly enjoying asserting her authority over Emma and enjoying the perfect physical control that Thruster provided. She clearly enjoyed summoning the frustrated girl to do her bidding, with the red button there ready for use at the slightest sign of recalcitrance. She also enjoyed kicking the still frustrated girl out of her bed, once she had performed satisfactorily, and ordering her to return to her hard little bed so that she, her mistress, could return to sleep without the bother and annoyance of having a girl trying to sleep in her bed as well.

Once Emma had seen the key to her chastity belt and the bottle of special liquid sitting on Ursula's bedside table. Her heart had leapt with excitement. Her hated belt was going to be removed! She was going to be allowed to yield! But remembering her beating she did not dare raise the subject and, to her dismay, Ursula made no move to unfasten the belt. On the contrary, she clearly enjoyed teasing the girl and keeping her in a state of wild arousal and utter frustration. Ursula had clearly decided to start in the way she intended to go on.

The next day was Emma's first in her new role. It was to be the first of many similar days.

She had to get up early, whilst Ursula was still asleep, and creep downstairs to ask Rafaela's permission to use the bathroom. Washed, refreshed, prettily made-up and dressed in her candy-striped maid's outfit, she then had to serve Ursula with her breakfast in bed, before bathing and dressing her.

Whilst Ursula dealt with her mail at her desk in the big long studio room, Emma had to make Ursula's bed, tidy and clean her room and bathroom. Half-an-hour later she was on her knees scrubbing the kitchen floor whilst Ursula and Rafaela watched her as they discussed the day's arrangements.

Soon it was time for Emma to change into her outdoor maid's uniform and accompany her mistress when she went shopping and then on to the health club. Emma found it acutely embarrassing having to walk respectfully behind Ursula in the street, carrying Ursula's parcels. She was constantly aware of her nakedness under the long dress and of her chastity belt. She would blush as Ursula told a shop assistant, 'Give that heavy parcel to my girl to carry.'

She was, however, even more embarrassed at the health club. Ursula pointed to a notice: 'Servants must remain with their mistresses at all times and must wear a servant's tunic.'

How different, Emma reflected, her situation was now from when she had innocently first visited the club and met Ursula. Then she had come to the club on her own as a free agent, wearing her prettiest clothes. Now she was being taken to it by Ursula, dressed and behaving as her servant girl, a horrible chastity belt locked round her loins. Then she still had her fantasies about meeting a rich and strong-minded older man who would control and dominate her. Now she was controlled by an older, rich and strong-minded woman who dominated her to an extent that she had never dreamed possible, and with whom she was besotted.

In the changing room Emma undressed Ursula and helped her into a leotard. She noticed, hanging in Ursula's clothes cabinet in the changing room, a grey short tunic of a thick calico-like material.

'Take off your maid's dress and put this on,' ordered Ursula, handing Emma the simple tunic. It rather reminded Emma of the short tunics she had seen slaves wear in drawings of ancient Rome. The top barely covered her breasts and the flaring skirt only just reached her thighs. Her little chastity belt, she thought with a shiver, would be well on display as she walked about. Indeed at that moment another woman came into the changing room, accompanied by a young woman wearing an identical tunic. The woman paid no attention to Emma, but greeted Ursula effusively. The young woman just stood behind her, her eyes lowered. She glanced up at Emma, and they exchanged a little secret smile, the sort of smile that tender young slaves in Rome might have hastily exchanged behind their mistresses backs.

The woman snapped her fingers and the young woman quickly ran forward to help her out of her leotard. Emma noticed that, like herself, the girl was naked under her skimpy tunic. She could not help noticing that although the girl's actual body lips were bare of hair, a little line of hair, like a thin moustache had been retained running across her mound. It gave her a strange and very unusual look.

'Come, Emma,' said Ursula. She led the way into the gymnasium. 'Just remember that there is a strict club rule that maid servants are not allowed to speak to members. Except when you are in the servants gymnasium, where I am taking you now, you must be in attendance on me at all times. We don't like young girls wandering about on their own and gossiping about their mistresses. Understand?'

'Yes, madam,' replied Emma, feeling awed by it all.

Ursula led the way to a door marked 'Servants Gymnasium'. She pushed open the door and pulled Emma in behind her.

Several girls, all wearing similar tunics, were being put through their exercises by a familiar looking figure. She turned towards Ursula. It was the dreaded Miss Perkins, the woman who had thrashed her at the weekend at the health farm!

Miss Perkins looked Emma up and down.

'I see that you've still got the same young lady,' she said to Ursula with a smile.

'Yes, she's just back from the school I sent her to. It seems to have been a great success, but I'd like you just to check her out. Weigh her and measure her and check her for any growth of hairs. You know how I like a little girl to look like one!'

'Yes, but . . .' laughed the odious Miss Perkins, pointing to where poor Emma's short little tunic met her thighs.

'Oh, I almost forgot,' smiled Ursula, handing Miss Perkins the key to Emma's chastity belt and the bottles of the special solvent and glue.

'Oh, incidentally,' said Miss Perkins, taking them both as if it was the most normal thing in the world for a woman to lock up a younger woman with a chastity belt, 'we are having a bicycle race here this afternoon for servant girls. Would you like me to enter your young Emma? After her stint at the school, she might do rather well. She should certainly be pretty fit!'

'Yes, do enter her. It should be amusing to see how she does. I presume that the girls' mistresses are allowed to stimulate their girls to greater efforts?'

'Yes indeed,' laughed Miss Perkins. 'Come, Emma, let's get your belt off.'

It was a chastened Emma who an hour later, wearing her chastity belt again, served Ursula with her light lunch. Ursula was laughing and gossiping to several other women, several of whom were also being served by young women dressed in the grey club tunics. Several women congratulated Ursula on Emma's much slimmed-down appearance and on her much greater submissiveness.

Suddenly Emma noticed that one of the girls wearing a grey tunic and serving her mistress was not a girl at all. She was a young man!

He wore long hair cut into a page-boy cut. His eyes and cheeks were painted like a girl. There was a hint of little growing breasts and of the soft skin that came from regular doses of female hormones. But when he moved the skirt of his short swaying tunic disclosed a young male, even if he was a completely hairless one. He was probably artificially hairless, Emma realised with a shock, just as she was herself, but there was nothing artificial about the male appendage that hung down under the skirt!

So, some of Ursula's set enjoyed having boys instead of girls in their service – or perhaps both. Indeed she saw that the woman in question was being waited on by a young girl as well as by the boy – and they seemed strangely alike, almost as if they might be brother and sister. Poor little Emma was indeed shocked!

Miss Perkins then arrived saying that the bicycle race would start in ten minutes time.

'Now,' said Ursula to Emma, 'you can see why I have not allowed you to have anything to eat yet. You won't win on a full stomach!'

Ten minutes later, half-a-dozen girls, including the boy-girl, were pedalling away on their exercise bicycles. A big dial behind each girl showed how far she had travelled. The race was over five miles with a long built-in hill for a couple of miles during which time each sweating girl had to overcome the effect of the brake that was slowing down her efforts.

Unless a girl turned her head right round, she could not see the dials which showed how she was doing in comparison with the other girls and how far she had to go. But the mistresses, each standing by her girl with a little dog whip in her hand, could see it all very well. Each had to decide when to use her whip to drive her tiring girl to greater effort, and when to allow the girl to get her breath back by pedalling more slowly.

'Come on, you little slut,' cried the mistress of the girl pedalling away next to Emma, as she brought her whip down across the girl's back.

But Ursula was more careful to conserve Emma's energies for a spurt in the last mile when the other girls were more tired.

'Now,' she cried to Emma, bringing her whip down across Emma's buttocks, 'now pedal like mad. Go on! Go on! Faster! Faster! Keep it up! Faster! Go on, little girl, win for your mistress!'

Each word was marked by another stroke of her whip, driving Emma into making even greater efforts until she felt that she was about to faint with exhaustion.

Then suddenly it was all over. Emma had won!

Ursula kissed the utterly tired Emma and pocketed her winnings; £500 no less!

'You're a good little girl, Emma,' the delighted Ursula whispered to Emma, who was now soaked in sweat from her enforced efforts. No wonder, she thought, we have to wear these calico tunics. But Ursula's next words thrilled her and made it all seem worthwhile.

'If you behave yourself for the rest of the day, I might take your chastity belt off when you come into my bed tonight!'

Emma could think of nothing else for the rest of the day.

She was on her very best behaviour when Ursula returned to her house in the afternoon for a rest before going out to a supper party. Emma washed Ursula and helped her into a long satin negligée. She put her to bed and drew the curtains. Then she crept downstairs to her maid's room. The door locked automatically behind her. It could only, she knew, be opened from the outside, or by remote control from Ursula's bedside bell.

Emma quickly changed out of her outdoor uniform into her candy-striped indoor one. She must be ready instantly when Ursula awoke and rang for her. Meanwhile she just waited. There was no clock in the barely furnished bedroom, and of course Ursula had long ago confiscated her own wrist watch, saying that it was not necessary for a servant girl to know the time: she was there simply to do whatever she was told at any time.

The only window was high up in the wall, and gave out onto a well. It had bars across it – ostensibly to keep out burglars, but Emma realised they were really there to make sure that Ursula's maid servant did not try to run away. She wondered how many other girls Ursula had kept here before her. She had seen scrawled in tiny letters in the one cupboard in the room the name Vivienne and a date five years ago. Had Vivienne too been waiting tremulously here, waiting to be summoned by her mistress?

Exhausted by all that had happened that day, Emma lay down on the little bunk bed and in minutes fell asleep.

As on the previous evening she was brought suddenly to her senses by the ringing of the buzzer. She jumped off the bed and touched up her hair. She heard the click of the door lock being released by Ursula upstairs. She longed to touch up her make-up. She wanted to look her best in front of Ursula. But such ideas were cut short by Ursula's impatient voice on the intercom.

'Hurry up, Emma! When I ring for you, I expect you to come running.'

Four hours later Emma was sitting in Ursula's Mercedes outside the house in which Ursula was attending a supper party. Her orders were to remain there until the party finished, and to lock herself into the car.

It was already two hours since, wearing her outdoor uniform and her chauffeur's cap, she had driven Ursula to the party. She had driven right up to the door and had then opened the door for Ursula to get out. She had been wearing a gorgeous, priceless silver lamé dress, the mere sight of which had driven Emma mad with jealousy. She had never owned such a dress in her life.

Then she had parked the car in front of the house and settled down for a long wait.

Through the curtains Emma could catch glimpses of the beautiful dresses, the exquisitely groomed women and the delicious food. How different it was from the awful dungeons and cages of the 'school'. How different it was from her own position of having to sit outside in the cold waiting for her mistress to leave. Unthinking she put her hand down, only to encounter the hard and unyielding chastity belt, or as Ursula often preferred to call it, Purity Belt.

'Remember, Emma, I shall be thinking of you sitting out here in the car, alone and fustrated,' Ursula had said as she got out of the car. 'It will make the party all the more enjoyable.'

Emma knew that it would once again be a strangely thoughtful and subdued Emma who would travel home the following morning and greet her husband when he returned from his office in the evening.

The quite extraordinary intensity of her submission to Ursula, typified by having to wait outside whilst she enjoyed the party had made a deep impression. It drove out all thoughts of making a break with Ursula. It made her realise, as perhaps never before, that what she wanted above all else was to be Ursula's slave and that the pleasure she received from being dominated by her outweighed all other considerations.

She was indeed more besotted with Ursula than ever. The fact that Ursula had paid a large sum to have her trained and had taken the trouble to lock her into a devilishly cleverly designed chastity belt all in some strange way made her feel happy. Her mistress bothered about her! Her mistress was jealous of her having any relationship with a man!

She could not also help admiring Ursula's brisk efficiency. She had thought of everything and had indeed reduced Emma to the status of a serf.

And that damned chastity belt! It was never out of her mind, not because it was uncomfortable, but simply because it was there, a degrading and humiliating secret sign of her status and of her acceptance of Ursula's utter dominance.

Moreover, she now realised with growing dismay that Ursula seemed to obtain nearly as much pleasure from Emma's very realistically soft new artificial body lips, as she did from Emma's own real ones. Indeed, when you include the intense mental satisfaction Ursula obtained from knowing that Emma could feel nothing, and was therefore being kept deliciously frustrated, then the pleasure was greater.

Tonight's removal of Emma's chastity belt was likely to be the exception rather than the rule, even when she was summoned to London expressly to give Ursula pleasure and to perform in her bed.

She thought about Henry. There would now be no question, she realised, of meeting him again behind her mistress's back. She really was, now, completely under the control of her mistress. What a fool she had been to have gone to Ursula's wearing, out of sheer misplaced bravado, Henry's little so-called chastity belt which had given Ursula the idea of having an improved version made to her own design in Morocco. And as for arranging to meet Henry again in Bruges after all that had happened when she met him in London – well she must have been mad! And it was that meeting that Ursula must have finally decided to send her to the training school in Paris and to have the real chastity belt made, and to put her in it.

She compared Henry's approach to that of Ursula. He was one of the most dominating men she had ever met, but mainly in the bedroom and for short periods. Ursula's domination, by comparison, was complete and continuous. For Henry it was an amusing game to be played from time to time. But Ursula never let up, ever. The difference had, Emma supposed, much to do with the different attitude to sex that men and women had. For men, sex was a sideline. They could be quickly satisfied and then turn their attentions to other things. For women, however, for really passionate women like Ursula, sex never stopped. It was in her mind all the time – like her domination of Emma.

But above all she remembered her horrific experiences at the hands of the terrifying Achmet. That was something she would never forget as long as she lived. To be so degraded by a man had been unbelievable. It had, she realised, made her fear all men. Was that the real reason Ursula had sent her to that school? To put her off men for ever? And then put her into this dreadful chastity belt just to make sure?

Suddenly the car phone rang.

'Is that you, Emma? Bring my car to the front door, at once!'

Later that night Emma stood naked in front of her mistress, clasping her hands tightly behind her neck. Her chastity belt had been removed, but Ursula, smiling cruelly, seemed to ignore that. Instead her fingernails were running up Emma's arm and down the sides of her breasts, up her thighs and across the small of her back, before occasionally squeezing her now very erect nipples.

It was all very exciting, but not what Emma was almost screaming for.

Desperately, she found herself constantly thrusting her beauty lips forward for Ursula's attention, but to no avail.

Then suddenly Ursula ordered: 'Keep quite still and quite silent. Stand up straight and look up! Keep your eyes fixed on the wall.'

Emma felt Ursula's fingernails running down her belly and then along her bare beauty lips – up and down her beauty lips. At last, thought Emma. At last! Her breath was coming in short gasps. She was finding it almost impossible to obey Ursula's orders to keep still.

'Now concentrate on keeping your head up and your eyes fixed ahead, little girl. That's better. Concentrate!'

Ursula's fingers were now probing inside her lips. Emma could feel herself becoming very wet with excitement. She bent forward.

'Stand up properly, or I'll beat you,' warned Ursula. 'That's better. Now slowly part your legs and bend your knees . . . Yes! Now let's see you.'

With a sudden shock, Emma felt Ursula's finger on her beauty bud. 'Ah!' she screamed with delight.

'Silence!' warned Ursula, still tickling the girl's almost throbbing bud. Emma gripped her hands tightly behind her neck and gritted her teeth in a desperate attempt not to move or cry out.

'Oh, you are an excited little girl, Emma,' laughed Ursula, pulling the girl towards her. 'Perhaps I should put the purity belt back on you after all!'

Emma gave a little moan of despair.

'All right, little girl, but you are going to have to earn your pleasure . . . Now, for a start, let's feel what it's like to have some real body lips under me for a change.'

Ursula pushed Emma down onto her back on the huge bed, and mounted her. She kicked the girl's legs apart.

'Raise your knees,' she shouted. Then pushing her own legs down between Emma's, she pressed her beauty lips against Emma's soft little wet ones.

It felt so good! The feeling of power over the girl was wonderful. It felt even better as Emma started to respond. But Ursula was in no hurry. She would keep the girl wriggling in a frenzied attempt to seek relief. She would put Emma though all the little tricks that she had been taught by Achmet at the special French 'school'.

'Lick!' she ordered harshly.

Seconds later she felt the tip of Emma's soft little wet tongue straining up to reach her chin, her neck, and below her ears . . .

Soon she would enjoy the feel of Emma's well-trained tongue sucking her hard nipples . . . Soon, kneeling astride the girl's face, she would enjoy the thrill of feeling the tongue working away under her, whilst she played nonchalantly from time to time with those now prettily exposed beauty lips, bringing the girl to ever greater heights of excitement.

And what of Emma? Oh, she was in a seventh heaven! She was thrilled and aroused as never before, as she lay wriggling under Ursula's hard body, held tightly by her strong hands.

It was so good to be Ursula's slave . . . so totally Ursula's slave. Nothing else mattered . . . nothing. Her job, her house, her husband and even Henry were forgotten. Oh God, the sheer ecstasy of it . . .

# NEW BOOKS

## Coming up from Nexus and Black Lace

### Sherrie by Evelyn Culber
May 1995   Price: £4.99   ISBN: 0 352 32996 3

Chairman of an important but ailing company, Sir James is having trouble relaxing. But in Sherrie, seductive hostess on his business flight, he has found someone who might be able to help. After one of her eye-opening spanking stories and a little practical demonstration, money worries are the last thing on Sir James's mind.

### House of Angels by Yvonne Strickland
May 1995   Price: £4.99   ISBN: 0 352 32995 5

In a sumptuous villa in the south of France, Sonia runs a very exclusive service. With her troupe of gorgeous and highly skilled girls, and rooms fitted out to cater for every taste, she fulfils sexual fantasies. Sonia finds herself in need of a new recruit, and the beautiful Karen seems ideal – providing she can shed a few of her inhibitions.

### One Week in the Private House by Esme Ombreux
June 1995   Price: £4.99   ISBN: 0 352 32788 X

Jem, Lucy and Julia are new recruits to the Private House – a dark, secluded place gripped by an atmosphere of decadence and stringent discipline. Highly sexual but very different people, the three women enjoy welcomes that are varied but equally erotic.

### Return to the Manor by Barbra Baron
June 1995   Price: £4.99   ISBN: 0 352 32989 0

At Chalmers Finishing School for Young Ladies, the tyrannical headmistress still has her beady eye on her pretty charges; the girls still enjoy receiving their punishment just as much as Miss Petty enjoys dispensing it; and Lord Brexford still watches breathless from the manor across the moor. But now there's a whole new intake for Miss Petty to break in.

BLACK
*lace*

*The Devil Inside* by Portia da Costa
May 1995   Price: £4.99   ISBN: 0 352 32993 9
Psychic sexual intuition is a very special gift. Those who
possess it can perceive other people's sexual fantasies – and
are usually keen to indulge them. But as Alexa Lavelle dis-
covers, it is a power that needs help to master. Fortunately, the
doctors at her exclusive medical practice are more than willing
to offer their services.

*The Lure of Satyria* by Cheryl Mildenhall
May 1995   Price: £4.99   ISBN: 0 352 32994 7
Welcome to Satyria: a land of debauchery and excess, where
few men bother with courtship and fewer maidens deserve it.
But even here, none is so bold as Princess Hedra, whose quest
for sexual gratification takes her beyond the confines of her
castle and deep into the wild, enchanted forest . . .

*The Seductress* by Vivienne LaFay
June 1995   Price: £4.99   ISBN: 0 352 32997 1
Rejected by her husband, Lady Emma is free to practise her
prurient skills on the rest of 1890s society. Starting with her
cousin's innocent fiancé and moving on to Paris, she embarks
on a campaign of seduction that sets hearts racing all across
Europe.

*Healing Passion* by Sylvie Ouellette
June 1995   Price: £4.99   ISBN: 0 352 32998 X
The staff of the exclusive Dorchester clinic have some rather
strange ideas about therapy. When they're not pandering to
the sexual demands of their patients, they're satisfying each
other's healthy libidos. Which all comes as rather a shock to
fresh-faced nurse Judith on her first day.

## NEXUS BACKLIST

All books are priced £4.99 unless another price is given. If a date is supplied, the book in question will not be available until that month in 1995.

## CONTEMPORARY EROTICA

| | | |
|---|---|---|
| THE ACADEMY | Arabella Knight | |
| CONDUCT UNBECOMING | Arabella Knight | Jul |
| CONTOURS OF DARKNESS | Marco Vassi | |
| THE DEVIL'S ADVOCATE | Anonymous | |
| DIFFERENT STROKES | Sarah Veitch | Aug |
| THE DOMINO TATTOO | Cyrian Amberlake | |
| THE DOMINO ENIGMA | Cyrian Amberlake | |
| THE DOMINO QUEEN | Cyrian Amberlake | |
| ELAINE | Stephen Ferris | |
| EMMA'S SECRET WORLD | Hilary James | |
| EMMA ENSLAVED | Hilary James | |
| EMMA'S SECRET DIARIES | Hilary James | |
| FALLEN ANGELS | Kendal Grahame | |
| THE FANTASIES OF JOSEPHINE SCOTT | Josephine Scott | |
| THE GENTLE DEGENERATES | Marco Vassi | |
| HEART OF DESIRE | Maria del Rey | |
| HELEN – A MODERN ODALISQUE | Larry Stern | |
| HIS MISTRESS'S VOICE | G. C. Scott | |
| HOUSE OF ANGELS | Yvonne Strickland | May |
| THE HOUSE OF MALDONA | Yolanda Celbridge | |
| THE IMAGE | Jean de Berg | Jul |
| THE INSTITUTE | Maria del Rey | |
| SISTERHOOD OF THE INSTITUTE | Maria del Rey | |

| | | |
|---|---|---|
| FANTASYWORLD | Larry Stern | |
| WANTON | Andrea Arven | |

## ANCIENT & FANTASY SETTINGS

| | | |
|---|---|---|
| CHAMPIONS OF LOVE | Anonymous | |
| CHAMPIONS OF PLEASURE | Anonymous | |
| CHAMPIONS OF DESIRE | Anonymous | |
| THE CLOAK OF APHRODITE | Kendal Grahame | |
| THE HANDMAIDENS | Aran Ashe | |
| THE SLAVE OF LIDIR | Aran Ashe | |
| THE DUNGEONS OF LIDIR | Aran Ashe | |
| THE FOREST OF BONDAGE | Aran Ashe | |
| PLEASURE ISLAND | Aran Ashe | |
| WITCH QUEEN OF VIXANIA | Morgana Baron | |

## EDWARDIAN, VICTORIAN & OLDER EROTICA

| | | |
|---|---|---|
| ANNIE | Evelyn Culber | |
| ANNIE AND THE SOCIETY | Evelyn Culber | |
| THE AWAKENING OF LYDIA | Philippa Masters | Apr |
| BEATRICE | Anonymous | |
| CHOOSING LOVERS FOR JUSTINE | Aran Ashe | |
| GARDENS OF DESIRE | Roger Rougiere | |
| THE LASCIVIOUS MONK | Anonymous | |
| LURE OF THE MANOR | Barbra Baron | |
| RETURN TO THE MANOR | Barbra Baron | Jun |
| MAN WITH A MAID 1 | Anonymous | |
| MAN WITH A MAID 2 | Anonymous | |
| MAN WITH A MAID 3 | Anonymous | |
| MEMOIRS OF A CORNISH GOVERNESS | Yolanda Celbridge | |
| THE GOVERNESS AT ST AGATHA'S | Yolanda Celbridge | |
| TIME OF HER LIFE | Josephine Scott | |
| VIOLETTE | Anonymous | |

## THE JAZZ AGE

| | | |
|---|---|---|
| BLUE ANGEL NIGHTS | Margarete von Falkensee | |
| BLUE ANGEL DAYS | Margarete von Falkensee | |

| | | |
|---|---|---|
| BLUE ANGEL SECRETS | Margarete von Falkensee | |
| CONFESSIONS OF AN ENGLISH MAID | Anonymous | |
| PLAISIR D'AMOUR | Anne-Marie Villefranche | |
| FOLIES D'AMOUR | Anne-Marie Villefranche | |
| JOIE D'AMOUR | Anne-Marie Villefranche | |
| MYSTERE D'AMOUR | Anne-Marie Villefranche | |
| SECRETS D'AMOUR | Anne-Marie Villefranche | |
| SOUVENIR D'AMOUR | Anne-Marie Villefranche | |

## SAMPLERS & COLLECTIONS

| | | |
|---|---|---|
| EROTICON 1 | ed. J-P Spencer | |
| EROTICON 2 | ed. J-P Spencer | |
| EROTICON 3 | ed. J-P Spencer | |
| EROTICON 4 | ed. J-P Spencer | |
| NEW EROTICA 1 | ed. Esme Ombreux | |
| NEW EROTICA 2 | ed. Esme Ombreux | |
| THE FIESTA LETTERS | ed. Chris Lloyd | £4.50 |

## NON-FICTION

| | | |
|---|---|---|
| HOW TO DRIVE YOUR MAN WILD IN BED | Graham Masterton | |
| HOW TO DRIVE YOUR WOMAN WILD IN BED | Graham Masterton | |
| LETTERS TO LINZI | Linzi Drew | |
| LINZI DREW'S PLEASURE GUIDE | Linzi Drew | |

Please send me the books I have ticked above.

Name        . . . . . . . . . . . . . . . . . . . . . . . . . . . . . . . . . . . . . .

Address     . . . . . . . . . . . . . . . . . . . . . . . . . . . . . . . . . . . . . .

            . . . . . . . . . . . . . . . . . . . . . . . . . . . . . . . . . . . . . .

            . . . . . . . . . . . . . . . . . . . . . . . . . . . . . . . . . . . . . .

            . . . . . . . . . . . . . . . . Post code . . . . . . . . . . . . . . .

Send to: **Cash Sales, Nexus Books, 332 Ladbroke Grove, London W10 5AH**.

Please enclose a cheque or postal order, made payable to **Nexus Books**, to the value of the books you have ordered plus postage and packing costs as follows:

UK and BFPO – £1.00 for the first book, 50p for each subsequent book.

Overseas (including Republic of Ireland) – £2.00 for the first book, £1.00 for the second book, and 50p for each subsequent book.

If you would prefer to pay by VISA or ACCESS/MASTER-CARD, please write your card number and expiry date here:

. . . . . . . . . . . . . . . . . . . . . . . . . . . . . . . . . . . . . . . . . . . . . . . .

Please allow up to 28 days for delivery.

**Signature**   . . . . . . . . . . . . . . . . . . . . . . . . . . . . . . . . . . . . . .